GHOST
MONEY

STEPHEN
BLACKMOORE

DAW BOOKS, INC.

DONALD A. WOLLHEIM, FOUNDER

1745 Broadway, New York, NY 10019

ELIZABETH R. WOLLHEIM
SHEILA E. GILBERT
PUBLISHERS

www.dawbooks.com

First Printing, April 2020
1 2 3 4 5 6 7 8 9

DAW TRADEMARK REGISTERED
U.S. PAT. AND TM. OFF. AND FOREIGN COUNTRIES
—MARCA REGISTRADA
HECHO EN U.S.A.

PRINTED IN THE U.S.A.

ACKNOWLEDGMENTS

You ever leave something to the last minute? You know, a paper, car repairs, colonoscopies . . . or, as I have discovered, acknowledgments!

Yeah, so I got like two minutes to throw something together and I had this whole thing planned where I would wax philosophic of the need for support and the collective effort of friends and editors and artists, and it was going to be fucking awesome. Like, I had illustrations, charts, fucking Voltaire quotes ready, too. VOLTAIRE. IN FRENCH.

Instead you get this.

My wife, Kari. That's a gimme. Betsy Wollheim and Sheila Gilbert and everyone else at DAW. Friends Kevin Hearne, Delilah Dawson, Chuck Wendig, Kace Alexander, Meghan Ball, Kelli Butler, Annie Lynsen, Jeff Macfee, Peter Clines, Lish McBride, ML Brennan, Teresa Frohock, Paul Weimer, Margaret Dunlap, and basically anybody I happen to see in my Twitter feed right now.

Assume if you're not on here, you actually are. AS A ROAMING GHOST UNSEEN AND TORTURED BY THE VOID.

Wait. No.

Look, if I know you and you're not an asshole, guess what, you helped. The support I have gotten from fans and friends has been mind-blowing.

Thank you. You complete me.

Now go read the book.

GHOST
MONEY

Chapter 1

Dying is easy. Grieving is hard.

Necromancers get a lot of questions about where the dead end up. Did Auntie Fiona go to Heaven? Is that Nazi being ass-fucked by demons? Are they getting what they deserved? Happiness? Peace? Punishment? My answer is usually along the lines of, "I dunno. Let's ask 'em." So far nobody's taken me up on the offer.

It's probably just as well that they don't. Actually contacting a soul in its afterlife? Hardly ever works and fuck knows I've tried. Maybe that's by design. A small kindness in a universe that doesn't give a good goddamn about any of us.

Grieving is about not knowing, not having answers. Answers collapse possibilities, bring out unpleasant truths. Who wants to risk that? No, sorry, Auntie Fiona is burning in a pit of liquid hellfire. That murderer who took out a school with an AK is in Valhalla yukking it up with Odin and Thor. Yes, your true love is being reborn right now, but come on, stop obsessing about them. They're a baby, that's just creepy. Get over it already.

Like it or not, souls go where they're supposed to go. Heaven, Hell, Mictlan, Elysium, whatever. Not even their ghosts, if they've left one behind, know. The ghosts are just cast-off shells, a thin veneer of the person who's gone.

Grieving is about being in the question and looking for the answers. Sometimes that means denial, alcoholism, sex with strangers, Ouija boards, phone psychics, talking to guys like me. If you're lucky, it means acceptance and moving on.

In the end a soul's destination is all uncertainty and doubt. And ultimately nobody really wants to know.

The air inside the house smells like grief and smoke. Everything smells like that now. A month and a half on and though most of the fires are out, the smoke hangs heavy and thick over Los Angeles like angry clouds threatening to rain down flames. Most of the freeways are still collapsed, or impassable, like parts of the 110.

When the small industrial city of Vernon exploded all at once, so many toxins got thrown into the air that they blanketed South L.A. The place is still toxic. It'll be months before the air is breathable and years before anyone can live there.

It's not just the stink of smoke that fills the air, it's the rot underneath it. It's that back-of-the-throat taste of shit and piss and Febreeze. Cholera waiting to happen. I doubt this house has running water. There's sure as hell no electricity beyond the handful of portable solar chargers they're using to keep their phones working and the LED camp lanterns lit.

"Didn't know you ever came out this way," Keenan says. A wiry man with skin like teak, Keenan Mitchell has taken up in an abandoned two-story Craftsman off Figueroa in Highland Park. From the look of things it started as a flophouse, or maybe a hotel in the twenties. Now it's a run-down apartment building with shoebox-size studios on both floors. It's one of the few buildings on the block that isn't a charred ruin.

Two of Keenan's cousins, Aaliyah and Indigo Wayne,

twins, hover on either side of his chair like an honor guard. They're younger than Keenan by about ten years or so, a little lighter skinned, but the family resemblance is obvious.

The only way I can tell the twins apart is the attitude. Indigo is all spiky-edged, don't-fuck-with-me energy, Aaliyah is more—subtle's not the word—coiled, like a spring, or a snake on the hunt, waiting.

"What can I say? I'm a roamer."

When the towers came down in Manhattan on 9/11, killing almost three thousand people and injuring more than six, the sheer number of people in the tri-state area who knew one of the dead or were close to someone who did was staggering. Twenty-eight million people were suddenly playing a game of Six Degrees of Holy Fuck What Just Happened. The grief was like a lead blanket crushing everyone under its weight.

How do you grieve for that many people? How do you even process it? Surrounded by that much heartache, that much sorrow? Some people buckle under the weight, some prop up others and damage themselves in the process. Grief grinds you down, leaves you in shock. Even the professionals, the people who get paid to deal with it, they're hammered by it, too. Three thousand deaths in an afternoon is going to break people.

Now up all that by a factor of thirty.

The Los Angeles Firestorm, or Firepocalypse depending on which news sites you read, swept across the entire county, from Long Beach to Lancaster, Malibu to Claremont. Almost a hundred thousand people died in one night, three times that many injured. Not enough hospitals, beds, doctors, medical supplies—a guarantee that the death toll was going to increase in the coming days, and it did. First responders were spread too thin, or dead at the scenes. The fires hit men, women, boys, girls, infants. Straight, queer, black, white, Asian, Latino, it didn't care. Fire is an equal opportunity killer.

Worse, it was magical fire. Fire that the Aztec god Quetzalcoatl stole from Xiuhtecuhtli during the invasion of the Spanish five hundred years ago, when Quetzalcoatl betrayed his brothers and sisters. Fire so hot it burns bodies to ash, melts steel, tears through concrete, destroys buildings, freeways, lives.

And why did Quetzalcoatl do it? Why did he burn a city that he shouldn't care a rat's ass about? He did it partly because he wanted to goad me into bringing him an artifact I didn't even know I had. Almost worked, too. Which would have been a whole other kind of nightmare.

But mostly he did it because I defied him. I refused to burn Mictlan, the Aztec land of the dead, to ash and destroy all the souls there for him. For that act of disrespect he wanted to hurt me, so he burned L.A. to the ground.

He didn't care that it killed a hundred thousand people. He didn't care that the people he murdered were innocent. He didn't care that he left behind ash, corpses, and heartbreak.

Gods are assholes.

"Somehow I don't think you just roamed on over to our neighborhood. So, to what do we owe the pleasure of your company, Mister Carter? Or can I call you Eric?" I showed up on their doorstep about half an hour ago and announced myself from the street by taking a small draw from the local pool of magic. Mages can feel that sort of thing, and they'll know where it's coming from. It's the magical equivalent of ringing the doorbell.

"Eric's just fine," I say. They didn't want to talk to

me at first, but instead of simply ignoring me, they upped the challenge by drawing more power from the pool. I was just trying to say hello and be all non-threatening about it. But since this had suddenly turned into a dick waggling contest, I saw their bet and raised them. I pulled more power. And kept pulling more power. A lot of power.

You're only going to know a mage when they do something with magic. We don't walk around with pointy hats that say MAGIC BOY in neon letters. But once you know they're there, a few things can give one mage an idea how powerful another is.

How much power can they draw? How fast can they draw it? How much can they hold on to? If you're really unlucky you might find out how much they can disperse, like, say, with a really big fucking fireball.

We go back and forth a bit. There's more than one mage in the house and they're all getting in on the act. But I'm tired and just want this over with, so I end the contest by pulling so much, so fast, that it blocks them from getting any more.

That's when they opened the front door and let me in.

I lean back on the couch. I came here with no weapons; no straight razor, gun, or pocket watch. I have my messenger bag, but there's nothing in it that could be considered an immediate threat. Everybody here knows who everybody else is and bringing weapons would just send the wrong message. I won the pissing match. That's humiliating enough. There's no need to be insulting, too. I'm here to have a conversation.

I can tell they're on edge, and in their position I would be, too. Keenan and his cousins are all largely untrained mages. Born to normal parents, they've had to scrape whatever they can from the mage community, too many of whom see them as some kind of normal / mage half-breeds, which should tell you pretty much all you need to know about the mage community.

For all their lack of training they've done remarkably well for themselves. They finally got the attention of some established mages when they made what was basically a DMZ around their neighborhood in South Pasadena. Crime pretty much disappeared within a two-mile radius. They won't start a fight, but you bet your ass they'll finish it.

After the fires and the riots calmed down a little, they pulled together a caravan of family, friends, and neighbors looking for someplace a little more defensible amid all the chaos. They found this empty stretch before the National Guard came in to lock down chunks of the city that were deemed uninhabitable, shutting off the grid, turning off the water. The Guard makes periodic patrols, but L.A.'s a big place, and they're easy to avoid.

"I hear you're having some trouble," I say. Indigo stiffens, Aaliyah looks away from me. Keenan merely nods.

"A bit. Some folks want to . . . what was it that guy said?"

"Bring the flock into the fold," Indigo says.

"Yeah," Keenan says. "Man came here saying we need 'protection.' And then showed us what we needed protection from."

"How many died?"

"Three," he says.

"One of them was our momma," Indigo says. She's been getting steadily angrier, puffing up, hands a little shaky. It's like watching the Incredible Hulk in slow motion. I know that feeling. It's powerlessness and sorrow, and no idea what to do with it all, so it just comes out as anger.

"Any survivors?" Indigo's laugh is filled with bitterness and rage. She shuts off like a light switch when

Keenan gives her a look. Keenan cocks his head at me and frowns.

"What do you want, Mister Necromancer?" he says. "I don't see anything here that might interest you. I hear you don't care much about the living, and all the dead are outside."

"I want to know if there are any survivors," I say. "And how they're doing."

"Why? What are you looking for?"

"I'm not sure," I say.

"Not sure to which question?"

"Both." I'm not lying to him. I'm not sure what I'm looking for, or why exactly I'm looking for it. I've got a lot of suspicions on what I'll find, but certainty's in short supply these days.

Keenan takes a deep breath. "Two," he says. "We got a boy in the back named Damien. We don't know what's wrong with him. Had a doc come by and look at him, said she needed to call in a speciali . . . Shit."

"Yeah," I say. "I'm the specialist."

"She never told us who." Probably a good idea. They might not have let me in if they'd known.

"I'm not a real popular guy these days," I say. "So thanks for seeing me."

"With what you were doing out there? Shit. If half the stories we hear about you are true, you're not somebody to piss off even on a good day."

Huh. I hadn't realized my reputation had gotten to the "let me in or I'll blow your house down" level.

"Okay. So there's the boy. Who else?"

"Sonofabitch who tried to make us pay for protection," Indigo says. "He's in even worse shape."

"Exactly what happened?" I say.

"Guy comes in," Keenan says. "Asian. Some lawyer type. Suit, briefcase. We didn't even spot him until he was already in the front room. Had one of those 'Don't Look At Me' spells up. Dropped it inside and we felt the magic go. Figured that was his version of a calling card."

That's just rude. At least I stayed outside.

"Then he starts making demands," Aaliyah says. "Like we're fucking peasants. Not even giving us time to figure out who the fuck he even is."

"First he made offers," Keenan says. "Get us someplace with electricity on, running water, medical attention."

"He give you details? Where it was, who's footing the bill, that kind of thing?"

"Nope. Just a clean, safe place."

"That doesn't sound so bad. Not to criticize, but you seem to be lacking some basics."

"Yeah, but there was this tone to it. Felt like a trap. And the offer was only for the talents. He didn't come out and say it, but I think he wanted us to kill the normals and come with him. No way that was gonna happen. So we respectfully declined."

"He wasn't happy," Aaliyah says.

"Asked us to reconsider," Keenan says. "Our decline was . . . less than respectful that time."

"We told him to go fuck himself," Indigo says. "I was gonna kick his ass. But then he lights up a cigarette and, fuck, I don't know what happened after that."

"Lots of noise," Keenan says. "All these wispy-looking nightmares with claws and teeth just explode out of his face." He smiles. "And man did they fuck his shit up."

"You saw them?"

"For a bit," Keenan says. "Some of them disappeared right away, a few lingered before they did the same thing. But I could tell they were still there because they were fucking this guy up good. Whatever those things were, he didn't have any control over them. Seemed like since he was the closest target they mostly went after him. Few other people got tagged." He lifts his shirt and shows me a long, familiar-looking wound on his abdomen that looks like freezer burn. "Saw a few of them fly out the windows."

Terrific. "And the boy? Damien?"

"He was sleeping upstairs. His momma said she saw five, maybe six of those things converge on him and then went all up his nose, down his throat. He woke up screaming, then passed out. You want to see 'em? We got the lawyer type in the same room."

"If I could." My next question's always touchy. I haven't figured out a good way to ask it and I never know the kind of reaction I'm going to get. I watch Indigo out of the corner of my eye. If it's gonna piss off anybody, it'll be her. "What happened to the ones who died?"

I see Indigo start to turn that rage on me, but Aaliyah touches her shoulder, barely brushes it, and she simmers down like boiling water taken off the stove.

"Nobody saw," Keenan says, "but when we found 'em, looked like they'd been sucked dry. Freeze-dried mummies. They started to crumble when we moved them. Took a while, but we buried them in the back."

"And soon as we can we're going to dig them back up and give them a proper burial," Indigo says.

"We talked about this," Keenan says. "We agreed we wouldn't do—"

"You agreed. Nobody asked me shit."

"Enough," Aaliyah says, and the others quiet down. "We'll talk about it later." She turns to me. "You want to see them, right?"

"If I could," I say. I'm not sure about the dynamic in here. One second I think Keenan's in charge, then I think it's Aaliyah, but I get the feeling that when the shit hits the fan everybody looks to the biggest bad-ass, and that's Indigo.

"I'll take you," Keenan says, getting up. "It's at the end of the hall." He leads me through the house to the back. There's a sound in a place like this that's full of misery. It's not crying or wailing for the dead. It's not even quiet. I can hear almost everyone in the house moving around, floors creaking, doors opening and closing. But it all sounds hollow, empty. Like everything good has been scooped out of it. It's the sound of too much taken away too soon.

"What's the story with you and the doc?" Keenan says.

"Vivian?" I say. "We used to be friends." And a lot more, but I don't get into that.

"Used to be?"

"I killed her fiancé," I say. Who also happened to be my best friend growing up. "It's complicated."

"Complicated. I had a girl who was complicated," Keenan says. "Shot me in the leg. We made up."

"I wish it were that easy."

We stop at a door at the end of the hallway. The smells of bad sanitation have followed us here, but they stop at the door and are replaced with the smell of meat left in the freezer too long. The temperature is several degrees lower here than the rest of the house. I touch the door. Frost spreads out from my fingertips at the contact.

There are definitely ghosts in there, I can feel them, but I'm not sure how many. Since the firestorm killed so many people the ghost population has exploded, making it harder to separate them all. In some places the concentration's so thick it's like trying to see a star when you're looking at the sun.

"When did this happen?"

"Two days ago. Doc came out here yesterday. She's been doing the rounds and we got lucky, or maybe she just knew we needed her. She got Damien hooked up to an IV. Left the other guy alone. She brought us some basics we hadn't been able to scrounge up ourselves. Water, food, blankets."

"Yeah, she's good that way." At least I assume she is. I haven't seen Vivian in over a month. At the time she'd been, not broken—I don't know that anything can break that woman—but bent. More cynical than I'd ever seen her before. Chain smoking, not sleeping.

Whatever was going on with her wasn't helped by my presence. She's made that abundantly clear on several occasions. So once I didn't need to be around her, I made sure not to be. Right now any communication is strictly through third parties.

"Anybody go in there besides Vivian?"

"Sure," he says. "We go in three, four times a day to check on things. So far, nothing's changed."

"The kid a talent?" I don't ask about the guy. I'm going to operate on the idea that he's a mage and dangerous until I see otherwise. Safer that way.

"Nah," Indigo says. "He's a normal. Neighbor of ours. I'd watch him sometimes when his mom needed to go out, but he's twelve now. Doesn't need a sitter. Good kid."

"What about the guy? He got a name?"

"I'm sure he does," Keenan says. "But when the shit hit the fan everything he had sort of . . ."

"Froze," Aaliyah says. "It was like he'd been left out in the ice for a couple of years. His whole wallet disintegrated when we tried to pull it out. Briefcase, too, when we tried to open it. Leather, locks, screws and all. Just flaked away."

"Huh. That's new. If it's what I think it is, better if nobody else is in the room but me." Indigo and Aaliyah share a look and a terse nod of the head.

"Nah, man," Keenan says. "I need to know what the fuck happened."

"It'll probably get messy."

"Since when is anything not messy?"

"Fair enough." I grasp the doorknob—it's bitingly cold—and open the door. The inside of the room feels like a meat locker. My left hand starts to throb from the cold immediately, particularly around the three through-and-through puncture scars where I took three shots from a nail gun. I got it taken care of by a mage doc I know in Venice, but he could only do so much. It's functional, but parts of it are numb, stiff. Hard to make a fist, and when it gets cold, it aches.

Most of the furniture has been moved out of the room, dust and skid marks on the old hardwood floor showing where it used to be. Now there's just a folding card table, a chair, and two cots with bodies on them. It's worse than I thought.

It could be easy for someone to think that the boy was asleep. But when I get a closer look I can see that his eyes are open, the irises rapidly changing color. Various shades of blue, green, and brown, in no particular order. Just below hearing I can make out whispers of jumbled sentences.

I had hoped the creatures the guy had released had been imps, minor demons, something like that. When a mage summons one it's usually for a specific task and when they're done they're sent away to whatever hell they crawled out of with whatever payment was agreed on. But sometimes a mage isn't paying attention, just doesn't care if they hang around or not, or really screws up and gets eaten. Bored demons do things like possess kids, but looking Damien over I can see that it's not that simple, and it's far more dangerous.

Ghosts exist in their own world overlaid on top of ours, or maybe the other way around, with a barrier that keeps them on their side, and us on ours, which is good, because they're ravenous for life.

Seen from this side of the veil they're indistinct, jittery, like old film. If I go to their side they're more solid to me. That barrier is all that keeps them from wreaking havoc, draining the life from everything they can get hold of. They absolutely cannot, one-hundred percent, no way, no how, cross that barrier.

Except when they can. I've only seen ghosts cross over three times. Two ended in a ghost possession, and both of those were special situations that had taken me weeks of preparation. This isn't that at all.

One time in Hong Kong a dozen or so ghosts crossed the barrier over the space of a month. Two, maybe three a week. That might not sound like much, but one ghost alone was responsible for fifteen deaths. By the time it was all over about a hundred people were dead.

I can see four, maybe five ghosts just under Damien's skin. They flow into each other, faces looking frantically around, some trying to pull themselves away from the unconscious boy, others dragging them back in, holding them in place. The ghosts don't have that ethereal quality they have when I see them through the barrier. The fact that they're also very clearly taking up space inside the kid is also kind of a giveaway. This feels a lot like Hong Kong, but there weren't any possessions. And there weren't nearly this many escaped ghosts at one time.

I lean in to get a closer look and one of them screams and takes a swipe at me. I back up quickly, barely missing getting ghost-bit. Keenan jumps back when I do.

"What happened?"

"Nothing good," I say. "Maybe don't get too close." There was something wrong with the way that one moved, the way it looked. But I can't tell what, in the sea of ghosts swirling through one another inside the kid's body.

"I didn't see anything," he says.

"You wouldn't." But it's weird he saw anything at all when they first appeared. I cross over to the other cot, keeping a little more distance.

The man is in much worse shape. He lies covered with a thick blanket up to his shoulders, long black hair falling out in clumps. Sores on his face, particularly around his lips. Like the boy, his eyes are open, but they're changing color more rapidly.

He has so many ghosts attached to him that I stop counting when I reach twenty. Some of them seem to want to possess him, moving their limbs as if trying to will his to move along with them. Others are feeding off him, taking nips at his soul, as if there isn't enough to go around. And maybe there isn't, because some of them look to be fighting with each other.

This kaleidoscope of the dead is giving me a headache. I press the heels of my hands into my eyes in an effort to stave off a migraine. A wave of dizziness washes over me. It's been happening a lot lately.

"You know what this is?" Keenan says.

"Maybe." I'm not gonna tell him what I'm seeing, not yet at least, not until I know I can do something about it. Besides, he'll tell somebody else, and they'll tell somebody and then somebody who actually understands what the hell it means that there are ghosts breaking through to our side and eating and/or possessing people will lose their shit completely and I'll have an even bigger headache to deal with.

This is so much worse than Hong Kong. Used to be this place just outside the city proper, Kowloon Walled City. What had started as a collection of squatters in an old fort in World War II had grown over the decades, residents building on top of each other until it grew to fourteen stories, covered about six acres, and held fifty thousand people. Shopkeepers, criminal gangs, doctors, dentists, and on and on. Water and electricity stolen from Hong Kong, it was as real a city as it needed to be.

The government of Hong Kong tore it down in 1993, built a park in its place. Nice, peaceful. Unless you can see all the ghosts, then it's a fucking nightmare. Kowloon still stands there on the other side of the veil, its psychic footprint so strong that it may never go away. Inside is a rat's warren filled with the dead. The decades of death, countless murders, assaults, accidents, have left behind thousands of ghosts.

I was traveling through Southeast Asia for a year when I was eighteen, nineteen years old, bouncing from country to country for a bit. It's easy when you have magic. You don't even need a passport. I was in Hong Kong just after they finished demolishing Kowloon.

I don't know if it was the act of tearing down the city that did it, or something else, but I discovered the hard way that when you get that many ghosts in too tight a space the veil thins. Holes appear. Sometimes it just tears completely.

Hong Kong was invaded by ghosts that summer. Not too many, but more than enough to cause havoc wherever they went. Like mages everywhere, the mages of Hong Kong didn't really care. It didn't affect them, so fuck it, right? Besides, only a handful understood how to handle the dead. Nobody else stepped up, so I did.

Pissed 'em off, too. Here's this tourist who's spent the last several months hanging out in the seediest red-light districts getting tattooed and smoking as much Thai stick and Afghan heroin he could get his hands on coming in and solving their little ghost problem. It was messy, it was ugly, and I never, ever wanted to see anything like it again.

Yet, here we are.

Chapter 2

"So that bit I said about how it's better if nobody is in the room but me?"

"Yeah."

"I'm thinking maybe out of the house. Or a few blocks over," I say. The look on his face tells me he thinks I'm joking. "No, really."

"Jesus, seriously? The hell happened?"

I weigh the pros and cons and finally decide to tell him the truth. Pretty soon one of the more knowledgeable mages out there is going to hear about this, put it together, and realize just how deep the shit is. But on its way there the message is going to bounce through a lot of other people who might take the hint and leave town.

"Keep a secret?" I say, guaranteeing that, of course, he won't. He nods. "Ghosts. A fuck-ton of ghosts."

"I—But . . . Okay, you're the expert, but I heard somewhere they existed in some freaky ghost world we couldn't see. I mean, people who aren't like you."

"Yes."

"And that they couldn't get over to our world."

"Also yes."

"Then how—"

"I don't know yet," I say, taking off my coat and

rolling up my sleeve. "But if I don't take care of these ones right now the kid's dead. Worse, there won't be anything left of him but meat. Do you understand what I'm saying?" Not every mage believes in souls, oddly enough. These are the ones who have no problem with summoning demons, working with nature spirits, and bending reality to their will, but believing in gods and souls is a bridge too far.

Keenan's face goes serious. "Yeah, I get it."

"Then give me a hand, or get out of the way."

"What can I do?"

"I need a bunch of containers," I say. "Ones I can close. Jars, Tupperware, anything." I open my messenger bag and rummage around until I find a sealed paper packet, a handful of vacuum stoppered test tubes, a syringe, and a roll of duct tape. The syringe needle is crusted over with old blood, but that's fine. It's not going into anybody.

"Would one big container do it?"

I think about that for a second. It'd certainly cut down on the amount of bleeding I'm about to do. "Iffy, but I think that'll work. If I can close the lid fast enough, I can—" Before I get any further he bolts out the door, yelling to his cousins to give him a hand. Whatever he's getting, I hope it'll work.

One of the things about necromancy is that it often works better with blood. Part of that, I think, is psychological. Some of it's tradition. A lot of it is that you're connecting with death on an intimately visceral level. For necromancers death is as an obstacle to overcome, a door to open, a friend to betray, an enemy to seduce. It takes a part of you whether you want to give it or not. It's usually easier to do it willingly.

One thing all ghosts have in common is that they're starving for life. That's what makes them so dangerous to me when I'm on the other side of the veil. They're hungry sharks and I'm the idiot scuba diver who was stupid enough to get in the water with them. They see me as a walking smorgasbord. And now that these ones are out here on this side, it's a lot more dangerous, and even more so for everyone else. At least I can see them.

I have protection spells inked into my skin from throat to wrists to ankles, except for one heavily scarred-up patch on my left forearm. Normally, I'd use my straight razor to make a quick cut there for some blood. Only a few drops will get a ghost's attention, but for what I'm going to try I'll need a hell of a lot more than that.

While I'm getting things prepped, I'm keeping one eye on the ghosts. A couple of them try to break free, but something's got them anchored. At first I thought it was the other ghosts that were pulling them down, but I don't think that's it. Whatever it is, I don't think it's going to hold them in place for long. Each time they pull, they get a little bit farther.

I'm not one to depend on things I don't understand, so I pull a can of red Krylon out of my messenger bag and spray a circle around each cot, then pour a mixture of salt, grave dust, and ground-up bone along the edge. I push a little magic into it and I can feel the circle close. Until I break it, they're not going anywhere.

Something rattles down the hall. Keenan and his cousins throw the door open and wheel in two black, plastic trashcans with hinged lids. Huh. Okay, yeah, that might actually work. I spray paint some sigils on the inside of each lid, on each of the external sides, and at the bottom of the cans. I toss in some of the salt, grave dust, and bone mixture.

I tear open the paper packet and pull a rubber tourniquet and a venipuncture kit out of it. Tourniquet goes on, tap the arm, find the vein, slide in the single-use needle. Long time back when I was learning how to do this shit, this is how I got blood for spells. Didn't occur to me that most of the time I only needed a drop or two. Every time somebody saw my arms they figured from the needle tracks that I was shooting up.

Please. Like I'm gonna pump shit into my veins to get high like some street junkie. I take pills for that.

I pop a tube into the holder and release the tourniquet, letting the blood flow in. The ghosts can smell it, stop to stare at me. That's right, you little bastards, it's lunch time. I fill two more. Should be enough. I pull the needle and wad it up with the packet and toss it into one of the open trashcans. A cotton ball for the bleeding and I'm good to go.

I fill up the old syringe with one of the vials and squirt a long line of blood from the edge of the circle around Damien's cot and over to the trashcan. I empty the rest of the vial inside the can and repeat the process with the other two at the circle surrounding the dead man's cot. What's left in both vials goes into the second trashcan.

"Okay," I say. I'm feeling a little woozy, but that goes with the territory. "Everybody hold hands. This part's gonna suck, but without it you're going to be more vulnerable. At least with this you can get out of the way." Nervously, they do until we're in a small circle, each holding the hands of the people next to us. I don't do this often. It won't be fun for any of us.

"Nobody lose your shit." It's a parlor trick. A terrifying parlor trick, and fortunately it doesn't last very long. I snap off a quick spell. At first it's like nothing's happened. Then Indigo gasps as she catches sight of Damien and the dead man.

"What the fucking fuck is that?"

"Those are the ghosts," I say. "You'll be able to see them for a little bit. Honestly, I don't know how long, so let's do this quick."

The last time I did this was to a serial killer cab driver who was screwing and murdering street kids. I showed him the other side, all the Wanderers who'd come far and wide to see this man when I called. Some of them, I'm sure, were ghosts of his victims. After that I bled him like a black ram at midnight and let the ghosts sup on his blood. But I keep that to myself.

Blood and the dead are a weird situation. They're not crossing the barrier when they feed off a sacrifice, whether it be drops in a cup, a bleeding ram, or a serial killing sociopath with his throat slit. It's an energy transfer, but I've never understood how.

"This is the shit you see every day," Keenan says. "Twenty-four seven."

"Great. We can see them. If something goes to hell, can we do anything about it?"

"Run. Okay, this is what's gonna happen." I point to the circle and trace the path in the air with my finger. "I'm gonna break the circle, the ghosts are gonna go for the blood, and dive into the can for the rest of it." I point to Aaliyah and Indigo. "When I tell you, slam the lids shut. There's gonna be a lot of noise and shaking, maybe some screaming. I'm pulling ghosts out of these two and they're not gonna want to go. But you need to ignore it and just keep the lid closed while I finish the spell.

"Keenan, take the duct tape and wrap the shit out of those lids as soon as they close. Do not let them open. I don't care how you do it, but if those cans open before I finish, we're all fucked. Damien here is probably going to look like he's having the mother of grand mal seizures as the ghosts leave, but no matter how much he bounces around, leave him alone. Got it?"

"What about him?" Aaliyah says, gesturing at the man on the other cot.

"He's already dead. Been that way since he set off his spell. The ghosts are trying to animate him, but

they're not very good at it. They have him breathing
and his heart pumping but that's about it. It's a good
thing the ghosts in him were too busy chowing down;
otherwise when you moved him in here they might
have gotten you, too." That's right, kids. Don't play
with ghost-possessed corpses without a trained necromancer around.

"You sure this is gonna work?" Keenan says.

"Oh, hell no. I'm making this shit up as I go."

"Wait, what?" Keenan says.

"Everybody good?"

"What do you mean you're making this up?" Indigo says.

"Then let's get this party started." If I give them
time to back out this whole thing's going to fall apart.
Don't question it, just do it. Let it be what it is, shift,
improvise, ride the magic and see where it takes you.

"Wait, I—" Keenan starts, but before he can get
any more out I throw out a spell that blows the pow-
der of the circles away, leaving bare floor.

Everything explodes at once.

At first the ghosts do exactly as I expect them to.
They burst out of both of the bodies like water from a
firehose, a deafening shriek filling the air. The temperature in the room plummets a good ten degrees as
they slam into the lines of blood leading to the cans,
traveling along it like fire on gunpowder. I had thought
about doing one set at a time, but some ghosts are
smarter than others, and I didn't want to take the risk
that the remaining ones would catch on and stay put.

The kid, Damien, is bucking on the bed like he's
lying on a fallen power line, the ghosts tearing themselves free. They've had their hooks into him for two
days now. It's a miracle he's even alive. It looks like
they've been feeding on him slowly, though why, I
couldn't tell you. I honestly don't know how much of
him will be left once this is over. Damien collapses as

the last ghost leaves his body. I signal Indigo to slam her lid shut, which she does, and secures by jumping on top of it. Keenan's right there with the duct tape, wrapping fast as he can.

The dead guy is, well, dead. He doesn't so much as twitch as the ghosts come pouring out of him. But I've been so focused on Damien that I haven't noticed that the firehose of ghosts coming out of the corpse has turned into a busted dam. There are so many of them that they almost look like a single long blur of shrieking color hitting the blood and traveling into the can.

Aaliyah is holding it together, but barely. Her can is bucking as the ghosts fight each other for the blood in the bottom. Indigo, her trashcan taped up, jumps over to her sister and helps keep it steady.

The stream is becoming unstable. There's only so much life contained in blood, and with this many ghosts going after it, it's going to be exhausted soon. When that happens there's gonna be trouble. I channel magic into a barrier that circles the body and the stream of ghosts, stabilizing it and forcing them into the can. It's like sticking a cat in a box. The ghosts slam against the barrier, clawing and chipping away at it as they go past. Seeing them all, I'm noticing that they all have the same feral expression, the same talon-like hands. That's not normal for any ghost. It's something to think about later, because as the final one comes through, it claws at the barrier where its buddies have been carving a weak spot and the whole thing collapses.

"Close the lid." Aaliyah slams it shut and Keenan starts to run over and freezes. The final ghost is free. A little stunned, very confused from the look of things. That won't last long. Any features that identified it as a person are almost completely gone. Its ectoplasmic mouth is full of awfully sharp-looking teeth, and those claws are even bigger and sharper than I thought when I saw them all passing through. There's a void where its eyes should be. Whoever it used to be is gone. It might as well be a wild animal.

"You hungry?" I yell. "Come on. Come get me. I'm right fucking here." I don't have my razor on me to cut myself and get some blood, so I'm gonna have to do it old school. I bite at the scarred patch on my forearm and spit out a chunk of blood and flesh onto the floor in front of me. The effect is immediate. The ghost homes in on me, ignoring the chunk of skin on the floor for the bigger meal in front of it, and dives straight for the wound in my arm like a shark smelling prey.

It doesn't realize that I'm a much bigger fish.

I channel a spell that pulls on it like a vacuum cleaner. It doesn't notice at first. Then, as bits and pieces of it keep tearing free, it turns its attention from the blood to my face. I open my mouth wide and inhale. The single ghost, clawing at the air and shrieking, gets pulled in and I swallow it whole.

Silence.

Then puking. Vertigo sweeps over me and my stomach lets go of whatever food it had and doesn't stop until I'm on my knees, dry-heaving over a pool of vomit. The ghost is still in me. It's not like I physically swallowed it. It latched onto my soul. For lack of a better term, it's dead. I catch glimpses of memory, bits and pieces from its life, but nothing after. Its entire existence as a ghost is wiped clean.

The last time I did something like this, the fallout was terrible. I had devoured a ghost that had managed to protect itself in pieces of hundreds of other ghosts all stitched together and wrapped around it like bubble wrap. They all came with it.

It was too much, and I couldn't break them down fast enough. For the next few months I kept waking up in new places, or having blackouts only to find that some stray bit of personality had taken over. Coming to in the middle of the Mojave desert in a burnt out shack, naked, covered in blood, and screaming is not a great way to wake up. Especially when you can't remember any of the events leading up to that, and have no idea where the blood came from.

But this one's easier. For a given value of easy, of course. I hadn't puked the last time, but then I don't know how this really works. Maybe this ghost was so twisted that it gave me some kind of existential food poisoning. But I can't just lie here in my own sick. I've still got shit to do. I get to my feet, vertigo swimming up to pull me back down, but I fight until I can stand without falling over.

"Cans," I say, voice rough, breath ragged, "Outside. In the street. Now." Complete sentences are not exactly my jam at the moment. While I was puking my guts up, the others were doing what needed to be done, sealing the second trashcan.

They don't need to be told twice. They wheel the cans down the hall and out of the house, careful not to let either of them tip over, but not taking their time about it either. I stagger behind, feeling like shit, but I've had worse. I almost fall down the stairs when a spike of pain lances through my skull, but I fight through it and it fades away by the time I reach the bottom of the stairs.

They get the cans out to the middle of the street, their wheels making tracks in leftover ash from the fires. I wave them aside. My stomach is still pissed off at me, but that's okay, the feeling's mutual. I stand between the cans, one hand on each. I've done this variant of the spell before, and that was while hanging on to the side of a speeding SUV with the people inside shooting at me. This should be a piece of cake.

I can move over to the other side, but it wasn't until the SUV that I realized I could send things over without me, too. I concentrate, the spell harder to construct because of my queasy stomach and skull-piercing headache, but after a few seconds I have it. I let it loose and the trashcans disappear with a loud pop. The ghosts are on the other side now. Back where they belong. Okay, stuck in a trashcan and thrashing around like pissed-off alley cats isn't exactly where they should be, but it's the other side of the veil, so I'll take it.

I stagger when the cans disappear, not realizing I was using them to hold myself up. I fall backward into the street looking up at a sky of gray clouds and ash. This is my fault. The whole thing. If I hadn't defied Quetzalcoatl, so many people would still be alive. All of these buildings would be just fine. We wouldn't be invaded by all the ghosts created when a hundred thousand people died.

I'll get up in a second. I just need to rest here a minute. I feel awful. I—

Chapter 3

My eyes snap open to the same gray clouds I closed them to. I try to sit up and my head tells me that no, really, lying down is my only option here.

"It's all right." Indigo. She's pulling me out of the street and onto the burnt patch of grass at the edge of the sidewalk. "You did it. You've only been out for less than a minute. Everything's fine." Is she telling me that, or is she telling herself?

"Damien—" I start.

"Keenan and my sister are in there," she says. "If they can't do anything for him then there won't be anything to be done. You gonna be okay here for a minute? I'll get you some water and a towel. I'll be right back. Just chill, okay?"

"Works for me." I close my eyes, but instead of chilling, I'm putting out feelers, trying to get a more focused idea of how many ghosts there might be around, and specifically if any of those feral ones might be nearby.

I see a lot of Echoes, a couple Haunts, and a whole hell of a lot of Wanderers. But they're all over on the other side of the veil. There's no sign of the feral ones who got away. I have no idea how I'm going to track them down.

Where did they come from? I knew some ghosts would start crossing over eventually, and I've been keeping an eye out for it. A hundred thousand dead in a city would leave twenty-five, thirty thousand new ghosts. Some of those are going to be in an area concentrated enough to at least weaken the barrier a little, if not break it.

But this? Jesus. This many did not come out on their own. They were pulled out. But did the act of crossing them over change them into those nightmares, or was that done afterward?

And then there's the cigarette. Whoever the guy was who came over to shake these people down must have really pissed off somebody something fierce. The cigarette was a spirit jar the same way I used the trashcans. They don't have to be jars, it's just a useful way for me to think of them. Magic and metaphor have a lot in common.

I've used paper as a trap a couple of times. Did it in Hong Kong, but I took precautions. Nobody's ever seeing those traps again. This is similar. More similar than I'm comfortable with, actually. But the differences are pretty important.

My traps collected one ghost per piece of paper. The cigarette held dozens. Also, I didn't make a ghost trap out of something that somebody's going to burn in front of their face. Seems a bit hazardous, assuming you care who gets caught in the whirlwind. Hell of a terrorist weapon, or one hell of a prank to slide into somebody's pack of Camels.

Indigo comes back, Keenan along with her. I've managed to sit up, the vertigo fading. Indigo hands me a plastic bottle of water and a towel, and I clean up as best I can.

"How's Damien?" I say when I'm reasonably sure I'm, if not presentable, at least not a vomit-covered horror show.

"He seems to be okay," Keenan says. "Talking, not sure what happened. Doesn't have a lot of energy."

"He know his own name?"

"Yeah."

"Keep asking him. He had those things in him for a couple of days. No telling what that did to his head. He might remember things that didn't actually happen to him. Also, he's probably going to be weak for a while. Those ghosts were feeding off his life." I don't know why they were taking their time. I'm honestly surprised he didn't die in the first thirty seconds, which has me wondering what was different about him. Or what was different about them.

"How about you?" Indigo says. "How are you doing?"

"Feel like hammered shit, but that's nothing new." I put my head between my knees, waiting for another wave of vertigo to pass. "How's the other guy? I mean besides already dead."

"Crumbled into dust," Keenan says. "Body, clothes, shit in his pockets."

"Pockets? I thought you said the wallet disintegrated when you took it out."

"Yeah, but when that fell apart we figured we'd just leave the rest of his shit in there. He had a set of keys, a cellphone, couple other things I couldn't figure out." Keys. Of course he'd have keys. It's not like he took the bus to get here. I get to my feet. All of the cars on this block but the one I came in, a Mercedes I stole in Beverly Hills the other day, are burnt-out hulks, nothing but frames of melted metal.

"You guys check the area very much? Patrol it, that kind of thing?"

"Yeah," Indigo says. "We got three people with walkie talkies walking around. Why?"

"Wondering if they've seen any working cars nearby, or noticed anything new on the streets."

"Hang on," Keenan says and heads back inside the house.

"What now?" Indigo says.

"I got a lot of questions," I say. "I want to know where that guy came from. I can tell you he's not on his own. If anything I think he came out here because he was expendable. He sure as hell didn't make that cigarette. And why you guys? Was the offer of a clean place to stay legit, or was it a trap? Was this even about you? Or was this some kind of test run of the ghosts? Because if nothing else, that was a weapon in there."

"And if there's one, there's more," Indigo says. "Yeah, I was wondering about that."

Keenan comes back outside with a yellow walkie-talkie in his hand, talking to someone on the other end of the line. He presses a button ending the signal as he comes up to us.

"There's an SUV about three blocks away. Wasn't there three days ago and it looks way too clean."

"That would be it," I say. "Which way?"

———

The SUV is a white Escalade and it stands out like a Disney princess in a pool full of hog shit. Keenan and Aaliyah stayed back at the house but Indigo insisted on coming with me. Fair enough. This fucker killed her mother.

When somebody dies it's the people left behind who get the raw deal. They have to pick up the pieces, patch up their lives, fill a hole that can't be filled. Some fill it with alcohol, some with sex, some with hardcore narcotics. Indigo, it seems, is the sort who fills that hole with beating the fuck out of whatever is standing in front of her. She heads down the street with the stride of a machine. She has a purpose, and god help anything that gets in her way. She gets to the Escalade about a minute before I do. I feel the magic as she unlocks the door. Only that's a lot of magic for a simple unlocking spell.

She grabs the driver's side door in both hands, rips it off its hinges, tosses it aside.

"I see you found a spare set of keys," I say as I come up to the car. Her breathing is ragged, and she won't look at me. She stalks off a few feet away to seethe in private. Just as well. I'd like to get some information out of this car before she turns it into scrap.

I do a quick once over and come up with a livery registration and a Starbucks cup that has what could be John, Yani, Lee, or, if I squint, Carl, scrawled on the side. No help from either of those. I pull out my cell phone, walk around until I find a spot with something resembling reception and make a call.

"Tell me this is you calling me to say that you're dead and I don't have to deal with your shit anymore."

"I love you too, Letitia. And when have I ever asked you to deal with my shit? You're the one joined the Cleanup Crew." Letitia Washington is a mage and a plant in the LAPD. She works with a loose group of mages called the Cleanup Crew, who miraculously haven't killed each other yet, trying to sweep magic under the carpet. They do a disturbingly good job.

"Fine. Then go clean up your shit and leave me alone."

"Somebody's cranky," I say.

Letitia has had her work cut out for her since the fire. Not only is she one of the Cleanup Crew, but since she's a police detective, she's working double shifts. Almost a third of all law enforcement in the County died in the fires. LAPD and LA Sheriff took the brunt, but every city has lost people.

"What do you want, Eric?" She's tired, and who wouldn't be? She's now officially in charge of the L.A. Cleanup Crew by dint of being in the most information-rich hub in the city. Stuff happens, she'll likely hear about it first and can let some of the Crew know in case they're needed.

It's a toss-up which of her jobs is more fucked up. Policing in a city where people have turned almost feral out of fear and desperation, or trying to cover up the biggest magic disaster ever recorded. I don't know how they did it—called in favors in other cities, got hooked into media and the science community, blackmailed officials, who fucking knows—but they managed to spin a horseshit tale of cluster earthquakes, old, ruptured oil wells and natural gas vents, and people bought it.

They doctored records, seismic activity reports, death tallies, and more throughout the nation and in a few other countries to back it all up. Sure, there are discrepancies, but the overwhelming evidence supports the story.

"Couple things," I say. "Let Vivian know the kid's all right, more or less. But she'll want to check him as soon as she can. I've got his people watching for any weird behaviors or personality shifts."

"Why don't the two of you just get over it?" she says. She's been playing intermediary between me and Vivian for weeks now and she's tired of it.

"I am over it," I say, though I honestly wonder sometimes. "She's the one who doesn't want to talk to me."

"Fine. I'll let her know. What was wrong with him?"

"Ghost possession," I say. Silence.

"Did you say—"

"Ghost possession, yes. Yes, it's possible. Yes, it's ridiculously rare. No, it didn't happen on its own and yes, it's a problem. Bigger than I really want to get into right now. The other thing I need is a check on a fleet vehicle." I give her the license plate and livery numbers. I hear typing.

"Stolen," she says. "About two weeks ago." A thought gnaws at the back of my mind.

"Isn't that kind of weird? With everything else going on, taking the time to call the police and file a report for a single SUV?"

"Need it for the insurance claim."

"Huh. Okay." Still, it seems like there would be more important things to do. Nothing stops the wheels of commerce, I guess.

"You gonna tell me what's going on?"

"Gimme a couple hours. I'll swing by your place and we can talk."

"No, that's not gonna work," she says.

"Your wife is still pissed off at me?"

"Does the Pope shit in the woods?"

"She does remember that I'm the one who saved her life, right?"

"Can we talk about this later? Got something I need to show you."

"That can't be good. Sure. Where do you want to meet? Parker?" Parker Center is the old Downtown police headquarters that was replaced a few years ago by a nicer, more modern building. It was supposed to be demolished, but since the LAPD's shiny new headquarters was one of the first structures to burn down, they've had to move back in.

"There's a noodle shop up on San Pedro just inside Little Tokyo I've been hitting lately. Let's meet there."

"There's a noodle shop that didn't burn to the ground?" Little Tokyo got hit hard.

"A few. This one's built around a taco truck. You'll know it when you see it. It feels like a you sort of place."

"That's not scarily cryptic or anything. Fine. I'll see you at your mystery noodle shop. In the meantime, can you give me the address of the livery company? I want to check it against the registration in the glovebox." She does and it's a match. A place up in Burbank, Imperial Car Service. Thank god it's not down near LAX. Huge chunks of the 405 are still gone and calling the standstill parking lot in West L.A. a traffic jam is like saying Caligula was a little kinky.

"Thanks. I'll meet you for noodles in a few hours. I want to check this out."

"No problem. I got more shit on my plate than I can handle anyway. But if you're involved it's gonna bite me in the ass eventually, so don't get yourself killed until you tell me what's going on."

"No promises," I say and hang up.

"Who was that?" Indigo says, coming back from her Anger Corner.

"Friend. Called her to let Vivian know the kid's all right so she could come check on him, and to see what I could find out about this car. It was reported stolen a couple weeks ago from a livery company in Burbank." She looks at the devastation around her. We've passed maybe a half dozen habitable houses on our way here, for a given value of habitable. Almost everything else has burned to nothing but foundation and ash.

"You'd think folks would have higher priorities than stolen Escalades."

"Yeah, it sounded weird to me, too," I say. "I'm gonna go pay them a visit. Probably a dead end." Indigo starts to say something, then stops. She looks behind her, brow furrowing.

"I better get back," she says, though I suspect what she wanted was to ask if she could come with me. She wants to punch something. I can relate. If this gets her closer to the person responsible for killing her mother, she wants to be part of it.

"I'll keep you updated," I say. I get her mobile number, give her one of mine. I use a lot of burners. I've got tattoos that help me not be tracked, but if somebody can hunt me down through a cell tower it kind of defeats the purpose.

"Thanks," she says. "Hey, I was wondering. That one ghost that got out. Did you . . . did you eat it?"

"Something like that, yeah. I don't recommend it."
It was different from the last time I did it. This one felt
like I was trying to swallow razor blades. And it felt
wrong. The fact that its memories of life were a shredded mess isn't surprising. A lot of ghosts are like that.
But that it had no awareness of what had happened to
it since it was created is.

"That's fucked up," she says, and begins walking
back to the house.

Yeah, no shit. Welcome to necromancy.

———

Montecito Heights to Burbank is a slog on the best of
days. Now that there's a chunk of the 5 Freeway missing, it takes twice as long to get anywhere, and that's
with fewer cars on the road. After the fires a lot of the
people who could up and leave, up and left. Most people just stayed where they were, shell-shocked, with
no options they could see.

Homeless camps popped up like Hooverville me-
tropolises along the street, across burnt out lots. Tents,
lean-tos, trailers, cars. Within a couple of weeks
fed, state, and city aid moved in, but it just wasn't
enough. No one has dealt with something of this
magnitude before. And it could have been so much
worse. I managed to stop it, but a good quarter of
Quetzalcoatl's fires went off, and they still killed a hundred thousand people.

I take surface streets most of the way and I get to see
the devastation up close. L.A. is a city where every few
feet could be a different culture, a different language.
Million-dollar homes on one block, slummy apartment
buildings the next. What's left is a twisted reflection
of that. Everything is burnt to hell here, completely
untouched there; the ruins of a mansion one second, the
next, an unmaintained apartment building from the fif-
ties looking like the Taj Mahal in comparison.

Imperial Car Service is up near the Burbank airport off of Glenoaks. It's seen a little damage, but not much. The cheap Rent-A-Car that couldn't afford digs closer to the airport right next to it is gray ash, blackened beams, burnt-out cars. The only thing surviving is the brightly colored, rotating sign in the parking lot that says DEPENDABLE RENTAL CAR. It's still lit up and spinning lazily on its pole.

Imperial is about twice the size of its neighbor. It's a stuccoed storefront with no windows, bearing the Imperial name and a logo of a pair of green Chinese dragons facing each other, making a circle. An office with a glass door sits at the corner for customers to go in and order up a car. Presumably the building is more garage than office with all of the fleet vehicles inside.

I park the junker of a Nissan pick-up that I stole in Dependable Rental's ash-covered parking lot. Shitty car. Manual, bad brakes, cracked windshield, needs a ring job something fierce and I swear I've seen flames peeking out from under the hood when I take it over sixty. But it's what I could find that wasn't either burnt all to hell or sitting on melted tires.

A light up sign in the corner of the office tells me it's open, but it's dark inside. It's only about three in the afternoon, but even with the airport still operational, I can't imagine they're getting much business. The door's locked, of course, but a simple spell takes care of that. I push the door open into the office, noticing the thick layer of dust on everything. Must not get a lot of walk-ins.

I can hear faint mechanical noises in the background. I ease open the door in the back to a darkened hallway and the noises are much louder. Someone is working on cars. Sounds like a lot of someones. Three or four cars, maybe more. I don't have to see any more to know what I've stumbled into. The untouched office, the closed-in garage, the sounds of hurried car work. I've stepped into somebody's chop shop, and Imperial's their cover.

Some part of it must be legit or they wouldn't have a livery license or report a stolen car, which I'm still having trouble figuring out. Was it reported by someone hoping it would be tracked here? It would have had to be someone who works here. They had the livery number, the license plate, and the VIN.

I'm thinking this through when the door at the end of the hall opens, flooding the hall with light, and a wiry Asian guy in coveralls smoking a cigarette steps through and sees me.

And it was going so well.

"Hi," I say, as brightly and stupidly as I can, and start walking toward him. "I needed to hire a car service and I saw your sign and the door was open and since I didn't see anybody I came back here looking for someone who could help me out and—"

At that point I'm close enough to him to grab him behind the neck, pull his head down, and bring my knee up into his nose. There's a loud pop. Before he can make a sound I hit him with a push spell that slams his face into the floor hard enough to give him a concussion, and he's out.

I drag him back into the hallway a bit. Now I have a choice. Leave, since there are definitely more of them in there than there are of me, or go forward and find out what the hell's going on, and probably get shot at.

Well, I haven't been shot at in at least a week, so I suppose I'm due.

I give up any pretense of stealth, draw my Browning out of my messenger bag, and fling the door open. There are about ten people in here working on cars, none of which are livery vehicles. There's a surprise.

They're all Asian. Chinese, maybe? There are only a

few Chinese gangs in the Southland, and most of them report up to one of the Hong Kong triads, like Sun Yee On, or 14K, or to one of the stateside Tongs, like Ghee Kung. Puppets being yanked around by bosses they might have never seen. Whose operation this is is anybody's guess. Hell, maybe they don't even know.

The closest one has his head under the hood of a yellow Charger. He glances up, sees me, and realizes that I'm definitely not his buddy who went out to grab a smoke. He goes for a wrench sitting on the engine. I press my hand to the side of the car. I let him grab the wrench but before he can lift it I throw an electricity spell through the car, bursting into him and locking all his muscles. I release it a second later and he falls to the floor unconscious and smoking.

I now have everyone's attention. This might not have been a good idea.

"Hey. Sorry to interrupt, but I'm trying to find out about an SUV you guys reported stolen a couple weeks back. I ran into it a few hours ago and the guy who was driving it was a little, uh, dead. I was wondering if any of you fine gentlemen might know who—"

I'm surprised they let me get that far before the shooting starts. I duck behind the back end of the Charger, the engine block soaking up the gunfire, bullets shattering the glass. I look under the car and see the feet of only a couple of the mechanics. The rest are behind other cars or equipment. I consider shooting at the ones I can see, but I doubt I'd hit anything. They're jumping around too much.

My gun disagrees and lets me know through a wave of angry disappointment. It's a Browning Hi-Power my grandfather got off a psycho necromancer during the war. The gun's original owner had been doing experiments on prisoners in concentration camps. He'd murdered enough people with this gun that it pulled in all that cruelty and suffering, storing the power like a massive magical battery and giving it a bit of a mind of its own. A normal person uses it and it's just an antique Nazi gun, albeit one with a nasty personality they're unaware of that whispers thoughts of murder into their subconscious, but a necromancer uses it and it's a hell of a lot more.

Every time I pick it up I feel like I'm sticking my hand in a bucket full of cockroaches. The death energy I can handle; it's the cruelty I have trouble with. But it's hard to argue with results. My aim's better with it than with any other gun and it makes holes bigger than any 9mm has any right to make.

That said, one of these days I'm going to melt the fucking thing down for paperweights. It picks up on my thought and keeps its opinions to itself. I'm told that as long as it doesn't start talking to me, I should be okay. So far, it just throws angry emotions my way. Fine by me. I don't want to talk to regular Nazis, much less their animated psychotic firearms.

I don't want to kill these people. I have questions that need answering. If one of them leaves a ghost behind, and there's no guarantee, that's one thing, but getting information out of a corpse is a colossal pain in the ass. But I doubt they'll give me much of a choice.

There are three exits to the garage. The garage door with a padlock on it, a barred door next to that, and the door I came through. I consider backing up into the hallway and using the door as a choke point. I can do it with a shield spell to cover me, but getting there means walking through a bunch of flying lead and the chance a bullet will get through goes up pretty dramatically. Are these guys even aiming?

The firing stops as everyone reloads. Okay, so they're not coordinating with each other very well. Makes sense. They're all grease monkeys. I pop up and get off a couple shots from the Browning just to remind them I'm still here and get a better idea of where everybody is before ducking back down. I see seven of them, so two of them are hiding. I haven't felt any magic, so that's a plus. They're just normals with guns.

I need to even this out. Take a lot of them down at the same time. I dig around through my messenger bag and pull out a small drawstring bag. I picked it up in a storage building in Van Nuys. The place is a vault hiding in plain sight, filled with magical crap collected over a couple hundred years. I don't have a lot of details on it other than that my grandfather was involved at some point, and it's got items ranging from the incredibly dangerous to the outright stupid in it. I've got a ledger listing the items in there, but it tends to be light on the details.

This one, though, I've tried. I open the bag and pour a handful of prisms, each the size of a small bead, into my palm. One of them is larger than the others, about the size of a die. A mage designed them in the forties for instant, widespread communication. The downside is that the beads burn out after one use.

I holster the Browning and pull the drawstring closed with my teeth before dropping the bag back into the messenger on the floor. I throw the beads under the car to scatter, and give it a second for them to reach as far out into the room as possible.

When the firing stops a second time I stand up point my finger at them like a gun and say, "Bang." I let loose another electric jolt, the power pouring through the prism in my hand and into the beads all over the floor. The room fills with a blue and white light show as lightning pours through the beads. A few guns go off as trigger fingers spasm, and bodies hit the floor. I stop when the room starts to fill with smoke.

Everything I see is charred with jagged lines from the arcs of electricity. I can smell burnt hair and charred meat. I wonder if I overdid it. I come out from behind the Charger to check my handiwork and it seems I didn't go big enough. One of the mechanics staggers to his feet. I get ready for more gunfire, but he's not holding a gun. He's holding a burning lighter. And in the other hand he's holding a cigarette. Shit.

Before I can so much as yell out a warning, he touches the lighter to the paper. The room explodes with nightmares.

Chapter 4

The ghosts are jagged things, broken and screaming. About a dozen of them boil out of the burning paper. The mechanic who lit it is totally unprepared for this and lets loose a shriek that suddenly goes silent when they all tear into him and start to feed. I've seen ghosts eat. I've seen ghosts kill. I've never seen this.

It's like watching a pack of starving jackals tearing through a gazelle. I can see them ripping at his insides, their claws shredding the body as well as the soul. And all the while his body gets leaner, skin goes leathery, face falls in against his cheekbones.

I watch in fascination for a few seconds as they devour him. But I already know how this play goes and I'm not about to hang around for the ending. I duck out through the door I came in. I don't know what sorts of senses they have, but I'm banking on the fact that there are a bunch of unconscious blood bags lying on the floor between me and them to take their attention.

The guy in the hallway who I slammed into the floor is still out. I grab his arms and start pulling him toward the exit. I need one of these bastards alive so I can find out what the hell is going on. Inside the garage I hear the screams of the others as they wake up only to find they're being eaten from the inside out.

I get the unconscious man into the office, and I'm almost through the door with him when the ghosts find us. Two of them have separated from the main pack. They look at us like we're the prime rib special at a Hometown Buffet. I don't stop moving, just keep dragging the man toward the door.

I don't know why I think getting outside will be safer. These two just phased through the wall. If they were on the other side, they'd bump into anything that had left a strong enough psychic footprint as if it were solid rock, but out here the rules are different, and I don't know what they are. I get the guy outside and over to the car, never taking my eyes off them. I lay him on the ground to get the door open.

Apparently, that's their cue. The ghosts dive bomb us, shrieking spirits with ectoplasmic claws and teeth. And that's when I realize what I've been missing. The rules are different for these things. But not all the rules. They're ghosts. Whatever else they've been twisted into, they're still just ghosts.

I put up a hand and channel my will through the magic. A glowing green wall appears between us. They don't care, or they can't see it. Doesn't matter, they're not slowing down. They hit the wall at full speed. And stop.

Hanging, suspended in air, caught by my wall of will. I squeeze my hand into a fist and they implode like a torpedoed submarine. Okay, two down. Will that deter the others?

Apparently not. As I lean down to pick up the unconscious man and get him into the car, the rest of the ghosts appear, bursting out of the ground and straight up through his chest.

It's the sort of show I never want to see again. Flashes of blue light burning through his eyes, mouth, and nose. They travel over and through him, tearing him apart the way they did the mechanics inside.

Yeah? Well, fuck you, too. I'm a goddamn necromancer.

I throw my senses wide, my mind tagging them all, and squeeze. They pull together, slamming into a single space, a cube too small for a mouse to fart in, much less move. I'm not sure if they notice. Can they? Is there anything left of a person in any of those things? Even the oldest Wanderers, who've been around so long and faded so much, remember who they were.

I weigh options. I could devour them, which I really try to avoid even with regular ghosts. I could banish them back to the other side, but I'm not sure I can do all of them at once. I can't let them go. And if I take my attention off of them for even a second, they'll strike.

None of them have very discernible faces. Anonymous shards of rage and hunger, their personalities ripped away. And where that's happened, a ragged thread hangs off every one.

I've seen something like this before, on a mage who was stealing Voodoo Loa and stitching them into his soul like a serial killer's skin suit. Once I found the thread it was easy. I just had to pull. I do the same here, yanking on those threads and spooling them all up at the same time, unraveling the ghosts from themselves, from each other. Bit by bit, they're exposed. The few memories of their lives caught in their shredded ghosts scattered and twisted.

Somebody made these, and I have to say, I'm not impressed. It's sloppy work, rough. I don't know for certain that these ghosts didn't wander over from the other side, but my gut tells me somebody pulled them here. There's just too many of them. Once they arrived, they were stripped down until they were nothing but pure hunger, crazed sharks ready to feed, locked away until they were set free with a flame. But like a grenade, they don't discriminate.

They struggle against the bond, against the process, but bit by bit I pull them all into a rapidly evaporating ball of toxic energy, unfocused magic that I shunt into the local magic well. It's not a good feeling. I'm like that kid who shits in the shallow end of the public swimming pool.

I check on the mechanic back at the car. It's too late. He's dead like all the rest, nothing but a desiccated corpse, freezer-burn gouges around his eyes and mouth. I nudge him with my foot and he collapses into dust, clothes and all. I bet if I looked inside the garage I'd see the same thing. All of the moisture in those bodies will have been drained out along with the life still in them. I lean against the car, slide down to the ground, and bang the back of my head against the rear door over and over again.

"Goddammit." I stand back up and kick the car door until it dents, screaming obscenities. I punch the side mirror, the silvered glass shattering. The firestorm was bad enough, but at least that just left people dead. Dead is not gone. Our souls are who we are. Our personalities, our memories, everything that makes us *us* goes into them. And when we die, we go wherever we're supposed to go.

But not the people these ghosts killed. Ghosts don't leave anything behind. They're ravenous and they make great murder weapons. All I have to do is push somebody from our side to theirs and the ghosts take care of the rest.

I look at the pile of ash that was the mechanic, the ashes of the building next door, on the street, in the parking lot. Coating everything. Ash so thick even the wind can't blow it all away. Of course nobody's cleaned up over here. Why would they? There are more important places to deal with, right?

I punch the pick-up's passenger window, cracking it, cutting my knuckles. Blood pouring from my fingers, I snap the side mirror off its base. Rip the door handle off. Follow it up with the door.

Even with the magic in my tattoos that makes all that possible, I'm gonna feel it later. I stop, breath ragged, back and shoulders already starting to ache. So much of the city is simply gone, and there are so many dead, and there's not a goddamn thing I can do about it but get pissed off.

How many know I was involved in the fires? How many blame me? From what I can tell, that secret's pretty much still under wraps, and of those who know, I can't tell if they hate me for it or are just pissed off at me on general principle. I've had few active attempts on my life lately, so that's a good sign?

I try to tell myself it isn't my fault, and that just pisses me off more. How? How is this not my fault? I brought Quetzalcoatl down on all our heads. A hundred thousand people died in a fire I was directly responsible for. A. Hundred. Thousand. And you know what's happening now? They left behind so many goddamned ghosts that they're bleeding through the veil and some asshole is sticking them into cigarettes to go off like a fucking ACME cigar in a Bugs Bunny cartoon.

Yes. This *is* my fault.

Quetzalcoatl is trapped in a hole in Mictlan; his pet assassin is a pile of ash. Everybody else who made this happen is gone. I'm the last man standing. This all starts with me, it all ends with me.

And the hell of it is, it wasn't even about me. It was about Darius. An 8,000-year-old djinn who somehow made his way into the possession of one Hernán Cortés, who waged a war against the Aztecs and used Darius to wage a war against their gods. During a fight in the tunnels below Mictlan, Darius was trapped inside his bottle and Mictlantecuhtli, the king of the dead, was entombed as a jade statue.

From there, the bottle hitched a ride with one Juan Rodríguez Cabrillo, who a few years later died on Catalina Island off the coast of California. The bottle disappeared. No one outside a very small circle realized that it was dug up during an archaeological expedition looking for Chumash and Tongva relics on the island. As far as everybody was concerned it was still hiding somewhere.

Which is true. It's hiding on the dining table in my grandfather's safe house that he built on the other side of the veil inside the ghost of the Ambassador Hotel. Don't ask me how it works, I don't fucking know. And I don't plan on telling anybody it's there, either.

The last time I saw Darius was the night of the fires. I limped to the motel I was staying in, battered, bruised, and with a hand wrapped up in enough gauze that it may as well have been a boxing glove. And just as I was about to open the door, it wasn't my door.

Darius doesn't have a lot of power outside of his prison, but one thing he can do is make entrances to it for other people. And you can tell it's his door. He goes for a high-class lounge aesthetic. The doors are always red leather with large brass tacks in diamond patterns.

Inside, he has complete control. It's his universe in there. It's not a big universe, but he can make it look and feel however he wants. Lately he's been doing it up like a jazz bar and letting some people in, dreamers mostly, though I don't know how or why. He fills out the place with characters of his own imagination, spends his time pouring drinks, flirting with the patrons. And always trying to figure a way out.

I figured I was going to have to talk to him at some point. Even before the night ended it was clear the fires were all to get me to find and retrieve the bottle so it could be stolen. Only I hadn't known I had it or even where it was. When I finally found it, instead of bringing it out, I brought out a fake and used it to trap Quetzalcoatl.

So I opened the door, went in, and the first thing he says to me after I limp up to the empty bar and share a couple drinks is: "I understand you found a bottle."

I told him it turned out to be a fake. That I had no idea what everybody thought it was. As far as I was concerned it was just some heavily warded spirit jar that I used to trap Quetzalcoatl. He didn't believe me, of course. He kept pushing, I kept denying. We went around in circles a few times like that. I didn't hide the fact that I was lying. There was no point. I just didn't explicitly admit it. Deny deny deny. Eventually, he stopped trying.

"We'll play it your way," he said. "You say you don't have it, you don't have it. But say you run into it. I'd surely like to know. It's not every day that someone gets to see the outside of their prison."

I told him, "Sure. I stumble across it, I'll give you a call," completely ignoring the mind-bending impossibility of bringing the bottle into itself so he could take a look at it. We finished our drinks and that was that. I haven't talked to him since, but I'm not stupid enough to think he's not keeping tabs on me.

I know he had his fingers in this disaster. Oh, Darius never does anything you can see. He nudges, whispers in an ear. Steers you in the direction he wants you to go and makes it feel like all your own idea.

So is it Darius's fault for existing? Cortés's for invading Mexico? Cabrillo's for coming to California? Spanish colonialism's in general for, well, Spanish colonialism?

Sure, why not. But it doesn't change the fact that I'm the one who made a deal with Quetzalcoatl and broke it. If that hadn't happened, who knows how this would have turned out. Maybe everything would have worked out the same, only without L.A. turning into a dumpster fire.

The wind kicks up a notch, picking up granules of the mechanic-shaped pile of ash, spreading him little by little across the pavement. Sorry, man. For what it's worth, I did try to keep you alive.

Chapter 5

After the firestorm I didn't dream of the dead. I dreamt of the survivors. The ones who had to pick up the pieces, figure out what to do next, come to grips with the fact that everything they thought they knew was gone. A grieving widow, a couple hysterical parents, a daughter left alone with nowhere to go.

It might make me an asshole, but those I can handle. They're one-offs, statistics, a rounding error. Shit happens and that was their turn at the wheel. But a hundred thousand dead leaves twice that many mourners at least. The pain and agony in the city is so loud I can hardly think.

I don't have a problem with death, obviously. At least, not bodily death. We're all just driving around in meat cars. Kill a man, he's dead. Kill his soul, he's gone. I fed Jean Boudreau, the man who killed my parents, to a crowd of ghosts and they tore his soul to shreds. They missed some bits and he came back, so I tore his soul apart myself.

I have no illusions about what the ghosts are eating. They're not just killing a person, they're ripping out their next life, they're destroying any chance of punishment, redemption, moving on to the bonus round, whatever.

Even when Quetzalcoatl demanded I destroy Mictlan and I saw all the souls it contained, knowing what would happen to them, I was still prepared to do it. I stood on top of a blood-soaked pyramid in the rain with the flames of Xiuhtecuhtli in my hand ready to burn it all down, myself included, as long as it took the king and queen of Mictlan down with me.

But the firestorm. That was different. A hundred thousand dead. A hundred thousand burning, suffering. There are no silver linings. There are no happy endings. They can all go off to an eternity of unicorns and hand jobs, and it wouldn't matter. No matter how I spin it I have to admit that without me it never would have happened.

If I'd burned down Mictlan, it would have been a truer murder than the fires. There's no after-afterlife. Would I feel the same way? I'm not sure I would have.

The living have potential, fluidity, the ability to change. We redefine ourselves every day. Who you are in the morning might be a far cry from who you are at night. But the dead are more static. They don't really go anywhere. It's almost like the gods couldn't figure out what to do with them, so they shoved them all into a warehouse.

In one night a hundred thousand souls scattered like petals on the wind. There were so many, and it was so sudden, that most of the ghosts they left behind are Wanderers: the ones that aren't tied to a place like Haunts, or just recordings of their deaths like Echoes. Couldn't say how much of a soul goes on and how much stays behind, but Wanderers are the most intact.

In Kowloon, when the ghosts tore through the veil, they were all Wanderers. They'd have to be. Echoes are mindless playbacks, and Haunts don't have enough willpower to pick up stakes and move around. There's no reason to think that these ghosts aren't the same.

Only in Kowloon the ghosts weren't twisted up into

whatever the fuck those things were at the house in Montecito Heights, the chop shop in Burbank. Somebody did that to them. Somebody took a chunk of a person's soul, tore out everything that made it unique or even human, and turned it into a fucking nightmare.

Weaponized ghosts. Whatever will they think of next?

I get off the freeway at Fourth Street, taking the bridge over the river into Downtown. Most of the westbound side collapsed during the fires, and a temporary barrier has been put up to keep cars from flying off the side of the bridge. There are rumors that nobody actually did any kind of engineering assessment, just threw up some cement barricades and hoped for the best. With so much destruction to deal with, I wouldn't blame them.

I send a quick text to Letitia telling her I'm in the area. I get a series of emojis, the only one of which I can understand being a thumbs up. English has gone the way of the Egyptians. We speak in hieroglyphs now.

Skid Row is a blighted wasteland. You know things are fucked up when reality makes a Tom Waits song sound glamorous. Most of the streets are cordoned off and National Guardsmen hang around a few of them with not much to do. Nobody wants to go down those streets anyway. There's nothing there but ash and bad memories.

I went through the area as the fires swept the neighborhood. No one's entirely sure how many people died in there, but with anywhere from five to ten thousand homeless crammed into four square miles, the current estimate is 'a fuck-ton.' The ghosts seem to agree. This is the densest concentration of them I've seen in the city.

This is where I've been expecting to see Wanderers break through the veil. The density is less than Kowloon, but where Kowloon's ghost population rose over several decades, most of the Skid Row ghosts were created inside of an hour. They're busting at the seams and there are a few spots where the barrier feels thin. They might not be breaking through now, but this is a place that bears watching.

I take San Pedro up through the remains of Little Tokyo. There are places that were hit worse, but not by much. Most of the stores are closed, boarded up, or burnt out husks. A few enterprising optimists have opened up again, ramen places mostly.

I see the one Letitia told me about. Somebody's set up what looks like a semi-permanent pop-up store based around an old taco truck. A roll of AstroTurf is spread out in front of it with a few plastic tables and chairs. A hand-painted sign above the truck reads APOCALYPSE NOODLES. Must be the place.

Parking is easy, which is not something I'd have ever expected to say about Downtown. One shop owner has swept away as much debris as he could, put a short ramp on the curb. He has a sign on the sidewalk with the price, and it's a lesson in correctly gauging your customers. He started at thirty, crossed that out, and went down until he got to five.

I see Letitia at one of the tables slurping up a bowl full of ramen and sit down across from her. "My kinda place?" I say. "I'll fit right in? You trying to tell me something?"

"Nothing you don't already know," she says.

"Yeah, well, you don't know how on-brand Apocalypse Noodles really is." I tell her what happened at the house and at the chop shop. I tell her about what happened in Kowloon, about how this is different, more dangerous. About my idea that someone is using the ghosts as a weapon but not bothering to tell the people who use it what it will do to them. She says nothing until I'm finished.

"Shit," she says. She looks down at her noodles. She hasn't touched them since I started talking. She pokes at them with her chopsticks. "They've gone cold. There are really that many new ghosts in L.A.?"

"Yeah," I say. "They're spread across the whole county, just like the victims were, but they're in clots. This place is crawling with them. I figured if any of them were going to bust through it'd be here. They still might." Letitia stares at me, eyes a little wide.

"Were you planning on telling me about this?"

"Sure. Eventually. You got a lot on your plate, Detective," I say. "And I didn't want to worry anybody."

"I'm worried now," she says.

"What a coincidence, me too. I don't think the ghosts I saw are breaking through. I think they're being pulled through. And something's being done to them to make them more dangerous. They're being tortured."

"Okay, setting aside that I was talking about the ghosts in Skid Row possibly breaking through to kill us all—torture? You can torture a ghost?"

"They're pieces of a person's soul. A shell, sure, and some of them are no more than a recording that plays back on a loop. But these are Wanderers. They're as close to the actual person who died as you can get. I've heard the idea that they might actually be the entire soul, or at least most of it, but I don't really buy it. So, yes, you can fucking torture a ghost."

"Whoa. Sorry to hit a nerve. Fine. I won't go around torturing ghosts."

"Sorry," I say. "It's just—never mind."

"I really wish I'd never met you," she says, looking a little ill.

"Hey, you had a chance to kill me when we were kids." Letitia and I go back a long time. Mage high school, if you can call it that. Less Hogwarts and more boot camp. If you survived to the end of it without killing too many of your fellow students you graduated. I almost didn't, largely due to Letitia. She stabbed me in the back. Literally.

"I can still kill you as an adult."

"But then you wouldn't have all this wonderful trivia about the sea of dead you're currently stewing in."

"However would I survive without that?"

"Watch out for the Skid Row ghosts. They might still break through, and if they do you need to be ready. Might want to spread the word that folks should brush up on their banishing spells. Quietly. I don't know who's pulling the Wanderers across, but I don't want them knowing I'm looking for them."

"Jesus Christ, Eric. How am I gonna even know it's happening? You're the only one who can see the damn things."

I've been wondering the same thing, and I can only think of one way. I unbutton my shirt, show her a scar across my chest that cuts through some of my tattoos. "Look for victims. They're either going to have wounds like this, or they're gonna look like they spent the last couple thousand years in an Egyptian tomb. Maybe both."

She peers at it closely. "It looks like chicken you left in the freezer too long."

"You should see them when they're fresh. Just keep an eye out. There are going to be more."

"Bad enough the city's a smoking crater," she says. "Now we have to worry about ghosts eating us. I don't know how many people know how to banish a ghost. I sure as hell don't. What do I do, call them bad names?"

"Seems to work for those ghost hunter guys on TV." I have to admit, I don't really know. It's just sort of something I do. Comes with the necromancy territory the same way an aeromancer knows how to fly, or how a diviner can look at coffee grounds and tell somebody's gonna shank you in an alley. Everybody's knack, that one thing we're stupidly good at it, is slightly different, but they tend to fall into broad categories, some more common, some less. Summoners are a dime a fucking dozen, but necromancers are kind of thin on the ground.

"Great. I'll let everybody know they're going to get eaten by ghosts and there's fuck-all they can do about it."

"Oh, come on. I can't be the only mage in the city who knows how to banish ghosts. You're in tight with the community, aren't you? Try Gabriela. She's probably got a spell or two for it." Letitia looks away, not meeting my eyes.

"Did something happen?"

"I'm . . . not really supposed to talk to her at the moment," she says.

Gabriela Cortez is in her late twenties. Masters in Sociology from USC. Helped out the homeless supernaturals like vampires and ghouls, who number a hell of a lot more than people realize. She's about five feet tall, maybe a hundred and ten pounds. One of the scariest people I've ever met.

A while back, when she decided she wanted to make the world a better place, she tried to give the city's supernatural community an actual home. Junkie vampires, wayward ghouls, lamiae who'd lost the ability to feed. If it's scary, inhuman, and hiding out behind a dumpster because it's terrified of being found by humans, she took it in.

And because nobody was going to give a twenty-something woman who looks like a teenager seriously, she invented La Bruja, a powerful old crone who lived in a hotel near Skid Row, and created a power base and a small army, mostly out of the local gangs. The inevitable happened and she had to go up against the likes of La Eme, Armenian Power, and 14K just to survive.

Gabriela has a simple philosophy of disproportionate

response. Be crazier and more ruthless than everybody else and they'll leave you alone. If something gets in her way, she kills it and makes sure it sends a message.

She's left skinned corpses on doorsteps, put heads on fence posts. Eventually everybody got the hint. Before she knew it, and without intending to, she was running one of the most successful criminal organizations in Los Angeles. Right under the LAPD's nose.

"Oh, thank fuck for that. I thought you were gonna tell me she was dead. You didn't try to arrest her, did you?" I say.

"What? No. Fuck no. That woman would turn me into a smear on the sidewalk. No, it's about Annie."

"Annie," I say. "Your wife Annie? Or are we talking a different Annie here?"

"Who the hell else would I be talking about? Anyway, Annie and I have been having trouble. The fires didn't help."

"The fires, or the years of lying to her about magic?" Letitia's married to a normal and—I have no idea how—managed to hide the fact that she's a mage, and that magic even exists, from her for their entire relationship.

Letitia narrows her eyes and keeps going. "That, too," she says. "With everything going on, she's . . . not needy? Needing more from me, I guess?" When it comes to relationships, I'm really not the most sensitive guy out there. And even I can see where she fucked this up.

"She learned magic's real," I say, ticking off points on my fingers. "Her wife's a mage. She got shot. L.A. burned down around her. All on the same day. I think more attention is a pretty reasonable thing to want."

"I know it is," Letitia says, frustration turning to anger.

"Honestly, I'm surprised she didn't shoot you."

She waves it off. "Whatever. The problem isn't me wanting to be there, it's that I can't. I haven't been home in two days. And when I am home, we fight. I had to talk to Gabriela a week back about some of the supernaturals that got burned out of their hidey holes. When I told Annie about it she went ballistic."

"Jesus, why'd you even tell her?"

"Because you told me to," Letitia says, her voice rising. She stops herself. "I took your advice and told her everything, and now I'm making sure to keep telling her everything."

"Well, that's your problem right there," I say. "You listened to me. Since when does Annie have a problem with Gabriela?" I say.

I understand why she has a problem with me. I'm the one who let the cat out of the bag about magic to her. She didn't believe me until later, of course, when Letitia finally came clean about it. All that ended with her getting shot and almost dying. If I hadn't been there to put her into a death coma, she wouldn't have made it. Of course, if I hadn't been there, none of that would have happened in the first place.

The only mage doctor around who could help was my ex, Vivian, who was working for Gabriela at the time, so I know they've met. The only thing I'd heard from Letitia since the fires about Annie is that she'd recovered, but that's all.

"She has a problem with thinking that I'm going to leave her for Gabriela," Letitia says.

"Come again?" I say.

"It's complicated. She doesn't trust me. Says that if I lied about the magic, then what else am I lying about. She's latched onto the idea that since Gabriela's a mage, and I'm a mage, that Gabriela and I must be fucking."

"Are you?"

"No. Of course not," she says. "Jesus, Eric. And it's

not just that. Annie was raised Catholic. Bad enough that she had to deal with that shit while figuring out she was gay, now she's trying to reconcile all of it with magic. She's been watching these witchcraft and demon documentaries online. She asked me if mages are blood-drinking baby murderers the other day."

"To be fair, I've known a few who are."

"Not helping," she says. "I try to explain to her how it works, what we are, but there's never enough time and we just end up fighting."

"Wow. You really fucked this one up, didn't you? Your entire relationship and you never told her about magic and then it all pops and you're surprised she's pissed off and confused? She's probably terrified."

And with good reason. We're terrifying people. I hope to hell Letitia hasn't told her anything about me other than that I'm an asshole. For a questioning Catholic, knowing Santa Muerte's real would be bad enough; I can't even imagine how she'd deal with Aztec gods.

Letitia shoves the heels of her palms into her eyes. "I know this," she says. "Nothing I try helps."

"That's why you're staying away from Gabriela," I say.

"Yes."

"Does she believe you when you tell her that?"

"Fuck, Eric, I don't know."

It makes sense, I guess. I can understand Annie being angry and scared. Magic's always been in my life, so it's no big deal. Even mages who realize they have talent late in life deal with it pretty well. Weird shit just happens around them, so actually finding a reason for it makes things easier.

Normals who learn about it react in one of three ways. They deny it, they accept it, or they fight against it. Sounds like Annie's still deciding between options two and three.

"Man, I thought I pissed people off."

"You're pissing me off," she says helpfully.

"Like that's new. Okay. I'll talk to Gabriela. See if she's got anything that can help protect against ghosts. Some charms, spells, something. I need to let her know what the hell's going on, anyway. Between the chop shop and the extortion attempt at the house, I'm getting a distinct 'crime family' vibe off of this. It'll end up on her doorstep sooner or later."

"Oh, shit. With all this about ghosts I almost forgot why I needed to talk to you." She pulls an envelope from her jacket pocket and hands it to me. It's a typical letter-sized envelope with my name written on the front.

"Arrest warrant?"

"I wish. I have no idea what the hell it is. I found it on my desk this morning."

"You opened it," I say.

"What kind of person do you think I am?" she says, voice full of outrage. "Of course I opened it. After checking it for wards and making sure it wasn't going to blow up in my face. You're welcome, by the way. Still don't know what the hell it means." I reach into the torn envelope, tug out a short stack of papers and a note with two words on it.

Billy Kwan.

Shit. This day just keeps getting better.

Chapter 6

"Is that money?" Letitia says. "Chinese yuan? It looks familiar."

Bright red and green banknotes, wrapped in a paper band. They're slightly larger than American dollars, with different portraits in the middle of both sides. The top note says that it's for one million yuan.

"Something like that," I say. For a moment I'm worried that these are more than they appear, but I'm not sensing anything unusual about them. They're just paper. "It's joss paper. Money for the dead. You burn it to honor your ancestors at funerals, festivals, give it to the bride at weddings. Real big during Zhong Yuan Jie. Chinese ghost festival."

"That's where I've seen it. Down in Chinatown. I've heard of it," she says. "Ghost money, right?"

"Ghost money, Hell money, it's all the same thing. One side's got Yù Huáng, the Taoist Jade Emperor, printed on it," I say, tapping the portrait on the bill, then flip it over. "Other side's got the ruler of Hell, or fuck, what are they called? Narakas? They're like individual Buddhist hells. Anyway, that guy's Yama, or Yanluo. Has a couple other names. Oversees the hells, but also passes judgment on the dead. The idea is that burning the money gives it to your ancestors so they can get by in the afterlife."

"This can't be a coincidence," she says. "The ghosts, these notes? Who's Billy Kwan?"

"When I knew him, he was a two-bit hustler selling heroin to Hong Kong tourists. Met him in a bar when a ghost slipped through the veil and came after everyone in there. Nobody saw it but me. After the bartender was killed in front of us, I was able to give everybody in the bar the ability to see it long enough to give them a chance to lose their shit and run. And Jesus fuck did they run. One guy went right through the front window. It was actually kinda funny."

"There is something wrong with your sense of humor," Letitia says.

"Oh, so many things," I say. "Anyway, Billy and I stayed."

"Guy's got balls," she says.

"That or he's monumentally stupid. I never really could tell." Billy always told me that he couldn't stand by and watch horrible things happen to good people. He even said it with a straight face. It was absolute horseshit, but who am I to judge? Guy wants to keep his reasons to himself, I let him.

"Anyway, Billy stuck around after I trapped the ghost in a cocktail napkin," I say. I remember hanging on to that napkin for a little while, though I honestly can't remember why. Pretty sure it was important, but I haven't thought about it in almost twenty years.

"A cocktail napkin?" Letitia says. "Seriously?"

"Yeah. You can use almost anything as a spirit jar, though actual containers are best. There's a possessed painting holding two demons in Chicago. That one, shit, what's it called? With the pitchfork and the farm?"

"American Gothic?"

"That's the one. They've been stuck in there since the forties. I knew someone who trapped a demon in a car a while back. That was a mistake. It wasn't so much trapped as given four wheels and a V-8. Why anybody would stick a demon inside some 1950s junker I have no idea."

"You didn't ask?"

"I would have," I say, "but the mage who did it was the first person it ran over." That one sucked. I flash to a memory of a moonless night running through a cornfield with a vintage Pontiac on my ass. Ended up taking it out with a combine thresher.

"I don't know what Billy's deal was, but he always had an angle he was working. He had some connections to a couple guys in the triads. He convinced them to help us out. It didn't take a lot of convincing. Whole different attitude toward ghosts over there."

I look over the notes, trying to find anything that might give me a clue as to who sent the package. The obvious answer is Billy, and if he's in town then this is more like Kowloon than I thought. The notes would be a reminder, I guess. Like I need reminding. You can get this stuff all over the city, not just Chinatown. Why's he being so cryptic? Afraid somebody will understand it who he doesn't want to? Maybe, but there's another possibility.

It isn't Billy. I'm sure a few of the triad guys he was dealing with to get us what we needed knew what it was for. And if it's a necromancer, then they might even have the original paper. There's a cheery thought.

"I had two problems when the shit hit the fan at Kowloon," I say. "The escaped ghosts and the holes in the barrier. The escapees were the easy part. I lured them with blood and then trapped each one in joss paper."

A flicker of worry crosses Letitia's face. "Is that—?"

"No," I say. "This is regular joss paper. No ghosts inside. Same stuff, though."

Letitia visibly relaxes. "So what about the holes the ghosts were coming through?"

"I couldn't figure out how to repair them, close them, anything. Eventually one of the other Kowloon ghosts would get through. I figured if I couldn't fix the holes, I could keep them stuck in there." Almost lost Billy in there. He helped me out and almost lost his soul.

"What, you built a cage to hold them all?"

"Pretty much, yeah," I say. "I got hold of a palette load of joss paper, turned them all into spirit bottles, dropped them in the center of the park and flipped the whole goddamn thing over to the other side. If I could pull the ghosts to the palette without dying, I'd be able to lock them away."

That was the first time I'd ever pulled something to the other side with me and it almost killed me. I didn't try it again for years.

"What'd you use as bait?" The look on my face must make it pretty obvious. "Seriously?"

"Who else was I gonna use? I climbed up and down the shadow version of the Walled City grabbing all the Wanderers' attention and luring them down." I traveled alleys that didn't exist, climbed roofs that had been torn down, crawled through ghostly duct work like it was Die Hard. And the whole time I'm trying to not pass out or throw up from the effort of the spell I'd used. I had some bad run-ins and had to stand my ground and fight a couple of times.

The worst was right after I got to the top. I'm trying to make my way back down with a fucking conga line of ghosts on my ass. No way in hell I'm going to outrun them. I'm a hundred and fifty feet in the air. I pop back over and I'll go crashing to the ground. If I don't, I get eaten by ghosts. I compromised by sliding over to the living side and then, as gravity yanked me down, sliding back. Back then that wasn't a spell I could do quickly or easily. It took me maybe thirty seconds to pull everything together any time I used it. A thirty second freefall before I could switch back would end with me making a nice little crater.

I had to run while prepping the spell, holding onto it in my mind, keeping it together, and prepping another one at the same time. So when I triggered the first one, I immediately triggered the second.

In the time it took I dropped about forty feet, impacting four stories down in Kowloon. Broken hand, dislocated shoulder, cracked clavicle. But hey, I was alive enough to bitch about it, right? Harder to complain if you're eaten by ghosts.

"Once I got most of them to the bottom, I needed more time for the rest to show up. I was barely holding them back. Fortunately, I had help. I made some paper charms with the cross-over spell to pull Billy over."

Paper charms are kind of like spirit jars, but instead of demons they trap spells. They don't have to be paper, but it's easiest that way. You can jot them down and let them loose with whatever you decide to use as a trigger. Throw it to the floor, set it on fire, whatever the designer wants. I wasn't great at that kind of magic. Any ones I created would most likely fizzle out. The only way to test them was to use them. I made half a dozen or so for him to try. Chances were at least one of them would work.

"You made him be bait?" Letitia gives me a look like she's just seen me shit out live scorpions.

"Made him? Fuck no. I *let* him be bait. That was the plan. Hell, it was his idea. I was against it from the start. He got tagged a couple of times, but not too seriously. When the rest of the ghosts finally showed up, I set off all the traps. Looked like somebody'd tossed a road flare into a fireworks factory. Like the goddamn Death Star."

I honestly can't tell if these notes are a trap to make me think Billy's in town or an actual message from him. Maybe they're a warning about him. Shit, I don't know.

I'm having trouble seeing him behind this. Billy's not a mage, and he never really struck me as the kind of guy who could pull off something that involved more planning than which bar to set up shop in. But then, that was twenty years ago. People can change a lot in twenty years.

I must have said something out loud because Letitia says, "Whether they're from him or not, one of the triads has to be in on it."

"I agree, but how do you figure that?"

"They're the only common denominator here. No way in hell that chop shop was an independent outfit, they don't work that way. And the guy at the house? He was connected to the chop shop. And what you did in Hong Kong? You had triad help."

"Okay," I say. "I can see that. But which one? I'm a little rusty on who's who these days."

"The ones out here all have a mage or two," she says. "I know of a few who work for Sun Yee On and Dub C, couple in 14K and Four Seas. Pretty low level, though. They keep it on the down low. None of these guys are powerful enough to stand on their own."

"Or it might be completely unrelated to any of them," I say. "The guys in the chop shop were working for somebody, but even they might not know who. You know how these things go. One guy knows the guy above him and that's it. They could have been poached out of their organization and not even be aware of it. I'm not sure what this whole thing is yet."

"I'll look into it," she says. "We're short staffed, but

we still have a gang unit. And most organized crime is being handled by Vice these days. They might have heard something." She looks at her watch and stands. "Speaking of which, I have to head back. Some of us have real jobs, ya know." She pauses and starts to say something.

"No," I say, cutting her off.

"You don't even know what I was going to say."

"Sure I do. You were going to ask me to tell Gabriela what's going on with you and Annie because obviously you haven't told her about the whole situation and you want to know whether she's mad at you or not, though I'm not quite sure why you care and don't really want to know. It is, as they say, not my circus, and not my monkeys."

"Fuck you, Eric," she says.

"Am I wrong?" She answers me by turning on her heel and walking away, giving me a raised middle finger. "So that's a no?"

———

I leave the car parked in the impromptu lot and take a walk to clear my head. The ghost money and the note have me rattled. It tells me that this is related to what happened in Hong Kong, at least, but not much else. If Billy left me the note, he didn't give me any way to get hold of him. And if it's a warning from someone else about him, it's irritatingly cryptic.

So it's an interesting data point, but that's about it. Right now I have other concerns—the Skid Row ghosts, though in light of everything else I have to wonder how closely related they are to each other. The ghosts are thick in Skid Row, just like they are everywhere, but as I head farther south the numbers shoot up dramatically. A lot of Echoes, a lot of Wanderers, not many Haunts. Fitting. Most of the people who died here didn't exactly have a fixed address.

Some of the Echoes are old enough that their deaths are shootings, stabbings, beatings, getting run down by cars. But a lot of them are from the fire. I can see them burning to death in agony before looping back to the beginning and doing it all over again. Fire is an ugly way to go out. At least the Echoes don't have any sort of consciousness.

The Wanderers and Haunts are the ones in bad shape. Some of them think they're still burning and run around screaming and slapping at themselves, trying to beat back phantom flames. Others are little more than walking skeletons, charred skin and bones, still surprised by what's happened to them.

Most of them will never understand, just go on being confused, perpetually surprised. Short-term memory isn't their strong suit. But others will remember. They'll go feral in fear and agony, and those are the ones I have to watch out for if I cross the veil. Haunts are usually not a big deal, since they can't follow outside of their pretty restricted areas. But Wanderers will come at me like a fucking zombie horde. It's a sight to see. If you like shitting your pants, that is.

The barrier between our worlds isn't usually something I can feel. Like your own heartbeat, you only notice it when it's not there. I come across a few spots where it's definitely thinned. The largest is outside a building that's nothing more than charred sticks and fire-blasted masonry. A clot of Echoes, Haunts, and Wanderers crowd inside and outside all the way down the street. This was probably one of the homeless shelters. If you couldn't get a bed, at least you could get a shower, maybe a meal. On a typical night the street would be lined with tents, blankets, abandoned grocery carts. Everyone here was caught unawares.

I'm not sure how it's going to play out here in Skid Row. The thin places where any holes would open up seem to be mostly at ground level with a few just a couple stories up. Skid Row buildings aren't very tall. The area's not nearly as dense as Kowloon, but I think there might be more holes scattered across a wider area of Downtown. I want to map them out, get a better idea of what I'm dealing with, and see if any of the ghosts I ran into at the house or the chop shop came from here.

The ghosts I dealt with in Kowloon were pretty tightly constrained. Most of the Wanderers didn't stray too far from the place. But everyone who died here was used to picking up stakes and moving on to somewhere else. They're already pretty dispersed, so I'm not sure trapping them is much of an option. Maybe if I set traps so that the effects overlapped each other?

An easier alternative might be to get them to disperse. That should get rid of the thin spots, but I don't know for sure. The Wanderers could just as easily create new ones somewhere else if they move in a group.

Aside from the ghosts the street is mostly abandoned. All but the most hardened homeless have moved on, either into one of the shelter camps or to some other bolt hole. Some of them have carved out a niche for themselves here, and they're not going to move no matter how dangerous it might be. The police and National Guard don't come in here very often, they're stretched too thin, only making occasional forays to see if there are any more bodies to pick up.

About an hour later I've gotten a good idea of where the thin spots are. The fact that the city has closed off so many streets and the National Guard is patrolling outside is a good thing. Not many people on the inside. Slipping past the few Guardsmen I run into is a snap with a HI, MY NAME IS sticker where I wrote "I'm not really here," and pushed some magic through. With it stuck onto the front of my coat, nobody pays any attention to me.

I tag the scorched sidewalks where I find any holes with silver Krylon spray paint. This way, I can find them easily enough. If it goes like Kowloon, the ghosts are going to be clustered around the gaps, either trying to push through or else drawn to the life they feel leaking over from the other side.

I need to have some conversations and I want to make sure that anything I'm talking to stays on that side of the veil. I find a roughly clean patch of concrete inside a burnt-out shop well away from any of the thin spots, and sit cross-legged on the floor. I take my jacket off, roll up my sleeve. Small silver bowl in front of me, straight razor in my hand. One quick slash, not too deep. I let the blood drip into the bowl and immediately have the attention of every single ghost in a quarter mile radius.

The Wanderers rush in, circling me, hovering over the blood. Men, women, children, Asian, Latino, black, white. They stare at the blood with a desperation in their eyes that will only grow as they get older. Some of them can exist for centuries. Those can be the most dangerous.

"All right, back the fuck up," I say, pushing them back with my will. They shift farther away, but none of them leave. "I need some space. Now, who wants to tell me about anything weird that's happened recently?" Hands shoot up into the air. I pick a woman whose skin is charred black, her face a bare skull with melted skin and shattered teeth. She points at me, reinforcing the fact that they're not the sharpest knives in the drawer.

"Okay, maybe a little earlier than now? Two, four days ago?" Ghosts are horrible timekeepers, so I might hear about something that happened last week or a decade and a half ago.

One of the ghosts, a man in a torn-up track suit

with no shoes and severe burns on one side of his face, says, "Excuse me. Chinese guy? He was trying to talk to us like you, but not doing a very good job of it."

"How so?"

"He couldn't talk well. Not like you." His voice is a thin echo on the wind, and self-aware he might be, but all there he's not. "He asked if any of us wanted to . . ." He trails off then seems to wake up. "He couldn't do it. Not for all of us."

Asked? Now that's weird. Nobody asks a ghost for anything. You want a ghost to do something, you make it. Doesn't always work, but asking would be pointless. They don't have much in the way of drive. They're more likely to forget or lose interest halfway through. Might as well ask a tree if it's okay becoming firewood.

"Couldn't do what exactly?" I say. The ghost isn't looking at me anymore, just staring at the bowl of blood. I snap my fingers under his nose, catching his attention.

"Open a door for us. He could only get it to work for a few of us. He couldn't get it to work for the rest. A lot of us got angry and tried to get at him, and his people, but we couldn't. I'm hungry. I'm so hungry."

"The people with him. How many were there?"

"Three? Four? I don't remember."

"You got a name?"

"I'm Frank," the ghost says.

"I meant the guy's name."

"What guy?"

Ah, well. It was fun while it lasted. His attention is completely on the blood in the dish. I'm not going to get anything else useful out of him. I slide the dish toward him and say, "All yours, Frank. Enjoy it with my compliments." The ghosts descend on the dish, but only Frank has permission to take any of it. He goes at it like a starving hyena, the dish rattling as he laps it up. In seconds he's done; the blood is still in the dish, some sloshed over the side, but it's inert, completely devoid of life.

Chinese guy with some necromantic training, but I doubt he is one. Just like with any knack, necromancers can do some things instinctively without anybody to show us the ropes. Not being able to pull a ghost through the veil, I can understand. Not sure I can do that. But not being able to talk to the dead very well? That's shit necros can do whether we want to or not. Unless I completely misunderstood what the ghost told me, there's no way that this guy is a necromancer.

And he had people with him. Bodyguards? An entourage? Either rich and paranoid or working for someone who is. Assuming the first, I can ask around about any wealthy Chinese mages in town. I know a few people I can ask.

If he's working for someone the triad theory becomes more likely. The only high point seems to be that he hasn't figured out yet how to compel a ghost. If he did, he wouldn't have bothered asking for volunteers. He'd just order them all to come with him and they'd have to comply.

It occurs to me that this might actually be worse than it sounds. This guy couldn't pull the ghosts out, yet that's exactly what's happening. Which might mean there's somebody else. One mage trying this shit is bad enough. Two is not something I even want to think about.

If the triads are part of this, I can see it getting messy fast. Let's say they are. It could create a necromantic arms race. First, they'd get the ghosts to actually target their kills rather than just the nearest thing at hand. Right now, letting them loose is like letting loose a bunch of pissed-off snakes in a crowded elevator. Everybody in there gets bit. But what else could they train them to do? Steal? Kidnap? Possess and influence someone? That seems a bit far-fetched for most ghosts, but then I didn't think a necromancer could yank ghosts into our world either.

My mind's spinning with too many questions and no answers. So much so that I haven't been paying attention to my surroundings. Somebody's tailing me. And that's never a good thing.

Chapter 7

White guy, a little overweight, kind of balding. He's wearing a windbreaker that's just this side of wrong for the weather, but it has deep pockets. I always worry about people who have deep pockets. You never know what's gonna be stuffed in them.

I pretend to ignore him and walk casually down the street and down an alley between two buildings that escaped the fires relatively unscathed. I pull a HI, MY NAME IS sticker from my messenger bag and write down THERE IS NOTHING BEHIND ME in black Sharpie before slapping it onto the side of a dumpster. I crouch low behind it and wait.

The guy tailing me doesn't disappoint. A couple minutes later he wanders past the alley, glancing in to see if I'm there. He stops when he can't see me. He rushes into the alley and looks around, completely bewildered that he can't find me. The alley is a cul de sac. The only way in or out is through the entrance to the street.

He spies a manhole cover, looks it over, and ignores it. He's clearly not *too* stupid. If he's got any brains then he can tell it hasn't been moved for years. The pavement is old, but it hasn't been scored by dragging out the heavy manhole cover in a really long time.

"The fuck," he says, turning around a couple more times, looking up, under, and behind things. He even comes over to my side of the dumpster and looks right at me. His eyes skip over me like I'm not even there.

I wait until his back is to me, then step up out of my crouch and get him into a sleeper hold. But dude's got some moves. The wily fucker drops to the side and twists, getting out of the choke and hooking his leg behind my knee, and I go down.

At this point the Sharpie spell breaks. It's hard to ignore getting choked out. He tries to curb stomp my head and I roll out of the way, reaching out with one hand to grab his ankle. His head bounces off the pavement when I pull him off his feet.

A second later we're both back. He's pretty good for an overweight, balding, middle-aged man. Probably a Marine. He reaches into his jacket pocket and yanks out an expandable baton, snapping it to its full length and taking a swing at my knee. I barely get out of range in time.

"The fuck, man?" I say. "I thought we were doing this all manly and shit, and you go and pull that out? Is that a penis replacement? This is all getting way too Freudian for me."

"What?" He pauses as he tries to parse what I just said, and I take advantage of this moment of confusion to decide that if he gets to bring toys to a fight then so do I, and I hit him with a force spell that slams him against the wall with the sound of breaking bones. I hold him up there for a minute, my spell pressing against his throat. His face turns purple, his struggling slows down. I let him fall to the ground just as he loses consciousness.

"All right, pal," I say, rummaging through his pockets and finding his wallet. "Let's see who you are." His driver's license says his name is Hank Wells, and his private investigator and concealed carry licenses say the same thing. Not surprisingly, he's armed. A hold-out on his ankle and a .40 Smith & Wesson in a belly holster. Nice guns. I don't need them, but I toss them into my messenger bag just to piss off the Browning.

In Hank's back pocket there's a shitty photo of me taken through a telephoto lens printed on cheap paper with the word TRUNK in big black letters, double-underlined. Well, that would be simple and straightfor-ward, except for the fact that his car keys are for a Honda Civic. Maybe Hank here knows something I don't, but I don't think I'm fitting into a Civic's trunk. I decide to test that theory.

I write up another don't-look-at-me spell in Sharpie on a sticker and toss Hank's dead weight over my shoulder. Almost takes me to the ground. Dude needs to cut down on the pizza and beer.

The only cars I saw were parked in the lot, and sure enough when I get there and hit the button on Hank's key fob, a blue Civic chirps and the trunk pops open. I lift it up to toss him in and stop. Goddammit.

The floor of the trunk is not the floor of a trunk. It's a door. Not a big one, but it takes up the entire space. It's brass-tacked red leather with a wide handle on it. I know this door. I've been through a whole bunch just like it over the years, but there's no way in hell I'm going through this one. This door goes to the inside of a djinn's bottle, a pocket universe under his control.

I'm not sure which pisses me off more, the fact that Darius is trying to kidnap me, or that he's using such a shitty amateur to do it. I'm really leaning toward the shitty amateur. I lift open the door with one hand and see nothing but black on the other side. I let it fall closed and toss the unconscious P.I. on top of it.

I've been wondering when something like this was go-ing to happen. I hadn't heard anything from Darius since I told him I didn't know where his bottle was and limped out of his bar. But I'm not stupid enough to think he would just give up. I'd been keeping an eye out for tails, and hadn't spotted any before. Doesn't mean they weren't there, just that I wasn't seeing them.

I'd assumed if he wanted to do something, he'd get a goddamn professional to do it. Now I'm rethinking that. Has he been looking for the bottle and finally decided that since he can't find it, he'd throw somebody at me to bring me in? Or was P.I. Hank a distraction, and the professionals have been on me the whole time?

Extreme paranoia never looks good on anybody, so I ditch that thought. What the hell would throwing this guy at me get him if he had better people already on the case?

The timing is interesting, though. Ghosts are popping through the veil and Darius is sending goons after me? Yeah, couldn't possibly be related. Darius has a way of manipulating events. When Quetzalcoatl came after me and it turned out it was just an excuse to get me to find the bottle, I wondered if Darius had somehow orchestrated it. The hell do I know about what goes on in his head? I can't prove it, but I can feel it in my gut.

Darius can't open his bottle from the inside, but that doesn't mean somebody he trusts can't open it from the outside. I've made a point of leaving it alone. I'm the only one who knows where it is, and now I'm certain Darius knows that. But the only way he's going to find it is if I tell him where it's stashed. But even if I did, it's useless information. I'm the only one who can get there.

I resist the urge to go back to the Ambassador Hotel to check on it. It's not likely anyone could follow me over to the other side or get into the ghost of the Ambassador without getting eaten by it, let alone into the room my grandfather bargained with the hotel's ghost to keep there. I don't know where the room's door goes, but from the view out the window it sure as shit ain't anywhere on this planet.

The site of the hotel is a now a school named after Robert Kennedy, who was assassinated in the hotel's kitchen, which really makes me wonder about the sort of message L.A. schools are trying to give kids. That's the safest point to shift over to the other side. It's within the bounds of the hotel, and the Ambassador is the biggest, baddest ghost in the area. So long as it doesn't turn on me, I should be fine.

Say someone gets past the hotel, gets into the room, gets the bottle. They still can't open it unless they know ancient Aztec death god rituals. Mictecacihuatl sealed it up five hundred years ago and nobody's been able to open it since.

Santa Muerte might be able to, but there's no way in hell she would unless she could take the opportunity to destroy Darius once and for all. Which might not be a bad idea, except for the fact that he kicked the shit out of all the other Aztec gods before he got to Mictlan, and she's not exactly herself these days.

If somebody more competent than P.I. Hank is tailing me, and I lead them to the school, that gets Darius one step closer to finding the bottle. Leaving it alone and watching my ass is the safest thing I could do.

I think Hank and I need to have a little chat.

I wake up Hank with smelling salts. He jerks, eyes popping open, rolling around in their sockets. He slips back into unconsciousness and it takes a few gentle slaps to bring him out of it completely. I have him wrapped in duct tape and chained around his middle to the hook of a two-ton cherry picker that has him a good four feet off the ground.

He thrashes around a bit, but all he does is manage to slowly spin himself in a circle. When his eyes focus, he doesn't seem happy to see me. His glance over my shoulder is more telling. He doesn't look happy to see all the bodies behind me either, but he doesn't seem terribly surprised.

"Hi," I say, big smile on my face, all sunshine and unicorns. "I don't think we've been properly introduced. I'm Eric." I gesture with my hands at the pile of corpses behind me. "These are some dead people. I understand you're Hank. Hank, dead people. Dead people, Hank."

"You did this?" he says, his voice somewhere between revulsion and awe.

I've brought him to the Burbank chop shop, dropping a sleep spell on him to keep him unconscious for the trip. I've dragged the desiccated bodies of the dead mechanics into a rough heap so Hank can get a good look at their sunken faces, their paper-thin skin draped over jutting bones.

"Oh, I didn't do anything," I say. "No, it was the ghosts."

"Ghosts?"

"Yeah, you know. WoooOOOooooo. Ghosts. One of these guys—uh, that one, with the face all half melted. He let a bunch of them loose. The ghosts ate him and then went to town on his buddies. It happens. Now it would be a real tragedy if those ghosts came back and ate you too, don't you think?"

"It wouldn't be my first choice, no," he says. All things considered, he's taking this pretty well.

"I'm really glad to hear that, Hank. So why don't you tell me why you're following me and I'll make sure they don't."

"How?" he says. "You can't control them. Not completely. They're all feral and shit."

"Really? Now this is interesting. What makes you say that?"

He laughs, but it's a hollow sound, the kind I've heard from men who know everything's gone to shit and they're not expecting to live much longer. "I was sloppy," he says. "I'll be the first to admit that. You should never have seen me in Skid Row. But I'd like some credit for the fact that you didn't see me here or back at the house in Montecito Heights."

"I think I would have noticed if you'd been here."

"Well, not *here* here," he says. "I was outside. But I did see you come out dragging that one guy. What happened to him? I saw him buck around like he was having a seizure and then he sort of . . . deflated. That what it looks like when a ghost eats you?"

"Apparently," I say.

"What, you don't know? I thought that's how you liked to kill people, by feeding them to ghosts."

"It does have a certain je ne sais quoi about it, yeah. But that's not on this side. Darius tell you that? I imagine he'd have given you some sort of briefing." He barely twitches, but I notice it anyway. "Oh. You didn't realize I know you're working for Darius. Yeah, that makes sense. You were kind of unconscious when I found the door in your trunk."

"Goddammit. I told him that was a stupid idea."

"Why are you following me, Hank? And don't tell me you don't know. Darius holds shit back, but he likes to give folks enough information to hang themselves with."

"He thinks you have something that belongs to him. He wants me to find it."

"And that thing would be?"

"Confidential," he says.

"Okay, look, we could do this all day, denying shit up, down, and sideways, and not get anywhere. So al-low me to speed things along. He wants you to find his bottle. He thinks I have it. I don't. He doesn't believe me. So you're here to see where I go and where I might have put it. That about the size of it?"

"Yeah," he says, resignation in his voice. "So what now? You gonna feed me to your ghosts?"

"Not if you answer my questions. Why you?"

"What?"

"If he wanted to find something of his, it seems a little weird that he'd send a person like you. Normal. No magic that I can tell. Obviously you know about this shit or we wouldn't even be having this conversation. But I haven't felt you do any magic or pull any power."

"Maybe I'm just that good," he says.

"No. If you were any good you wouldn't be skulking around in a Honda Civic as a private detective."

"That's rich coming from you. How many cars have you stolen in the last week?"

"I'm a big believer in Marxist theory," I say. "Collective ownership, common property, that kind of thing. Look, I don't know if you know what Darius is, but if you do, then you probably know that if he wants talent he can pretty much get whatever he needs. There's a reason he sent you. What is it?"

"I don't know."

"Okay. Let me go see if I can scare up some of those ghosts."

"Wait. Hang on. Jesus. I'm wondering the same thing. Yeah, I know about magic. I've dealt with it. But I don't know why he wanted me."

I can think of a couple reasons but none of them make much sense. It's easy to underestimate normals. Hank is clearly a professional. I didn't see him until he slipped up in Skid Row, but I still caught him. He could be a decoy. He could be a trap. He could be lying about being normal and just hasn't shown me he's a mage.

"Is there anybody else following me?" I say.

"Not that I know of. Haven't seen anyone, at least."

"Why do you have the door in your trunk?"

"I give him reports a few times a day and it's easier than tracking down an unlocked door. It's not like I can call him. He doesn't exactly get cell reception in there."

"And what do your reports say?"

"Mostly that your life is pretty fucking sad. I've been following you around for the last two weeks. You've spent every night alone, at eight different motels and three abandoned houses. You've stolen seven cars. You've worn the same clothes the last five days in a row and before that it was a different suit, but almost identical. That's all he knows right now. I haven't checked in since before you were in Montecito Heights."

"He doesn't know about the ghosts," I say. I ignore the jab about my life being sad.

"If he does, he didn't hear it from me. Same about this place, or you hanging out with the cop over at the noodle truck. What'd she give you?"

"None of your fucking business," I say. Should I kill this guy? I could leave him hanging here, but he might get out of all that duct tape. I can't just cut him loose. Or can I?

"Thanks for the information, Hank," I say.

"What now?"

"Now, I let you go."

"What? I—"

I slap my palm on his forehead and hit him with a sleep spell. I'm not very good with them unless it involves putting someone into a death-like coma, but it should keep him out for a couple of hours. He slumps unconscious. I cut him down and he falls heavily to the concrete floor.

I write my phone number on a nametag and slap it on

his forehead. There's no magic in it, but he'll notice it's there. He'll tell Darius what happened, though I'm not sure he'll say anything about the phone number. I don't think Darius will pull him off this job. He'll wonder why I let him go and want to see where that leads.

I'm kind of curious myself.

Chapter 8

My life is not sad.

I say this to myself from behind the wheel of a stolen pickup in the parking lot of a half-burned motel with a large handwritten sign out front: WE HAVE ROOMS.

Okay, maybe my life is sad. You know what it's like, right? Surrounded by ghosts, married to a death goddess, entire family murdered, plenty of corpses left in your wake, and you wonder where it all went wrong?

No? Just me?

There's fuck-all I can do about any of that and I'm goddamn tired so I pull up my big boy britches and go get a room at a motel so seedy even the low-end rentboys won't come to it.

After the fires, the hotels and motels still standing jacked up their prices by three, four hundred percent. Rooms filled up fast, making them even more expensive. Then it got worse when the state jumped in and shut a bunch of them down for price gouging. Pretty soon the only rooms to be had were people renting out their own property because they didn't want to be in it themselves, burnt-out houses and skyscrapers, or places like this.

The room is nothing special. Bed, closet, bathroom. Stinks of smoke, but everything stinks of smoke right now and besides, it's hiding the scent of whatever else there might be dug into the carpets. I lock the door, set my wards, and just as I sit down my phone rings.

I see who it's from and hit the answer button. "Tell me you didn't kill her," I say.

"The fuck is wrong with that woman?" Gabriela says.

"Annie?"

"Of course, Annie. Fucking normals. Have you ever dated a normal?" she says.

"I always figured they were more trouble than they were worth. Then again, they probably wouldn't try to eat my soul. So, trade-offs, I guess."

"At first you think, 'Oh, hey, I don't have to deal with all the political mage bullshit. But then you let 'em know magic's real because you're in love and they're 'The One,' like who fucking knows that at sixteen, and they're all butthurt because you can throw a fireball, so they have to prove they're all macho and better than you because you're threatening their penis, and then next thing you know their family's all pissed off because you had to skin him and stick his goddamn head in their fucking mailbox."

After a moment of collecting my thoughts all I can come up with is, "That, uh, that sounds like a pretty personal example."

"Yeah, well, there are some things you don't let go of."

All right. Moving on. "Did Letitia actually tell you what's going on?" I say.

"She left a message about the ghosts. I got the gist. You and I need to talk."

"And Letitia?"

"Yeah, her too. You both need to see this."

"What is it?"

"A body."

———

My motel's in Jefferson Park a little west of USC. I take the pickup and take surface streets across the Fourth Street bridge to East L.A. The sun dips below the horizon, turning the sky a brilliant orange fading through to purple as the sunlight passes through all the smoke and haze. L.A. always looks its best when it's at its worst.

Gabriela's warehouse has a gated parking lot. Two guys with AKs open the gate for me, which is either good (they're the welcome wagon), or very, very bad (they're here to box me in and kill me).

It's a calculation I always have to make. I like Gabriela, but I know mages. One of these days we're going to find ourselves on the opposite sides of a problem and it's going to end badly for one of us. Part of being properly paranoid is trying to judge which of your friends will turn out to be an enemy who was just waiting for you to lower your guard.

The warehouse is a large industrial building with loading docks, bright spotlights on the eaves to get rid of any shadows someone might hide in, and snipers on the roof. If it were anybody else, I'd say the snipers were overkill, but sometimes I think they're not enough.

The second story windows are all covered with sheets of plywood. About a day before the firestorm, Quetzalcoatl had the city of Vernon blown up, the whole thing. Sure, Vernon isn't big, about five square miles, but when I say he blew it up, that's not hyperbole. The whole place went up in a five-hundred-foot-tall fireball.

The blast collapsed nearby structures. Three miles

away and it shook the warehouse like an earthquake and blew out the windows. Worse, it let loose a shit-ton of toxic chemicals into South L.A. and down toward Compton. Until the rest of the city burned it was the biggest humanitarian nightmare the city had ever seen. Evacuating people, getting to the dead and dying. It was going to take weeks and a concerted effort to get the Vernon blaze contained. And then everything burned, and it was just one more fire.

Inside the warehouse looks like any warehouse. Industrial shelving, crates and boxes, forklifts. There are a couple of shipping containers in front of a loading dock in the back. I don't know what she's storing, and I don't really want to. But you go upstairs and it's a different story. It looks like a rebel stronghold. People rushing back and forth. Command center at one end, infirmary and surgical suite at another. The small space in front of the windows used to be a lounge, but it's been changed into a workshop for repairing body armor and guns.

Gabriela is standing by a map of L.A. on one wall, pushing thumb tacks into it. She had the same thing in her hotel Downtown. Helped her keep track of all the different homeless supernaturals in the city. There are a lot more pins than I remember. Ever since her hotel burned down, everyone she was sheltering scattered, went to ground. She's been trying to regain their trust ever since.

When I first met her, she had the look of a sorority girl turned executive assistant. Professional, smiling, an excellent cover to hide her role as the Bruja. Then she got outed and finally said fuck it.

She's short, little over five feet, but her glittering purple Doc Martens give her an extra inch or two. The shimmering green-to-blue hair and tattoos creeping down her arms from underneath her short-sleeve shirt are new.

"Rocking the Suicide Girl look there," I say.

She shrugs. "I'll do something different next week. How's the hand?" she says.

"Aches sometimes." More than sometimes. And more than aches. Making a fist out of my left hand isn't easy, and I may never get full use of it back. But with my good friend oxycodone I'll be just fine.

"Really should have had Vivian look at that."

"I didn't want to take the chance she'd just lop it off."

"She wouldn't lop off your hand. She's a professional. She'd lop off your head," she says, turning to me, dropping a handful of colorful push pins onto a table next to the map. She sinks into a desk chair. She's covering well, but I see the bloodshot eyes, dark circles, fingernails ragged from all the biting. Seems nobody's getting any sleep these days.

"You don't look good," she says. "I mean you never look good, but you look especially not good right now."

"Looked in a mirror lately?"

"Yeah," she says. "But I have better hair."

"Can't argue that." I sit in a chair opposite, stretch my arms over my shoulders, and several joints I didn't know I had pop back into place.

"Seriously," she says. "What's wrong?"

"Besides everything?" I say. I go on when she doesn't respond. "Not sleeping, migraines, dizzy spells. I mean, come on, I eat like crap and there are some days I don't eat much of anything at all. How about you?"

"Holding things together," she says. "I'm not sleeping either. Trying to coordinate taking care of my people and their families while getting as many of the homeless supernaturals as I can some shelter is exhausting."

"How's it going?"

"Slow. Getting pushback from some of my folks. They don't understand that as long as these people are on the streets, humans are in more danger from them than ever before. There's just so much to do."

"Where's Letitia?"

"On her way. I wanted to talk to you before she got here."

"Am I gonna regret this conversation?" I say. "Whatever's going on with you two is your deal."

She looks confused for a second before enlightenment dawns. "Oh, Annie. That's Letitia's drama. I don't have time for that. I feel like I'm everybody's therapist lately. Whole goddamn city's got PTSD. You ever try to get a vampire to open up about their feelings?"

"Can't say I've had the pleasure." Usually when I've had to deal with them the only thing they're feeling is hungry and pissed off.

"Lucky you. Anyway, I wanted to talk to you about our mutual friend behind the red door."

I had wondered about mentioning Darius to her, but had decided against it. She's on friendly terms with him, has deals I don't know about. Figured I didn't need to go shitting on her carpet. Now I'm thinking I need to.

She knows how dangerous it'd be if anyone got hold of his bottle and cracked it open, but that doesn't mean he can't manipulate her into doing something that brings this whole thing down on me. I haven't told her that I have the bottle or even that I found it. But I can still let her in on the fact that he's keeping tabs on me.

"I haven't talked to him lately," I say. I'm about to say more when paranoia kicks up a notch. What if she's working for him, too? I shove that down hard. That thinking will get me nowhere.

"Me either," she says. "I haven't used his door since he locked me out before the fires." Darius creates doors as needed and very few of them last more than a few minutes at a time. I know of half a dozen that are semi-permanent, in that he hasn't decided to close them yet. One of them is here in the warehouse.

"I thought you two were close," I say.

"Business partners from time to time. I only trust him so far. Lately I think that's bothering him. I've seen the door open a couple of times, but I haven't gone in. He's not the sort to make an invitation that obvious. Usually he just puts a door down, it's up to you to open it or not."

"That does sound unusually . . . needy."

"Yeah. And I figure it has something to do with you."

"Bit of a leap, don't you think?"

"Eric, everything in this town that's gone to shit since you got back has had you in the middle of it."

"Fair point. So what do you think I've done?"

"Really? We're doing this?" she says. She gives me a long, considering look. "Are we enemies?"

"Are we friends?"

"You tell me," she says. "Yeah, you're a pain in my ass. But you and I have seen some shit together. You were free and clear of Santa Muerte and then went running right back to her, and that's after she tried to fucking kill you."

I've had this argument with her before. And I can't say she doesn't have a point. She knows the new Santa Muerte isn't like the old one. She's heard the word on the streets, talked to some of her followers. Things have shifted. But the remains of the old Santa Muerte are fused into the bones of the new one. Is she really different? Has having Tabitha bound up with her made her better? Safer? I honestly don't know.

"You tried to kill me, too," I say, reminding her of the first time we met.

"Everybody's tried to kill you. My point is that I'd

hope by now I'd rank a little higher than the death goddess who set you up and murdered your sister."

She's right. I've trusted her with my life. She's trusted me with hers.

But this is different. This is explosive. It can, it *will*, change everything.

It's also not something I can handle on my own.

"I have Darius's bottle," I say.

She jerks back like I've slapped her, wide-eyed, un-believing. Silence stretches between us the size of the Grand Canyon.

"Oh," she says. "Does he know?"

"Strongly suspects. I've denied it, but come on, he knows I'm lying. He's got some normal following me around hoping I'll lead him to it."

"You kill him?"

"Let him go. Better the devil you know and all that. I gave him my phone number. If he's gonna be on my ass anyway, I might as well have him where I can see him."

"You can always kill him later," she says, ever the pragmatist. "I can see why you didn't want to tell me. Now I'm definitely not going through that door."

"I notice you're not asking me where the bottle is."

"That's because I don't want to know. Is it safe?"

"Safe as I can make it."

"Okay. Keep me in the loop if you can. I get that might not always work out that way, but if the shit is about to hit the fan some warning would be nice."

A noise behind us. Letitia coming up the stairs. Did she hear any of that? My worry must show on my face because Gabriela shakes her head and points to the floor. Silencing wards in a circle around us. I hadn't noticed them before—they're unobtrusive, hard to spot in general, and I'm pretty crap at catch-ing wards anyway. We've been in a cone of silence since I came up here.

"Hey," Letitia says. She nods to me, an afterthought. All of her attention is on Gabriela. If she's nervous about being here with her, she doesn't show it. "You said there's a body."

"I did," Gabriela says. "Want to see it?"

━━━━━━

Gabriela takes us downstairs to the back of the warehouse where she's stored a refrigerated twenty-foot shipping container. The hum of the compressor mixes with the ambient sounds around us, turning it all into a wall of white noise.

"You just happened to have a refrigerator container lying around?" Letitia says.

"I was going to be using it for a job later this week to ship in . . . well, that's not important. Come on." She grabs a pair of thick gloves off a nearby shelf and lifts the latch on the container, pulling the doors wide open. Inside, there's a gurney with a sheet-covered body on it.

"Ghoul found him in a dumpster in Monterey Park," Gabriela says.

"Scavenger?" I say. Ghouls look enough like humans to blend in. Until they open their mouths. Then you get to see the unhinged jaws, the multiple rows of hooked teeth. They prefer human. Some hunt. Most scavenge. A surprising number own butcher shops.

"Yeah. He only goes after roadkill," Gabriela says. Roadkill. A quaint euphemism for dead hobos, junkies, the occasional back-alley suicide. I've known a few ghouls. Decent enough people. Just don't go to dinner with them.

"They're a goddamn menace," Letitia says.

"You don't approve?" Gabriela says. Something in her tone has Letitia backpedaling.

"It's not that," she says hastily. "Not all of them are scavengers. Tired of having to clean up their messes."

Or put them down, I imagine. Like Gabriela, Letitia's a pragmatist. But they have differing views on what is and isn't acceptable behavior.

Gabriela drops it, and we follow her into the freezer. "Like I said, he was found in Monterey Park. Justin— that's the ghoul—called me up when he found him. I asked him to bring him here." She pulls back the sheet slowly, but even before she gets past the man's chest I know he's going to look the same all the way down.

It's hard to tell how old he is, how much he weighed, his ethnicity. All that's left is a sunken-eyed mummy with gray, dried-out skin tight against the bones. And wounds I'd seen before, but never like this.

"Your ghoul find him naked?" I say.

"Not a stitch on him," Gabriela says. Letitia looks from Gabriela to me and back.

"Is that what ghost bites look like?" Letitia says.

"Bites, scratches, gouges," I say. "I don't really know what you'd call them. That's not the part that worries me." I lean down to get a closer look. "Some of these are healed."

"I thought once they attacked that was it," she says. "Game over."

"Usually," Gabriela says. "But that's on the other side. Over here, I don't know how they'd act. It looks like the ghost left and went back a few times before finishing the job. Probably took a chunk of his soul with each bite."

"It's more than one ghost," I say. It's hard to explain, but my gut is telling me there were four, maybe five ghosts that went after him. I point to the ragged skin around his wrists. "Rope, maybe chains. Somebody did this to him. Tied him up, set these ghosts loose. And then pulled them back."

"How?" Gabriela says. She knows ghosts, she's dealt with them, and she knows that controlling them is a pain in the ass. They do what I want them to when

I talk to them because I'm on this side and I'm paying them in blood. But when we're on the same side, as far as they're concerned, I'm lunch.

"I don't know. But there's got to be another necromancer in town," I say. Goddammit. It'd be nice to find somebody I can talk shop with who I don't eventually have to murder. Especially when they could teach me a new trick.

"I'm wondering why," Letitia says. "Torture? That seems kind of complicated for torture." It's a good question, and when the answer comes to me it makes me sick to my stomach.

"He's a bait dog," I say.

"Fuck," Gabriela says. She closes her eyes and slides the sheet back over him. "Why didn't I see it?"

"What's a bait dog?" Letitia says.

"Dogfighting," I say. "It's how you train your dogs to attack. Get a smaller, weaker dog, tie it up as bait, and let the others at it. Or get something that can't fight back and let it loose in the pit. The weaker and more submissive, the better. Puppies are a favorite."

"Jesus," Letitia says. "Now I know why all the detectives on dogfight duty always look like they're about to throw up."

"Whoever did this," I say, "is pulling ghosts from the other side, trapping them, changing them, and then has enough control over them to train them."

In fact, I think I've seen some of the results. Damien in the Montecito Heights house. Those ghosts attached to him were nibbling at him. Instead of devouring him in a heartbeat, they were slowly taking him apart piece by piece.

"That's not good," Gabriela says.

Some people have a real gift for understatement.

Chapter 9

"I need to find Billy Kwan," I say. "Or at least find out what the fuck he has to do with all this." I drop heavily into a couch on the second floor that faces the windows. The last time I sat here, I was showered with glass when Vernon went up in a fireball on the horizon. One of the windows is still boarded up.

"I can put the word out," Gabriela says. "But knowing Justin, he's already spread the story about the fucked-up corpse he brought to me. Boy can't keep his mouth shut. It's going to get the attention of whoever did this. I should start hearing more in the next day or so."

"I checked around the station and nobody remembers seeing somebody dropping that envelope off at my desk," Letitia says. "Security footage was a bust, too. System's been down since we moved out of Parker and nobody's gotten it back up since we moved back in. Low priority."

"Anything on the triads?"

"Not yet. Organized crime is a backseat problem right now. Most of the force is just trying to keep riots from breaking out in the refugee camps."

I know it's bad out there. I see it every day driving through the city. More gas stations are closed than open, whole city blocks are piles of burnt timber and ash. Power is still out in almost half the city. But I still forget how bad most people have it.

The camps are the worst. People are afraid and confused and there are too many of them crammed into too small a space. Nobody's keeping them there, but where the hell are they going to go? If you're in a camp it's because you've got nowhere else to stay. They have to turn people away at the gates. Food and water trucks are hijacked on the daily.

The best the government can do is hold back the tide, and they're doing a shit job of that. And the mages? Well, we're just fine, thank you very much. We've got our ivory towers, our untouched pocket universes. We don't pay attention to the little people. We're the point-zero-one percenters, and most normals don't even know we exist.

I've never felt like one of us, the privileged few, the top of the heap, though I know I am. Sure, nobody likes necromancers. Especially other necromancers. But even if I don't acknowledge it, or wish it would go away, I've got power. Power grants privilege. I know this. Whether I choose to use it or not is a different story entirely.

I'm trying to save people. I'm making a difference. I'm pushing out the doubts that say I'm just going to fuck it all up, like I fuck everything else up. I'm a hatchet man. I cut down things that can kill everybody and they don't even know about it. And if I blow it, well, look around you.

But if I don't stop whoever's bringing ghosts across soon, it's not going to be a mage problem, or a normal problem. It's going to be an everybody problem. I'm doing something. I'm doing something that nobody else can do. At least I keep telling myself that.

"All right," I say. "I've got a couple ideas of how I can find Billy, but I need to sleep on it." I stand up from the couch and head toward the stairs. "I'll catch the two of you up later." Letitia stands to leave with me, but Gabriela stops her.

"Let's talk," she says.

I show myself out. One of Gabriela's boys is going up as I'm heading down. I stop him and shake my head. He gets it and goes down with me, stopping at the foot of the stairs to keep anyone else from going up.

I don't know the kind of shit Letitia's going through right now. I've never been in her shoes. Dating a normal I can understand. Marrying one, even. But keeping magic a secret from her this whole time? Why do that? Shit, how do you do that? I'm not judging, I'm just trying to figure out the logistics. I hope she can work out whatever it is she needs to work out. In this shitshow of a world it'd be nice to see somebody happy.

———

A black Mercedes S 560 says a lot about a person. It says they're wealthy, recognize luxury when they see it. When it's the only car parked in the lot of a half-burned no-tell motel, it also says they're probably that kind of asshole who likes to wave his dick around. Inconspicuous it isn't.

There's a particular type of person who has that much audacity, and they're the type who don't like waiting. There's another type of person who doesn't really like that type of person and is more than happy to keep that type of person waiting to see the type of person who doesn't give a flying fuck whether they want to see them or not.

With that in mind, I park in front of my room next to the Mercedes, kick on the pick-up's brights to shine into the room's curtained window, lean back, and see how much I can piss off a stranger.

Whoever is in my room isn't going to try to kill me.

Car's too nice for that. They might order me killed, and if experience is anything to go by they probably will—if not tonight, then soon. I'm not exactly in a hurry, but I am tired. I consider walking in shooting, but then I'll have to clean shit up before I go to sleep. And I really need sleep.

I take the time to look over the Mercedes. It's covered in wards so obvious even I notice them. Some deter thieves from even thinking about touching the car, some thwart the more determined, and others do some really nasty shit to those who haven't caught the hint.

Maybe I could take a nap here. I wonder if whoever's in my room would be polite enough to wake me up before they try to kill me. About ten minutes in, just as I'm about to drive the truck through the wall, the door to my room opens. A muscled Asian man with a crewcut and a blue suit that's just a little too small on him sticks his head out.

"I can't remember," he says. "Were you this much a pain in the arse in Hong Kong?" He's got an accent that's a little hard to place if you've never heard it before. Slightly British, maybe Australian, but not quite either one.

"Nice to see you too, Billy."

"Get in here. Someone needs to see you," he says. "It's too exposed out here." I look around the empty parking lot and the pools of darkness on the street—every third streetlight is missing, melted, or on the fritz. There are dead around: Haunts, Wanderers, couple of Echoes. Nothing new since I checked in.

"I don't remember leaving my door open, and I see you tripped my wards and you're not dead. So I think I'm good right here."

"Oh, is that all? The wards were easy. We went old school." He steps aside so I can get a look inside the room. There's a body on the carpet. Mostly. The com-

bination of the wards on the front door were designed
to incinerate everything besides the outer skin and the
skeleton. The skin hangs loose off the bones like a
sheet, little lumps here and there from the piles of ash
left inside.

"You're cleaning that up, ya know."

He waves it away. "I always tidy up after myself.
Plenty of room in the trunk. Look, my boss wants to
have a word. And he's here. He's one of you magic
types. If you don't come in, he's going to get cross. And
if he gets cross, you'll get cross, and then you're throwing around lightning and death magic and I'll be stuck
in the middle, which is something I would really like to
avoid."

Even if this is a trap, I need answers. Getting whoever is in there to come out here is turning into a pain
in the ass and I am too tired to deal with this shit.
"You first," I say. I follow him in, checking for any
magic.

Inside, in the room's single chair, sits a heavyset
man with pockmarked skin and a dour expression. He
wears a conservative black suit, kind of like mine, only
his doesn't have burns and holes in it and it probably
hasn't been slept in.

"Who are you?" I say. The man stares at me, face
impassive as stone, then looks at Billy.

"Uh, he doesn't actually speak English," Billy says.
The two of them have a conversation in Cantonese that
goes on for almost two minutes. I can hear a few words
I recognize, but not many. My name comes up a few
times, usually followed by Guǐ, the Chinese word for
ghost.

Finally Billy turns to me. "His eminence is known
by many names," he says, like he's reading off a script,
"but you may call him Bo xiānshēng."

"All that and you settled on Mister Bo?"

"I just do what do I'm told," Billy says.

Billy's made his introductions, so I make mine. I channel some power, enough to notice, but hopefully not enough to be seen as a threat. Mister Bo's cool enough not to react.

I address Mr. Bo, but I'm talking to Billy. "Why are you here?"

Billy translates, and I'm reminded of when I first met him. He'd change his accent based on who he was talking to. If he wanted to come across like a local, it was all Konglish all the time. Otherwise he was like this. My Cantonese sucks, so Billy translated for me. I had a tourist phrasebook, but that was pretty much it. I had meant to pick up a translation charm before I left the states, but I wasn't big on planning at the time.

"You have triad problems," Billy says after Bo's response. "One of your people is working for Sun Yee On."

"My people? A mage?"

"A necromancer," Billy says, not bothering to talk to his boss. "Name of Nanong Fan. You've got ghosts on the loose and he's scooping them up. So far he's only able to turn them into bombs. But he doesn't know how to make them anything else. He catches them but they all turn into, shit, I don't know what else to call them, xīqìguǐ. They eat qi, not like the ones we ran into that just eat life. These ones are—"

"Feral," I say. "I've run into a few."

The Chinese have a lot of different types of ghosts. Yǎnguǐ can turn into pure darkness, nǚguǐ are vengeful spirits of women who committed suicide, and on and on. In Chinese Buddhism everyone becomes a "ghost." They're not Echoes, Haunts, or Wanderers—I wouldn't even think of them as ghosts. Not saying they're wrong, just that maybe we look at things differently. By my lights most of their "ghosts" would be demons, or souls that have already moved on.

"Let me get this right. Some guy from Sun Yee On has figured out how to trap ghosts from across the veil, but they turn into something worse when they're over here."

Most of that jibes with what I already knew or suspected, but it's not syncing up with what the Skid Row ghosts told me. If Nanong Fan was a necromancer, he shouldn't have had any trouble talking to the ghosts. But somebody's doing it, so if it's not him, then who? Either we're talking about different guys, or the ghost got it wrong. Considering that most ghosts have the brainpower of a toddler blacked out on Benadryl, I'm thinking it's the latter.

"Exactly," Billy says.

I nod at Mister Bo watching our conversation and saying nothing. "So what's he here for?"

"Bo xiānshēng is 14K," Billy says. That explains a lot. Sun Yee On and 14K are the two largest triads in the world, and they're always looking for some way to fuck the other.

"And he wants to keep Sun Yee On from perfecting this thing?" I guess.

"If they do, it's not just the triads that are fucked," Billy says. "You think this won't get out and turn into some kind of nightmare cottage industry? And when it spills into my world there's not going to be any way to hide it." I've been trying to avoid thinking about that part.

"What about the other guy?" I say.

"What other guy?"

"The one who can't pull ghosts across the veil. At least that's what some of them told me. The way they talked about it, this guy could barely talk to them. Whoever he is, he's not a necromancer."

Billy fires off some rapid-fire Cantonese at Mister Bo, whose eyes go wide. He answers in a couple of short sentences. "First we've heard of it," Billy says. "This is not good. If it's not the guy from Sun Yee On, then who the hell is it?"

"Kinda hoping you could tell me." Billy shakes his head, worry clear on his face. "Okay, then how about the bait dog?"

". . . the what?"

"Bait dog. Dogfighting. It's—"

"I know what a bait dog is, Eric. The hell does it have to do with ghosts?"

"Found a corpse who'd been killed by some. Looks like he was tied up and left out for them to eat, only something pulled them back before they were finished. And then they went and did it again a few times over. Whoever it was had at least some control over the ghosts. Near as I can tell they were either torturing the guy or using him like a bait dog to train them."

"Jesus fuck." Billy sits hard on the edge of the bed. "What kind of sick fuck would do that?"

"I can think of a few," I say. "Like some mage working for 14K, maybe?"

"You think—"

"Cut the bullshit, Billy. Nobody in this room has clean hands. 14K's just as bad as Sun Yee On. All you fuckers are just mirror images of each other. Dub C, Four Seas, La Eme, Armenian Power, MS-13. Names are different but it's all the same shit."

Billy's trying to convince me he's the good guy here. That he works for the *good* thugs and murderers, not like those other *baaaad* thugs and murderers. There's no good or bad here, no lines separating one from the other. It's one big smear and we're all part of it, some closer to one end or the other, but not a goddamn one of us clean.

"It's not us," he says, eyes hard. When we were in Hong Kong he was outside looking in, though he had enough connections to get us an audience with somebody in 14K. But he always insisted he was independent. I wonder when he became an "us."

"I don't really care one way or another. I just want it to stop. So quit blowing smoke up my ass. We both know that if your Mister Bo over there, who's been surprisingly quiet throughout this whole exchange, got hold of the spell to pull ghosts across, he wouldn't hesitate to use it. So thanks for the heads up on some of the players in this little drama, but I don't think our goals are exactly mutual."

"Eric, this concerns all—"

He doesn't get a chance to finish the sentence. Automatic gunfire sweeps through the room, shattering the windows and stitching a pattern of bullet holes across the far wall.

Chapter 10

Billy and I hit the ground, but Mister Bo's not so lucky. He catches a handful of rounds and his head pops like a blood-filled balloon. The bullets are still coming, some of the shooters out there reloading as others empty their magazines. It takes a second for Bo's body to hit the ground after all the bullets he's catching make him dance like a spastic marionette.

Engines rev, headlights kick on, and the shooters peel out of the parking lot, leaving behind the stink of gunfire and burnt rubber. I blink, and the scene has changed more than it should have. Billy's moved. I don't remember seeing him doing it. And he's yelling at me.

"What?" I say.

"The fuck is wrong with you?" he says. "You spaced out. This is not the time to be spacing out."

"I'm fine. These guys are Sun Yee On?" I say.

"Yeah, they're Sun Yee On. Fuckers." Billy slowly sits up, glass and drywall falling off him like sand. He catches sight of his headless boss, the blood soaking into the carpet. "Oh shit."

"Yeah, I don't think he's gonna pull through."

"Oh shit," Billy says again. "This is fucked. I'm fucked. We've gotta get out of here."

"Relax," I say, getting up and brushing off debris.

I've got some small cuts from flying glass, but otherwise I'm unhurt. I'm not sure what happened back there. Did I black out? I feel okay, or at least no worse than normal. "This is like the ninth gang shooting in the last two days. Everybody's taking advantage of the fact that there aren't enough cops to settle old scores. We're not even gonna see a chopper for like two hours."

"No, you don't understand. I was supposed to protect Bo xiānshēng. With him dead they're gonna want my head. Oh, I am so fucked."

"Huh. Yeah, sounds like. What are you gonna do?"

"I don't fucking know," he yells, his voice reaching into registers I didn't think were possible for a guy his size. He's shaking, really freaking out here. I kind of feel sorry for him, but not too much.

"Gimme your number," I say, pulling out my phone. He does and I punch it into the contacts under Pain In My Ass. I tell him mine and warn him, "That's only gonna be good for a few days before I ditch this phone and switch it out. I'm assuming that's the same with yours?"

"Yeah, I know the drill."

The room is a total loss. There's probably more lead in here than intact drywall. The bed has exploded out in stuffing and coils, the curtains are so shredded they barely exist. Outside in the parking lot the pickup has four flats, no windows, and a shape that's barely anything you could call a car.

Billy's car isn't much better, but at least that one was warded, which protected it a bit. A couple of smoking bodies lie on the ground next to it. They were too close when the wards went off. But even with all that it's completely undriveable.

"Jesus, I don't even know where to go," Billy says. "I can't go back. They'll kill me."

"I'm sure you'll figure it out."

"What about you? Where are you going?"

"Like I'm gonna fucking tell you. I don't know if you've figured this out, yet, but the guys with the machine guns? They weren't after me. They were after your boss there, and maybe you, too. It's a little refreshing, actually. You led them here. Telling you where I'm going will shorten my life expectancy considerably. So you'll excuse me if I don't share."

I had a bag with some extra clothes and shoes, but that's just as destroyed as the rest of the room. My messenger bag's all right. I brought it in with me and it hasn't left my side. I need to find another car, and another place to sleep. A lot of hotels and motels burned down, and the ones that didn't are either shitholes like this one or stuffed to the gills with people who lost their homes. Some of them are coming vacant as people either leave the city or run out of money, but there's still no way I'm going to find a room on short notice. Which means there's only one place I can realistically go. Aside from making sure it hadn't burned down, I've been avoiding it.

"But—"

"Billy, I'm tired. This is the third time in less than twenty-four hours that I've almost died. I usually call it a day at the second. Now, I know we have a lot to talk about, but the way I'm feeling right now, I'm more likely to shoot you. I have your number. You have mine. If you don't die tonight, call me sometime tomorrow. If it's before noon I will cut off your fucking head and stick it in a bowling bag."

"What the hell am I supposed to do?" he says.

Adrenaline and survival instincts tell me to cut him loose, but he's the only solid lead I have and if I lose him I might not get him back. "Fuck. Hang on." I pull my phone out and dial up Gabriela.

"I was trying to sleep," she says.

"But it's not even dawn yet."

"What do you want?"

"Found Billy," I say. "Got shot at. His boss had his

head pulped and if he goes back to whatever Triad rock he crawled out from under they'll probably gut him for it. I can't really take him where I'm going, so . . ."

"There's no room at the inn," she says.

"Oh, come on. I leave him on his own, we're not likely to see him again."

"Take him with you," she says.

"And let him know where my secret lair is?"

"Oh, I get it," she says. "You're just fine with him seeing *my* secret lair."

"Everybody's seen your secret lair. Wait. Are we talking about the same thing?"

"Fuck you, Eric. Fine. Tell me where he's at and I'll have someone pick him up." I give her the address, tell her he'll be hiding across the street in one of the burnt-out buildings, and give her his number to call when her people get close.

"You're an angel," I say.

"If you call me that again I will cut off your balls and hang them over my desk."

"Love you, too." I hang up before she can threaten any other body parts.

"Who was that?"

"Somebody you don't want to piss off. Go hunker down in one of the burnouts across the street. Your ride'll call you when they get here. Think of it as Uber for desperate triad thugs. They'll give you a place to bed down."

"What are you gonna do?"

"Steal a car. Take a couple Ambien, get some sleep. And if I'm really lucky, not have anyone try to murder me before the sun comes up. Goodnight, Billy. Try not to get yourself killed."

———

I jack a grime-covered Honda from down the street and head south. There's no good way to get to the

Westside even before L.A. was a nightmare wasteland. By the time I pull into the driveway of the house in Venice I've been in the car almost two hours.

Venice is a weird little neighborhood of canals and bridges meant to evoke—yep, you guessed it—Venice, Italy. It doesn't. Everybody knows about the beach, but the houses facing the little canals are hemmed in by larger buildings and if you don't already know they're there you might just drive on by, which suits the locals just fine.

A lot of the houses in Venice didn't burn, though on the couple of blocks where they did the flames spread across the entire row of homes, turning the entire block into an ash heap.

My sister Lucy's place is one of the ones that made it. I pull up into the driveway around the back and kill the engine. The first time I'd been in it was a few weeks after her murder, and I got to watch her Echo relive the brutal last minutes of her life. Her killer used her broken and bloody hands to write a message on the wall that only I was going to see.

It wasn't until after I killed the first Santa Muerte, the one who'd ordered her murder, that I came back here. I exorcised her Echo, letting it fade away into nothing. That's the day I discovered I'd inherited the house and everything from her and our parents. It was a lot more than I had expected.

I unlock the wards and the door and head inside. I'd had the place furnished a while back. Abandoned houses, especially now, are great for squatters looking for a place to crash. The wards on the house aren't as nasty as the ones I'd usually set up at a hotel room, inducing nausea and feelings of dread instead of death, but they'd keep most people out.

Memories start to crawl out of the back alleys of my mind. The way she died, the way our parents died, the way I let her and everybody else down. I shove them back hard. I don't have time for this crap.

You can only hide from your memories and hold off grieving for so long before so much of your soul gets chipped away that you either deal with it or turn into a monster. I get the feeling I may have already crossed that line, and since I'm sure as shit not dealing with it, it's pretty clear which of those two I've shifted toward.

Mage life is complicated. It's amazing there are any of us still breathing, with all the in-fighting and murder we do. Friends might turn on you. Family might try to kill you. I've known of whole mage lines wiped out in a single night because everyone in the house assassinated each other, or groups of mages with the best of intentions taking each other out over petty disagreements.

We are not what you would call stable individuals.

I sit on the couch in the living room. I close my eyes and for a second I see it the way it appeared the first time I came here. White carpet soaked and crusted in blood. Furniture turned over and destroyed, blood and meat on the walls. Lucy being torn apart piece by piece until there was nothing left but her trauma to guarantee that when she died she would leave an Echo. All to get me to see a message, and make sure there wasn't anything left of her that I could talk to.

"Fuck, that night sucked," I say to the empty room.

"I remember." A gravelly voice at my back, a scent of roses filling the air. Okay, not-so-empty room.

"And here I thought I was going to get some sleep," I say.

Chapter 11

I turn my head to look at the tall skeleton in a red wedding dress behind me. The new Santa Muerte, only with less Mictecacihuatl and more Tabitha Cheung than the original.

"I am sorry for that night," she says.

"That's all right," I say, exhaustion weighing me down. "I murdered you for it already."

"I remember that, too."

"I suppose you're here to collect?" When I killed the first Santa Muerte, it broke the contract we had that tied me to her. No, let's call it what it was. We were married. When I killed her, that was a divorce. Then when the shit hit the fan I made the same deal with the new Santa Muerte, only with different strings attached.

I was wary, still am, but I knew she wasn't what she'd been. Tabitha's influence. Since I was going up against the god Quetzalcoatl and needed the kind of backup only a goddess could give, I took her hand and renewed my vows, so to speak.

"You told me a month," she says. "I am growing impatient." Her voice resonates uncomfortably in my skull. The pits of her eye sockets glow as if she's trying to bore holes into me. I've seen it before.

I got her help with Quetzalcoatl. In return I agreed

to help her rebuild Mictlan and officially take the role of her old husband Mictlantecuhtli, without the problem of him still being around and about like the last time. The place had gone to shit since the Spanish invasion of Mexico five hundred years ago, and the souls were backing up. Whole sections of Mictlan had been twisted into a nightmare realm of blood and bone. Not that some of those places weren't supposed to be slightly different nightmare realms of blood and bone, of course.

"I've been a little busy," I say. "Mictlan's been around a long time. A few more weeks isn't going to make things worse." She wanted me to be a full-time stay-at-home husband, which—yeah, not gonna happen. I was able to negotiate it down to three months a year. They didn't have to be all at once, but I kinda got the feeling that's what she was shooting for.

The skeleton shivers, shrinks. Muscle, flesh, hair bubbles up to cover the bones as the wedding dress shifts into jeans and a flannel shirt. Tabitha stands in the skeleton's place. A short Korean woman with hair cut in a bob. She slides over the top of the couch and sits cross-legged on it next to me. She does this a lot, I've noticed. It's a blatant attempt to manipulate me. Put on the human face when the big scary skeleton won't get her what she wants. The funny thing: I'm more comfortable talking to the skeleton.

"New haircut?" I say. "Looks good."

"Thanks. Thought I'd try something different."

"Same outfit, though. Weren't you wearing that when I killed you?"

"That was blue," she says, tugging at the lapel of the flannel. "This one's red."

"My mistake. You know I'm still not coming to Mictlan until I finish shit here, right?"

"I know," she says. "I'm not going to try to make you."

"That's . . . not what I expected."

"Eric, you are one of the most bull-headed people I have ever met, and I've got a millennia of memories to draw from. Not a lot of folks will crawl their way through the land of the dead to murder a couple of old gods and actually succeed. Trying to force you isn't going to work. But I do need to get things rolling soon."

"What's the rush?"

"You ever have backed-up plumbing, where you clear it but everything clogs somewhere further down that you can't get to?"

"What am I in this analogy?" I say. "Please tell me I'm not the wad of diapers stuck halfway around a tree root."

"We'll get to that. When you came in and opened Izmictlan Apochcalolca, that let all the dead into the mists. The problem is it didn't let them out again."

Izmictlan Apochcalolca is the blinding fog, a thick wall of mist that's one of the final steps in the soul's journey to Chicunamictlan, their final destination. When I was in Mictlan, it was locked. None of the dead who had started their journey could get any farther. They were all stopped, an uncountable sea of souls camped out at the edge, unable to go on. I needed to get through it. To do that, I needed to open it.

"So . . . I'm the guy who flushed the diapers? I thought all the souls were getting through now."

"So did I, except they're getting into the mists and no further. Some of them aren't worthy of passing through. But that's not a lot of them. The rest are just lost. Izmictlan Apochcalolca is Mictlantecuhtli's responsibility, not Mictecacihuatl's."

"Oh. I'm the plumber."

"You're the plumber."

"What do I need to do?"

"Come with me to Mictlan and fix it."

"And what exactly does 'fixing it' mean?"

"Oh, for fuck sake, Eric. You're Mictlantecuhtli. Out here you can barely touch your power, but in Mictlan, you're a god. You'll figure it out."

I'm still having trouble with that idea. I don't particularly want to be a death god. Gods are assholes. And though that might make me a perfect candidate for the job, it's not really my kink.

"Can we have this conversation later? On a day when ghosts aren't trying to eat me and the living aren't trying to kill me?"

"That day's never going to come," she says. "I'll make a deal with you. Three days. Get your shit together in three days and then you come to Mictlan."

"And if I don't have my shit together by then?"

"Then I drag your ass to Mictlan. Out here you're a pain in my ass, but I can take you down."

"If I say yes will you let me sleep?"

"I'll even cuddle with you, if you want."

"Fine. Yes. But no cuddling. I'm not a cuddler."

"That's not what I remember," she says, grinning.

"Just go away, please."

"Three days, Eric. I'll see you soon." She's gone as quickly as she appeared. No fade-out, no special effects. Just gone, a scent of roses and smoke the only hint she'd been there in the first place.

Three days. Shit. I'm not surprised. I've been putting this off as long as I can, and while, based on my relationship with the old Santa Muerte, breaking deals with gods is apparently a thing I do, I don't really want to break this one. I actually do want to help restore Mictlan.

When I was there it was a mess. The Aztecs didn't really have a concept of sin, but they had rules like any other religion, and the souls were judged by them. Whether I agree with those rules or not is irrelevant. At least at the moment.

If they were all just a bunch of mass murderers . . . Okay, a lot of them actually are mass murderers. The Aztecs were kind of murder-friendly. When Mictecacihuatl took on the mantle of Santa Muerte she gained a new following of cartel types, also known for their murder-positive philosophy.

Point is that those souls are suffering not because they've been judged, but because the system's broken. I don't like suffering in general, but I absolutely hate pointless suffering. And this at least I can do something about.

Part of doing something about it isn't just getting the pipes working again, but changing the rules. I don't know exactly what they are. I missed my "So, You're A Death God Now" orientation class.

Maybe the rules work in favor of cartel hitmen. Maybe they don't. I don't really know. And I won't know, and more importantly won't be able to do anything about it, until I get there.

Three days. Looks like it's time to kick things up a notch.

———

I wake up on the couch, soaked in sweat, smoky sunlight shearing through the windows. At first I don't know where I am. And then, more slowly than usual, I wake up enough to figure it out—but I feel like there are holes. What am I missing? I can remember . . . a few days ago? Something's happened in that time, but why can't I remember it?

The memory of the last few days comes rushing back as my body reminds me that it's all one massive bruise. Every movement feels like ripping muscle.

The wounds from the ghosts feel like burning ice. Bloodless and raw, with the look of freezer-burned chicken. They always leave ugly scars. I discover cuts from shattered glass, drywall, and bullet fragments that

I didn't know I had. They've bled overnight and crusted over, sticking to my shirt.

And to top it off my left hand is throbbing in time to my heartbeat. One of these days I'm going to have to see a better healer for it, which will probably mean breaking the bones the nails went through all over again. Yippee.

I get to my feet, my back cracking like snapping timber. I wonder if people in other lines of work feel this bad in the morning? Accountants probably have just as many back problems, but fewer instances of having someone beat on their kidneys for half an hour.

I change into a wrinkled shirt I have wadded up in my messenger bag. My pants and coat are dark enough that I can get away with wearing them a little while longer. This is one of the problems of having no fixed address. I lose a lot of shit. Burned, buried, stolen, left behind. To say I travel light is an understatement.

Which makes inheriting this house and all of my parents' properties a bit of a head fuck. I have a house in upstate New York that I got as payment for a job, but aside from one debauched weekend almost ten years ago I've never lived there.

That and the Venice house I understand. They're just houses. But I also inherited a handful of storage facilities dotted around L.A. filled with magical items collected over the last hundred years by different people. I can't be the only one who has access to it, but I don't know who else does.

And then there's the Ambassador Hotel, where I'd been spending a lot of time until recently. People aren't the only things that leave ghosts. With enough energy and history, the psychic footprint that makes old buildings a physical presence on the other side can develop a consciousness.

The Ambassador Hotel spent decades catering to presidents, ambassadors, kings, the elite of Hollywood, and some of the most ruthless criminals ever spawned. Long before it shut down and was finally demolished to make way for a school, the Ambassador Hotel woke up.

Sometime before he died my grandfather made a deal with the ghost of the Ambassador. I don't know the details, but it involved a sacrifice of a lot of blood, enough to sate the most massive ghost I've ever seen for decades.

In return, granddad got a room. Well, really, he got a door. The other side of that door is a room. It's physical, real. Not part of the dark ghost side of the veil. It's also, as far as I can tell, not on this planet, or time, or plane of existence.

All I know is that he made a hotel room that can only be reached by passing through the ghosts that surround the place and the ghost of the Ambassador itself, knowing the room number, having the key, and being a member of my family. That's why I keep Darius's bottle in it. If somebody can get through all that, I've got bigger problems.

I've started leaving things in there. Magic odds and ends, spellbooks, and the ledger for all those warehouses I inherited. Also, my clothes.

I haven't gone back because of Darius's pet private eye. He can't follow me to the other side, but he can see where I flip over. Doing it too far from the hotel will just get me killed. Too many ghosts in the way. Too close and anyone watching might figure out where I'm going. Ideally, I'd have something that could camouflage me so I could go in and out without worrying about it.

Only I suck at obfuscation spells. I can do them, but they never come out right. They don't last long enough, they fizzle out, or they backfire and make whatever I'm trying to hide glow like a spotlight. I could use a Sharpie and a HI, MY NAME IS sticker, but unless I dump a lot of power into it, it's not going to work on another mage.

I wonder if I could travel to Mictlan and come out at the hotel. I don't have a lot of Mictlantecuhtli's abilities out here, but I should be able to travel to and from Mictlan like I'm clicking my heels together and saying there's no place like home.

But if I go to Mictlan, I won't be leaving anytime soon.

I don't see any way around it. I'm covered in blood and drywall dust. I need a shower, a change of clothes, and some serious painkillers.

I'll have to be careful if I want to avoid notice. And if I see Darius's P.I., I'll just have to shoot him. That's a pretty solid plan.

Chapter 12

The school complex they tore the Ambassador down for is named after the hotel's most famous assassination victim, Robert F. Kennedy. I really have to wonder who came up with that idea. Do they have a plaque where the kitchen used to be, where he was gunned down by Sirhan Sirhan? Maybe a bust that says BOBBY KENNEDY MURDERED HERE?

Most of the buildings are closed. Some burned down in the fires, others took a lot of smoke damage. Classes are still in session, but I heard they were running them for entire grades at a time in an auditorium.

Even knowing that, it's weird to see any students walking between classes. It's just as well; I suspect I'm getting a reputation as that creepy guy who hangs around the school. If I don't run into the police at some point over it, I'll be surprised.

I shift over to the other side, the school buildings fading away to be replaced by the grounds of the Ambassador, grand and bright and bursting with activity. The hotel is more real than most things over on this side of the veil. It has a solidity that no normal ghost can achieve. The look is from the hotel's heyday. Guests stream in and out of the main doors, head over to the Coconut Grove to go dancing, take taxis out to places that don't exist anymore.

These ghosts aren't going to bother me. They're actually all just one ghost. The guests and staff are puppets, extensions of the Ambassador's consciousness. I've spoken with the hotel and it doesn't seem insane, but I don't really get why it runs this display. Maybe it's using it as an anchor to remember itself. Or maybe it's crazy in a way that only architecture can understand.

"Good morning, sir," a bellman says as I step into the foyer. He's generic in every way. White, mid-twenties, average height, average weight. Got that "Golly, gee!" attitude that screams 1920s Americana. And he looks exactly like every other bellboy in the hotel.

He looks me up and down. "Seems you've had quite the evening. Perhaps you'd like to spend some time in our spa. I can book you for any time you like."

"Thank you, Ambassador," I say, "but that won't be necessary." It pays to be polite to a ghost that dwarfs some towns I've passed through. I have whatever deal in place that my grandfather made, but I don't know all the details so I'm not necessarily going to trust it. Staying on the hotel's good side is just smart strategy.

"Very good, sir. If there's anything else I can do for you, please don't hesitate to ask." I start to walk off, then pause.

"Actually, I was wondering, can you see the other side?" I know ghosts can see me from their side of the veil, and when I'm over here I see the living as indistinct lights that are vaguely people-shaped.

"Oh, yes, sir. Sometimes it's clearer than others, but I can get a gist of what's going on out there, if that's what you're asking."

"I was more wondering about sensing specific people."

"More difficult, but I can try. Is there someone in particular you'd like me to keep an eye out for?"

I almost say "anyone suspicious," but what would a hotel consider suspicious? Instead I give him Darius's P.I.'s description, and after a moment's consideration the bellboy nods.

"I'll keep an eye out."

"Thanks."

"Don't mention it, sir."

I head upstairs to my room, walking through empty hallways like I'm in *The Shining*. I wonder if the doors are decorative, or if the Ambassador's puppet show extends into the rooms as well. Does anything exist behind those doors? Or would a room only exist if I were to open a door?

My door is easier to spot. It's in a different location on this floor every time, but I never have trouble finding it. Today it's at the end of the hall, set a little farther away from the others. I unlock it with my key and step through, my ears popping from the pressure change.

It's a comfortable hotel room furnished in a 1940s style. I don't know how it works. It has electricity, running water, a fully stocked fridge that refills on its own. The place even has cell coverage.

I'm not sure what my granddad used this room for, but I'm thinking safehouse. Given the level of security, it could just as easily be a bomb shelter. Either way, it's the safest, most secure place I've ever seen. Even if the sky outside the window is a sickly shade of orange and the landscape is dotted with herds of tentacled nightmares eating each other.

Which is why I keep an ornate glass bottle on the small dining table near the kitchen. People have been looking for Darius's bottle for five hundred years. Granddad got hold of it during an archaeological dig on Santa Catalina Island. He kept it in one of the storage facilities, just one more magical knickknack. When he discovered what it was, he brought it here. Or maybe he made this place to have somewhere secure to keep it.

I'm not sure how long I'll be able to use the room. It's not that I'm going to get kicked out. The hotel says the deal for the room is good for several more decades. It's me. This is the most stable location I've lived in for almost twenty years. And just knowing it exists is freaking me out a little. There's a lot knotted up in a tight little ball about having somewhere I can call home, and I haven't even tried to unpack it yet. I don't think I'll like what I find.

I shower, shave, put bandages on the worst of my injuries, and apply a balm I got from an herbalist in Florida that helps with the ghost wounds. One cut above my left eye needs stitches, but all I have are butterfly bandages, so I make do. I've stitched myself up plenty of times, but I'm not poking a needle that close to my eyeball.

So what now? Start with what I know, I guess. Ghosts are being pulled across and made into weapons. The cross-over ghosts that I've run into have no sort of discipline, but given the state of that poor bastard the ghoul found, it looks like someone's training ones that do.

That's two players right there. According to Billy one of them is a Nanong Fan, necromancer from Sun Yee On. Who's the other one? Was it Bo, the guy Billy was supposed to bodyguard? He says it isn't, that 14K's not doing anything like that, which I don't buy for a second. So that's player two.

Or is it? Bo's supposed to be another necromancer. But whoever tried to get the Skid Row ghosts to come over could only grab a few and did a piss-poor job just talking to them. That's rudimentary shit, up there with breathing. You can't talk to ghosts, then you're not a necromancer. Period.

So that's a third player in all this. Well, a second, really, since Bo took a bullet that popped his skull like he was an extra in *Scanners*.

And that's something else that bothers me. Why's Billy in town? According to him he's 14K and he and his boss are in L.A. trying to stop Fan from making ghost soldiers or whatever the fuck his plan is. Bo, I get. But why Billy? Why not use local talent? All Billy seems to be good for is speaking Cantonese and getting his boss shot to hell. I can find a guy like that in Chinatown in twenty minutes.

I sit down at the table, pick up Darius's bottle, and give it a shake, turn it around in my hands to look it over. I wonder if he can feel that. He's eight thousand years old and was originally trapped inside a gourd, so the bottle's a pretty fancy upgrade, but it would suck if he feels it every time somebody knocks it over.

I hope he likes it in there. He's been in it for the last five hundred years, and since it was sealed by spells only Mictlantecuhtli knew it's not likely anyone can—

I stop as my eye catches on something around the stopper. Faint etched pictograms glow along the edge. They're tiny, almost microscopic. They look familiar. Really familiar. But I don't remember ever seeing them before.

The more I look, the more of them I can find. The bottle is covered in them. And then, like those pictures of static that snap into a 3D dolphin if you stare at them long enough, the pictograms pop out from the bottle and I can read them.

They're binding spells, thousands of them, layered over and through each other, dropping into infinite depths and branching out into new bindings like a Mandelbrot set on acid. They all make sense. I can see how each one was set in place and locked into all of the ones around it, all the connecting points, the joins and overlaps, the threads wrapping around themselves in infinite knots, and if I were to pluck on that one right there and hold that one over there then the whole thing would unravel and disintegrate into dust.

It's some of the most complex magic I've ever encountered. I shouldn't be able to see it, much less see how to remove it.

I set the bottle carefully down onto the table like it's sweating dynamite. My heartbeat spikes and I break out in a cold sweat. Is the spell decaying? Darius said it had gotten weaker over the years. Is that what I'm seeing? Mictlantecuhtli put this spell on, and only Mictlantecuhtli should be able to take it off. But he's dead and I'm—

Oh. Of course.

I knew that since Mictlantecuhtli is, as the Munchkins say, not only merely dead, but really most sincerely dead, that I'm his replacement. I didn't realize I was going to get all his other shit, too.

There's too much I don't know that I don't know. Like what I can do with Mictlantecuhtli's powers outside of Mictlan, or hell, even what those powers actually are. I had a taste of them when he and I were trading places but the more I used them the closer I came to turning into a jade statue. Kind of puts a damper on the whole exploration phase of things.

I've been ignoring the fact that I'm flying blind on this, and I can't afford that. Especially now that I can see how to pull the binding spells off of Darius's bottle.

It's a problem that will fix itself in three days when I officially make my debut in Mictlan as a blood-soaked god of the dead. But I still don't know what that means. I feel like an understudy for the stupidest role in the worst Broadway musical ever, and I'm missing the script.

The only things that have been keeping the bottle safe have been that it's hidden, hard to get to, and that the only guy who could open it is nothing more than a bad memory.

But anything hidden can be found. Any lock can be picked, and now apparently I can crack this one open. If anybody finds out about that little trick I am going to be in some serious shit.

Or will I? Darius was doing Cortés's bidding. What if he was doing mine?

Dangerous. I know fuck-all about djinn. How true is the whole three-wishes thing? Darius took down almost an entire pantheon of gods for Cortés. He worked his way through all twenty-two different realms of the gods and tore through the most powerful of them like a rhino through tissue paper. That seems like a little more than three wishes worth of work to me.

Jesus, am I seriously considering trying to control Darius? I don't care if he can grant wishes or just give a decent handjob. I'll be the first to admit my usual response to bad ideas is "Hold my beer," but this is a bit much even for me.

A knock on the door makes me jump and I have a sudden urge to throw a blanket over the bottle, like that's going to do any good.

I've never heard a knock on the door. I wait a minute and it repeats. Who the hell could even be here?

There's no way to see into the hallway. I guess an interdimensional peephole in the interdimensional door was just a step too far. I draw the Browning, ready a shield spell, and yank the door open to see the Ambassador bellboy, smiling calmly at me.

"Oh," I say. "Hi. I didn't realize you could— You know what, never mind. Uh, what can I do for you?"

"Good afternoon, sir," the bellboy says, chipper as always. "The gentleman you were asking about is outside." The hallway shudders like a ship in high seas. I stumble, bracing myself against the doorjamb.

"What the hell was that?"

"He appears to be attempting to gain entry." The hallway shakes again. The bellboy isn't affected by it. He's rooted to the floor. I guess when you're part of the floor, the walls, and the whole grounds, you don't need to worry about pretending gravity exists.

"No," he says, frowning. "Oh, dear. He's trying to open a hole to pull me through to the other side. That's . . . unexpected."

That's one word for it. I could swear Darius's P.I., Hank, wasn't a mage, and sure as hell couldn't channel so much power that he could pull a ghost as formidable as the Ambassador through to the living side.

The bellboy winces. He flickers, jerking in and out of position like badly threaded film. His face shifts through a dozen different appearances in a second. Men, women, white, black, a kaleidoscope of faces.

"I think he's su—su—succeeding."

I close my eyes and throw out my senses. From the other side I see ghosts as faded, translucent figures. From here I can see the living, but with a lot less detail: featureless, human-shaped lights. I can sense them from here the way I can sense ghosts from there.

I filter out all the noise, the bucking of the floor, the flood of panic from the Ambassador manifesting all around me. I can't tell if the P.I. is casting a spell from here, but I can feel the pull that's yanking on the Ambassador.

It takes me a precious few seconds but finally I see him on the other side. He's right below me, four stories down. Shit. Stairs or the elevator will be too slow, not to mention dangerous. I don't want to be in an elevator when all of a sudden the Ambassador goes feral and tries to eat me.

I don't have time for any of that. I close and lock

the door, make sure there's a round in the Browning, and line myself up as best I can over Hank.

"I'll be right back," I say and shift back to the living side. There's no hotel over here, just four stories' worth of air between me and the blacktop below. Oh yeah, and gravity.

Chapter 13

One of the problems with being able to travel between the lands of the living and the dead is that they're not always in sync. What's here may not be there, and vice versa.

Airplanes, for example. They simply don't exist on the ghost side. They're too transient, move around too much to make an impression on the psychic landscape. Going from one side to the other on an airplane in flight is a good way to find yourself at 35,000 feet tossed forward at a couple hundred miles an hour. Not ideal.

This applies to everything over here, especially old buildings. They might be torn down on the living side, but completely untouched on the ghost side. Even if the Ambassador hadn't developed a consciousness, it would still be here. It's got too strong a psychic imprint not to be.

I am on the fourth floor. Hank, Darius's P.I., is on the living side, on what looks like a kickball court, on blacktop, on the ground. If you take the mass, acceleration, distance, and whatever other numbers you want to throw into the mix, the final answer comes out to: "This is really going to hurt."

I'm in midair the moment I flip over and gravity

yanks me down. Back when I did this same thing in the Walled City I was a lot slower. Now I can do it as fast as thought.

Apparently, I'm a slow thinker. Just as quickly I flip back, but falling takes next to no time at all and I slam into the hallway of the floor below. Even with tucking into a roll and my tattoos soaking up some of the impact, I've fallen more than ten feet. It's better than forty, but it still hurts.

I don't know if he's noticed me yet, but probably not. I was only visible for a split second, and most people never look up in their lives. It's kind of surprising we ever evolved past the prehistoric rodent stage.

This time, he's definitely going to notice me, and he's not going to be happy about it. I line myself back up to him, toss on my shield spell and throw myself at the floor while flipping back across.

I fall three stories, pumping as much energy as I can into the shield, trying to use it as a combination cushion and battering ram, neither of which it's intended for.

Hank catches sight of me just as I'm coming in, freezes in shock. He tries to dodge at the last instant, but he's too slow. My shield hits him before I do, slamming into him at an angle and more or less breaking my fall. There's a loud snap as we collide. Whether it's my shield collapsing or his bones breaking, I'm not sure.

He hits the ground hard, tumbling away like a bowling pin. I roll across the blacktop along the rough surface. I can feel blood welling up at the back of my scalp and the palms of my hands are torn and bleeding.

We both stagger upright, neither one of us at our best. He's holding his left arm close to his chest at a weird angle, his face and hands a mess of roadrash from his trip across the blacktop.

He puts his hand up, fear on his face. He's about to say something, but I don't give him the chance, running into him and taking him down in a tackle. We hit the ground and roll. Despite his broken arm, he's not one to give up. He manages to straddle me and hammers his fist into my face two or three times before I can throw him off and lurch to my feet.

The cut on my forehead has opened up and a wash of blood fills my left eye. Blood pours from my nose. He backs away from me, his left arm limp by his side. He can barely stand, much less keep coming at me. I'm about to hit him with a lightning spell, send a few thousand volts through him, when I realize there's something not quite right with this picture.

The spell pulling the Ambassador through the hole in the veil is still active. Something like that takes concentration and energy. I feel pretty comfortable saying that his concentration is pretty shot.

Things have happened so fast that it didn't occur to me to check if he was the one casting the spell. He's not. He hasn't tapped any power or thrown any out. Which means the real mage is nearby, but I can't see him.

I start to turn, throwing up my shield, but I'm too late. A lance of burning agony punches through my back and a glowing blue blade thrusts a foot out the front of my chest.

My heart stops. Every muscle seizes. My lungs feel like they've collapsed. I don't have enough air to make any sound more than a quiet wheeze. Something shoves against my back, pushing me off the blade. I'm unconscious before I even hit the ground.

———

Good news. I'm not dead. Bad news. I'm not dead.

The burning in my chest has receded to a four-alarm fire. My entire body feels like it's been rubbed

raw and dipped in alcohol. Breathing is agony. I crack
open my eyes and the blurry light stabs into my brain
like a pickaxe made of fire ants. I blink a few times
until my vision isn't quite so thick and gummy, but the
pain doesn't go away.

I've been stabbed before. More times than I'd like—
but then, once is more times than I'd like. I had some
guy in North Dakota punch a twelve-inch Bowie knife
through my left arm, once. That didn't feel nearly
this bad.

Jesus, what the hell did I get hit with? It clearly
wasn't lethal, though with this much pain I kind of
wish it was. I bet it could be dialed up and kill me just
fine. Whoever wanted me, wanted me alive. I'll re-
serve judgment on whether or not that's a good thing
for now.

I'm edging toward "not" as the light resolves into a
dentist's office. I'm strapped into the exam chair with
duct tape, a handful of roofing nails placed on the top
of my left hand, poking out from the tape such that I
can see them. Even if I couldn't see them, I'd know
they were there. You don't quickly forget pieces of
magic as nasty as they are.

The office is clean, bright. Music filters through wall
speakers. A potted plant sits in the corner. Posters show
anthropomorphic teeth demonstrating in rhyme how to
brush and floss correctly and the horrifying consequence
of a green gingivitis monster for not doing so. The only
personal item looks to be a framed diploma on the wall.
I can't read the name from here, but I'm pretty sure it
belongs to the woman on the floor in the corner with her
throat opened up from ear to ear, eyes staring blankly at
me, blood thick down her front. That's usually not a
good sign.

What worries me the most, though, are the nails on
my hand. They're the same type Quetzalcoatl's sicaria
shot into that same hand. These haven't punched

through flesh and bone like the other ones did, they're just laying directly against flesh, but that's enough to cause a problem.

They nullify magic. I can't feel it, can't channel it, can't pull energy, nothing. The effect feels weaker than when I had three of them shot through my hand, but it's there. Probably why I feel so hungover now.

The magic in my tattoos is for more than defensive spells. Some of them are to reduce pain, speed healing. They're weakened, though I can feel them trying to do their jobs. The nails probably work better when they're actually embedded in my flesh. If I can get them off me I should be fine, but as long as they're touching skin I'm nearly as magic-free as any normal out there.

"You're awake." The voice is raspy, with a little bit of a slur like somebody who's had a stroke. A man steps into view. Tall, wide shoulders, heavily muscled. He's wearing a blue pin-striped suit with a tie. Very professional. His blond hair is cut scalp-close on the right side of his head. If it's to hide the fact that it's all burnt off on the left then it's doing a piss-poor job, because everything below it is even more fucked up.

His right side is fine, All-Star American footballer type. Almost blazingly white skin, high cheekbones. An eye blue as cut sapphire. He could have been a model. But his left side. Jesus. He looks as though he's been split roughly in two.

The left eye is gone. Most people would cover it up with an eyepatch, but he doesn't seem the shy type. The skin around the empty socket is shriveled, bleeding into the waxy and mottled ropes of thick scar tissue on his face that make him look half-melted. The scars pull back the cheek muscles on that side, giving him a sneer showing a handful of cracked and charred teeth. His left hand is a burnt, twisted claw, two fin-

gers missing. Despite all that damage, he looks familiar. Where the hell have I seen him before?

"Holy shit, I've woken up in a Batman comic." My
voice is thick with phlegm and a nasal sound that I
really hope doesn't mean my nose is broken again.

"Hello, Carter," he says. He tries to smile and it just
pulls the left cheek into something more horrific.

"Don't take this the wrong way, but I think you
might have a skin condition." I didn't think he could
outdo the smile for the award for Best Supporting
Nightmare Fuel, but his face twisting in anger is definitely in the running.

"You know what I noticed about you when we met?
You don't take anything seriously. You just shit on
everything. Wherever you go everything goes to hell,
and you joke about it."

"Have you been talking to my therapist? Because
he says the same thing."

He leans down until he's eye level with me. "You
ruined everything. Everything. And now you're going
to pay for it."

"Did I sleep with your sister or something? Because
you seem really upset, and I'm not entirely clear on
why." His face goes red, twists into an even uglier sneer
as rage crawls across it. "Oh, shit. I did, didn't I? Look,
man, I'm really sorry but what goes on between con-
senting adults is really—"

He punches me in the face, snapping it to the side.
At this point it's mostly numb from all the pummel-
ing I took from Hank and falling multiple stories out
of a ghost hotel and yeah, I feel it, but it's distant
noise.

"You don't even know who the fuck I am, do you?"
he says.

"Harvey Dent?"

He punches me again. "Who am I, Carter? Say it.
Say my name. Who the fuck am I?"

"Not somebody who's ever punched me before, that's for sure. The fuck was that, a slap?"

"You destroyed my life, you fuck."

"You're gonna have to give me a little more to go on than that. It doesn't really narrow the field much. It's kinda my thing, you know. Destroying lives."

"Peter," he says.

I stare at him, my face a blank. "No," I say. "I don't think I know any Peters."

Punch.

"Sorry," I say, blood dribbling down my chin. "Still drawing a blank."

"Peter. I'm Peter. Peter Sloane, you fuck. You remember me. I know you do. Don't you fucking tell me you don't." He punctuates every sentence with another punch. Thank god there are no semicolons, and god knows what he'd do with an umlaut. "I was with David Chu when you brought the house down on us. When you handed him over to Attila Werther. I almost died because of you."

"Oh," I say. "Peter." I can barely recognize my own voice. Peter was Councilman Chu's lackey, the guy who was working with Quetzalcoatl to get Darius's bottle. His face settles a bit at being remembered. "I thought your name was Phil." He punches me again.

"Mister Sloane," says a voice behind me. I can only crane my neck around so much, but I recognize Hank's voice. "Do you need me for anything?"

"What? Oh. No."

"Nothing at all, sir?"

"Of course not. I've got this."

"Am I dismissed?" There's a subtle emphasis on the question, particularly that final word, that makes me think there's more to it than just cutting off early from work.

"What? Yes. Go do whatever the hell you want. I'm busy here."

"Thank you, sir. I need to make a phone call."

"Whatever," Peter says, waving him off, not even bothering to look at him. I hear the door open and close behind me. Even though I had thought I was alone with Peter before, having it confirmed by hearing Hank walk out is a little worrisome. The prospect of dental surgery from a half-burned psychopath is really not my idea of a good time.

"You know, this has been a hoot catching up and all," I say, "but what the hell do you want, Phil?"

"Peter."

"Right, right. Peter. Like Cottontail."

"I don't think you get the position you're in here, Carter."

"Oh, I don't know. Kinda hard to miss with all this duct tape. It's not exactly shibari, but whatever turns you on. Seriously, though. What do you want? Chu's dead, or if he isn't I bet he wishes he were. I get that you're the petty vengeance type, but you're ambitious, too. I'm thinking this isn't just you wanting to re-enact scenes from Marathon Man. This is about the bottle, right?"

"You know where it is," he says. "And you're going to tell me."

"Is that what Darius told you? I assume you're working for him now. Or you don't realize you're working for him. He's good at making people do things they thought were their own idea." He leans back a little, a slow frown crawling across his ruin of a face.

"Oh, please. Who did you think I'd go to? David's dead, Quetzalcoatl is fuck knows where. I just went to the source."

"Your source is blowing smoke up your ass," I say. "But let's play that game. Say I do have it. Let's say I can even get it to you. Put it in your grubby little hands. What the hell are you going to do with it? That thing's locked up tighter than a vicar's asshole. So unless you're looking for a nice objet d'art for your bookshelf, you're shit outta luck."

"Anything can be opened," he says.

"With what? Dynamite? Trust me, that's just going to blow it into the sky, and when it comes back down there won't be a scratch on it. The only guy who knew how to open it is Mictlantecuhtli. He's dead. I should know. I killed him."

"Bullshit."

I start to laugh but it turns into a coughing choke. "Darius didn't tell you about that little detail, huh? Yeah, not a shocker. He just wants it where he can see it, knows it's safe. He promise you three wishes? Some Hooters waitresses in short shorts and skintight shirts? Maybe fix your face up, make it so you don't look like a monkey's ballsac?

"Come on, Phil. He can't give you anything, and he wouldn't, anyway. He's spent eight thousand years locked up and dancing to somebody else's tune. The fuck makes you think the second he gets free he's not going to just fuck everything up out of spite? If he promised you anything for getting the bottle, I don't think it's going to be what you think."

"The fuck do you know about it?"

"Clearly more than you do. What I don't know is how you did that trick over at the school pulling ghosts through the veil. I don't know what your knack is, but you're not a necromancer. Who taught you?"

The shifty look on his face as he considers how to answer tells me everything I need to know. "Nobody taught you, did they? Darius give you a spell to use? A charm?" I was too busy getting punched to really notice it before, but Peter's got a ring on his right index finger. He catches me looking and steps back, putting his hand out of sight.

"Nice trinket you got there, Phil," I say. "Is that

what you used? What's it do? Open holes between worlds? Grab ghosts?"

"Where are you hiding it?" Peter says, leaning in, his face inches from mine. Shit, even his breath smells burnt.

"Up your mom's smelly asshole." I slam my forehead into his nose with a satisfying crunch, knocking him back. Blood wells from one of his nostrils.

"Fucker." That charred claw of a hand goes to his nose. He doesn't punch me this time, but grabs a dental pick off a tray next to the chair, shoves the hook end into the side of my face, and drags it down to my neck. Yeah, that doesn't feel good. "Where the fuck is it?"

"Bottle, bottle, who's got the bottle?" I say, my teeth grinding together through the pain. "Why do you think I have it, Peter? What makes you think I'd even want it?"

He stabs the pick a couple of inches into my left shoulder, just below the collarbone. He wrenches it out and my vision swims, going dark around the edges. He spreads my left eyelids wide open, shoving his forearm across my face to keep me from moving. He raises the pick to jam into my eyeball.

But then something happens. There's a scream that isn't mine, a blur of red, a fountain of blood, and Peter's head in my lap. His body slumps to the floor, blood pumping from the stump of his neck.

Chapter 14

It takes me a second to process what the hell just happened, and when I do, I'm still having trouble understanding it. I feel like a wide-eyed raccoon in the middle of the road, caught by an eighteen-wheeler's headlights.

I slowly try to edge Peter's head off my lap, but the duct tape is too tight and all I do is roll it over until it's staring at me, eyes fluttering before going still and wide. The pouring blood slows to a trickle.

Hank steps into my field of view, blood covering his shirt, his arms. It drips from his fingers like a leaky faucet. He shakes some of it off, spattering it across the walls, the ceiling, me.

He looks at the body, looks at the head in my lap. "Man, was he an asshole. Don't thank me or anything."

Okay. Hank did this. Middle-aged, balding, slightly overweight Hank, the semi-effective private eye working for Darius to keep tabs on me whose ass I've kicked twice. Hank, the guy whose arm I broke when I jumped on him from a non-existent four-story building, who just slashed somebody's head off in the blink of an eye.

I can work with this. Peter's head falling into my lap was a shock, but it's not like it's the first time I've seen a sudden decapitation.

"All right," I say. "I won't." My voice is steadier than I expected. I can't fight or magic my way out of this, so talking and keeping my head is the only thing that's going to let me, well, keep my head. "Hey, I notice your arm isn't broken anymore."

He looks at me, down at Peter's head, to the thick wash of blood dripping from his hand, then back at me. "That's what your brain snags on? My arm's not broken anymore?"

"Not the only thing," I say. "You're wearing loafers. Can you even still buy loafers? I thought they weren't making those anymore, like leaded gas or sodomy laws."

"What am I gonna do with you?" Hank says.

"That's a really weird word. Loafer. Like someone who makes loaves. But I thought that was a baker." He snaps his fingers under my nose to grab my attention.

"Hey. That wasn't a rhetorical question."

"You really want an answer?" I say. "Okay. Kill me, or let me go. Either one, I got shit to do." If I die here and now, Santa Muerte won't be waiting three days for her boy toy to come knocking.

He gets a pained look on his face, is about to pinch the bridge of his nose and catches himself, remembering the blood soaking his hands.

"You did break my arm," he says.

"Looks fine to me." He's moving it around like nothing ever happened to it at all.

"Okay," he says. "Here's what's gonna happen. I'm gonna cut you out of that tape, and you're gonna walk away. And you're not gonna ask me any questions."

"What the hell are you?" He's definitely not human, though I don't know why he didn't do to me what he did to Peter. I hardly used any magic on him and he just took my punches. Why did he wait to kill Peter? He could have done that any time he wanted to.

"What in 'You're not going to ask me any questions' was unclear?"

"I don't take direction well. All my teachers said so." Then it clicks. He didn't kill me and Peter because he couldn't. And it wasn't until Peter specifically dismissed him that he took his head off. That would explain why I was able to beat the shit out of him down on Skid Row.

"Darius had a lock on you," I say. "You're a demon."

He wipes his hands on his pants and then realizes his clothes are so soaked that it's working out the other way around.

"Yes, I'm a demon. Yes, I was bound. No, I'm not anymore. Does that cover it?"

"Not even close." Like why aren't I dead? "Peter let you go. He was either monumentally stupid—" I look down at the unblinking head in my lap and move on. "Which I'll concede is a distinct possibility, or he didn't know what you were. Much as I think the former, I'm going with the latter. So he wasn't the one to bind you, was he?"

"You talk too much, too."

"Yeah, I'm a real chatterbox when I'm wrapped up in duct tape in dentists' offices, my face all ripped up by half-faced men out for vengeance, talking with random demons who decapitate people in front of me. Darius couldn't have bound you. Unless he somehow got you into his little pocket universe. He can barely extend his awareness outside of his bottle, so I can't see him being able to even summon you. Somebody sold you to him."

"Congratulations. You figured it all out," Hank says. "Ya know, you're so good at figuring shit out, I'll let you get out of that chair all on your own. I'm leaving now. Have fun." He heads toward the door, stepping out of view.

"Darius really fucked himself making Peter his

proxy, huh? That's what happened. He gave you to Peter to help him get me in this room and when he said you were dismissed, the binding dropped. You're a free agent."

"Leaving now." I can't see him, but I can hear the door open.

"I know how to take Darius down," I say.

There's a long pause and then I hear the door slowly close. Hank steps back into view. "You have my attention."

I've been intent on keeping the bottle hidden, but I've known that couldn't last. Peter was right, anything hidden can be found, and any lock can be picked. Even if I don't know how, eventually someone would be able to. So I've been mulling over a Plan B. Maybe Hank is just what I need to make it happen.

"No," I say. "I need a few things first."

"Nuh uh," Hank says. "I don't do contracts, anymore. That's what got me into this mess in the first place."

"Fine, then. A simple agreement. No magical binding. No blood." I look at the dripping walls. "No new blood. No signed contracts or handshakes."

"I don't trust you people," he says. "Mages are nothing but trouble. Why am I even talking to you?"

"Because I'm a charmer."

"You're really not."

"That's what everybody tells me. So, you in or out?"

"What do you want?"

"We don't hurt or kill each other."

He laughs. "Scout's honor, huh? All right. I don't believe you, but I'll give it a shot," he says. "I got my own demand. You don't try to banish me." Banishing demons is one of the first things a mage learns or they don't last long enough to learn anything else. There's no one place demons come from. Banishing isn't a subtle or delicate type of spell. It's a brute force kick in the nuts and a shove out the door, and not necessarily back where they came from. It's like being deported to a country you've probably never been to.

"I can live with that," I say. And if it turns out that I can't, this isn't a binding agreement. At some point it will probably devolve into us trying to murder each other, but I've had relationships built on less. "Second, I want to know who the hell you are."

Peter's body lets out the kind of fart that only the dead can pull off. The stink overcomes the scent of blood. A lifetime of being around corpses is helping me maintain eye contact despite Peter's rapidly evacuating bowels.

"I'm kinda with Peter on this one," Hank says. "That's a pretty shitty proposal."

"The fuck are you, the demon prince of dad jokes? You already know more about me than I know about you."

"You're not getting my true name," he says.

"Good," I say. "I don't want it." I figured he wasn't going to give me his real name. That'd be one more thing that could be used to snare him again.

"Is that all?" he says.

"One last thing. Get me out of this fucking chair."

"I kinda like the idea of leaving you here for the cops to find and see how you get out of that with no magic." It's a show. We both know my lack of magic is temporary. As soon as these nails aren't touching skin, I get my mage club membership back. "All right. Deal."

Razor claws extend from his fingertips and he slices the duct tape away. I yank the tape off my hand holding the nails in place and feel the magic flow back into me. The pain in my face and shoulder diminish to an almost tolerable burning.

I push Peter's head to the floor where it splashes in

the still-spreading puddle of blood and rolls to his slumped-over body.

"This'll be the second suit I have to throw out today," I say. I'll never cease to be amazed at how much blood a human body can hold, or how much of it can soak into my clothes. I get out of the chair, peel the last of the duct tape off me. I bend down and grab Peter's hand. The ring on his finger is definitely magic. If this is what he used to attack the Ambassador, I don't want it lying around.

Hank is one of the few demons I've run into that isn't unimaginably stupid. Most of the time mages summon them and they're little more than rabid eating machines with no impulse control. Takes a lot to summon, much less bind, a smart demon.

"All right, so what do I call you?"

"Still Hank Wells," he says. "Been Hank Wells for two hundred years. Don't see any reason to go by anything else now. I was summoned and bound by a mage in the 1790s. I was locked into this form and used as everything from a courier to an assassin. I got sold to Darius to pay a debt around 1910 or so."

"And you're a private detective now?"

"Not really, but it's an easy way to be places I shouldn't be when Darius sends me on errands. This time he wanted me to track you down and help Peter pull you in for an extended question and answer session. I think Darius is getting a little desperate. He wouldn't normally give my leash to an idiot like Peter."

"Does Darius know you're a free agent?" If not, that could be really useful. Not sure how yet, but if Hank could play the loyal stooge it might give me an advantage.

"Who do you think I went out in the hallway to call?" He laughs. "I been waiting a hundred years to do that. Man, he was pissed." So much for that idea.

"Now I've shown you mine. Show me yours. What's this plan to fuck him over?"

I want to ask more. Why does he hate Darius so much? How did he get summoned? What got him bound? But that's probably pushing too much for the first date.

"We let him out of his bottle," I say.

"I know my hearing's just fine," he says, "but did you just say—"

"We let him out of his bottle. Not here, of course. Some backwater hell, or something. I'm sure between the two of us we can figure out a place."

"I was hoping for something that was more like tearing his heart out and eating it in front of his face."

"Does he even have a heart?"

"No idea," Hank says, "but I'm willing to find out."

"You know you can't take him. In his bottle he's in charge of that entire pocket universe. Outside, he's strong enough to take on gods and win. You think you can take him?"

"I can try."

"And get fried before you got close enough. You can't kill him. I can't kill him. But we can make sure he's gone and stays gone. This is a better punishment than anything you could do to him."

"That's a shitty plan," Hank says. "There's gotta be something better." I hesitate, try to look as wary as I actually feel.

"You're right," I say. "It is a shitty plan. And I have a better one. I just don't want to use it."

"How come?"

"Darius uses people. But he's never steered me wrong. That's only because we were pointed in the same direction, sure, but I owe the guy. Killing him is an option I'm really not up for."

"I respect that," Hank says, a dangerous edge coming into his voice. "Tell me anyway."

I need to give him a story that will not only be one he'll believe but also what he wants to hear. If he's on the level he'll argue with me about it. Probably a lot. If not, he might just go along with a minimum of fuss. This whole thing with Hank could be a ruse, another game Darius is playing.

"I know where the bottle is," I say.

"Yeah, no shit. Tell me something new." At this point I doubt there's much Darius doesn't already know, even if he doesn't have the details. But I think this next bit might give him pause.

"I know a guy who can shatter it like a bottle of Dom on a brand-new yacht."

Hank raises an eyebrow in surprise. "I thought that thing was unbreakable." He's right so far as I know, but I need to sell him on the possibility that it isn't.

"Sure it is, more or less. But the spells holding it closed are weakening. There are cracks forming, cracks wide enough that if you know what you're doing you can shove them farther apart. This guy isn't going to try to undo Mictlantecuhtli's spells. He's gonna shove in a wedge and crank them open. They're wrapped in and around the entire structure. He cracks those spells, the bottle goes with them."

"I see a flaw here," Hank says. "If we break the bottle, how is that different from opening it?"

Here's where things either come together or fall apart completely. "Because once that bottle breaks, Darius is done for. He's not just locked in that bottle, he's tied to it. The spells Mictlantecuhtli put on it to turn it into a prison have also turned it into a death trap."

"Whoa," Hank says. "Does Darius know this?"

"Don't know. He might, but not care because he thinks the bottle can't be destroyed."

"So let's go get this guy," Hank says. "Take him out now."

"Nope. I gotta arrange it first. He knows me, but the

timing's important. We try this at the wrong time, it not only won't work, it'll never work. There are rituals, sacrifices. I still need to get my guy the things he needs. Then there's the matter of where we do it. When that thing cracks, it's gonna leave a pretty big crater. We got enough ghosts in this city, I don't need to add another thousand to the list if I don't have to."

"This guy have a name?" he says.

"Leather Charlie," I say. "He sells passports and bondage gear out of the trunk of his Buick in K-Town. Of course, he's got a name. You fucking think I'm gonna tell it to you?"

"I could beat it out of ya."

"You really want to test that theory?"

He narrows his eyes. He's thinking about it. I might not be in great shape right now, but I have my magic back. Even odds who the fight would go to, but even if it's him he knows I'll go down swinging.

"Fine. Keep your buddy's name secret. This isn't a 'let's go get him now' sort of plan. I get that. I'm just not thrilled about it." Really? Or is this what you want so you've got time to report back to Darius and get your marching orders because you're lying to me almost as much as I'm lying to you?

"Me either," I say. "But we have time. Darius can't afford to kill me because he still doesn't know where the bottle is or how to get to it. He knows if he fucks with any of my friends I won't wait around to find a safe spot to break that bottle. I'll smash that fucking thing and take myself and anybody else out just for spite."

"So what, I sit on my ass until you say go?" Hank says. "Screw that." There's no heat in his voice. If he's really upset about it, he's sure doing a shit job of showing it.

"You telling me that after two hundred years on somebody's leash you've got nothing you want to do?

Go out. Live a little. Do demon shit. It's not gonna take me that long. If he doesn't know you and I are working together, he's got no reason to go after you except petty vengeance."

"He's pretty goddamn petty," Hank says.

"This is the plan. You in or out?"

"This one's a shit plan, too," Hank says. "Just so you know where I stand on things."

"Surprisingly, I agree with you. But I got nothing better. How about you?" He glares at me, but it's clear he's coming up blank.

"I don't like you," he says.

"That's okay," I say, knowing I've got him. "I don't like you much, either."

Chapter 15

Lying to Hank was easier than I expected. My gut tells me he's still working for Darius, and this was all a performance to get me to think he's on my side. Of course, he might just hate Darius so much he'll jump on anything that could take him out.

The fact that I don't actually have a plan isn't a big deal, so long as Darius or Hank think I have one. If Hank's on the take, Darius won't move on me when he hears about it. If he's not, then Hank will probably stay out of my way for a little while before he figures out he's been played. Either way, it should give me a little breathing room. Crossing fingers.

With that seed planted, I just have to wait to see which way it grows. Until then, I have to figure out what's going on with Billy. I didn't exactly plan for this little excursion, so I don't have my phone on me. Which is just as well, because I need to head back to the Ambassador, burn these clothes, take some oxy, and do something about this ragged gash in my face.

There are days I think I should just go around wearing a painter's smock or a hazmat suit. Maybe something plastic that's easy to hose off. Getting back to the Ambassador is easy enough with a little Sharpie magic to keep people from looking at me, but I feel disgusting.

My clothes are a lost cause, covered in so much blood that it fills my shoes. Even after it's gotten cold and stiff, it'll draw ghosts from all over if I'm not careful. I have to get into the Ambassador's space before crossing over to keep from becoming ghost chow.

Hank turning out to be a demon has me a little thrown. I've only run into one other demon smart enough to have a conversation with who didn't try to kill me outright, and that's only because it'd been trapped inside a henge in Wales.

I don't fully trust him, but I'm banking on being able to trust him long enough to see what side he's actually on. If he's telling me the truth, great. If not, I still have Peter out of the picture, some bad intel fed to Darius, and hopefully some time to not have to think about any of them.

I'm a little worried about how the Ambassador will react to all the blood, so I'm ready to pop back to the living side if I can move fast enough. So far it hasn't tried anything, but then, I haven't been here covered in gore like barbecue sauce until now.

"Good evening, sir," the bellboy says to me when I cross over inside the Ambassador's lobby. Chipper and proper as ever. "You're looking a bit put out. Do you need a hand with anything, sir? Medical assistance?"

"Could you actually help me if I did?"

"I do have the memories of a surgeon who resided in me from 1962 to 1968. As long as you're not hoping for anything grandiose I'm sure we can figure something out."

"Thanks, but I'll be okay. Mostly I just need a shower. Appreciate the offer, though."

"Not at all, sir. Not at all. After your assistance with the earlier unpleasantness it's the least I can do."

"How are you holding up?"

"Right as rain, sir. The moment the spell stopped, everything went back to normal. It's been a long time since I felt that."

"That's happened before?"

"Yes. Not long after your grandfather rented his room. I don't know the particulars, but it seems a German gentleman of your grandfather's acquaintance tried something similar. I can only describe the sensation as like water swirling down the drain."

Granddad was a busy boy. The German is probably a Nazi necromancer named Neumann with whom he had some bad blood from the war. Real piece of work. I met him a couple of times before I left L.A. Made my skin crawl. Before I came back, somebody'd killed him. Rumor is they ate him, too.

"Did it feel like you were being pulled out?" I say. Is it the same magic being used to pull the ghosts through? Peter all but came out and admitted that the ring I took off him was the source of the spell.

"No," the bellboy says. "It was as if someone had opened up a hole and I was falling through it. An odd sensation. Do you think it will happen again?"

I can feel the weight of the ring in my pocket. Opened a hole. Interesting. Something's cooking in the back of my mind but it's not quite done.

"Not if I can help it," I say. Was that Darius's plan? To create a hole to pull the Ambassador through? But then what? I don't know if getting rid of the hotel would get rid of the door to the room, but I sure as hell wouldn't want to risk it.

Like with diseases and symptoms, different spells can yield identical results. Can make figuring out who cast a spell, what spell was cast, or how they did it a real pain in the ass. Magic's all about will, intent, and the ability to negotiate with reality so it does what you want it to do.

I know ten different spells I can use to light a cigarette. One requires doing calculus and complex topology equations to agitate the molecules where you want the flame to be until they heat up enough to light. Another one just tells the cigarette that it's on fire. Guess which one I use.

Every mage has their own way of doing things, their own way of looking at the world. Prevailing wisdom is that that's what causes each of us to have a knack. Seeing the world a certain way tends a mage toward a particular type of magic, which doesn't say anything good about my outlook on life.

If the ring can make a hole between the living and dead sides, it may not be the same magic that's being used to pull the ghosts through, but in a pinch seems like it'll do the job.

The question is, is that what it really does? The hole might be a side effect of what it's primarily doing, or it might be designed for a completely different thing.

I knew a guy, real asshole, who, whenever he got into fights, he'd cast a light spell on his attacker's eyeballs, taking them down screaming before they could even swing a punch. Most of the time the blindness was permanent. Completely fried their retinas. Pretty soon nobody would try to get close to him. He thought he was invincible.

I took him out from a building across the street with a high-powered rifle. Problem with mages. Always thinking the only way to do anything is with their magic.

"I appreciate the assistance, sir," the bellboy says. "If there's nothing else?" I tell him no. He nods smartly and I swear almost clicks his heels together. He heads to the front doors, presumably in search of baggage, while I head up to the room.

There's no cell coverage on this side of the veil, but in the room, for reasons I can't even begin to compre-

hend, my phone works. It's on the floor with about a
twenty percent charge left. All the notifications have
vibrated it off the table and drained the battery. Every
call is either Gabriela or Billy. Good odds they're all
variants of "Where the fuck are you?" I don't bother to
listen to them.

I dial Gabriela and she answers with, "I'm going to
kill him." Not what I was expecting, but somehow not
all that surprising.

"Is this a general 'him,' or are we talking about your
houseguest?"

"You get that motherfucker out of here now or I am
going to skin his hide and turn it into book covers."

"What the hell did he do?"

"Asking questions of my crew he's got no right to
ask. Poking his nose where it doesn't belong. I caught
him trying to break into the freezer car."

"Did he get inside?"

"No. Wards knocked his ass to the floor, but he is a
nosy sonofabitch. Taught him a lesson, though. Didn't
try that shit on anything else in the warehouse."

"Thank you for not killing him yet. I do kind of
need him alive."

"You're welcome. Now come get him."

"As soon as I can. I'm covered in blood and need
to stitch up a couple things."

"Of course you do. Do I want to know?"

"Not over the phone, you don't. But if you see a
balding, middle-aged man with a gut snooping around,
he's a demon."

"Should I kill him?"

"Not sure, yet. But probably."

"Got it. Get your ass over here as soon as you can
or so help me I will murder this motherfucker."

"Noted. I'll be getting Billy out of your hair to go
put some heat on the necromancer who's making all
those ghost bombs. You want in on this action?"

"Do I have to talk to Billy?"

"Might be unavoidable."

"Thanks, but that's a hard pass. Watch your back with him."

"Will do. With Billy if he doesn't have an angle, something is terribly wrong. I just haven't figured his out yet."

"You could just let me shoot him," she says. "It'd save a lot of time."

"Is he worth the bullet?"

"Hell, he's worth a whole clip."

"I'll come get him," I say. "Talk to you soon." She ends the call.

Goddammit. Billy might not be able to go back to his bosses because Mister Bo caught a hail of bullets, but he's still Billy. And he's still part of 14K. Of course he's going to snoop around.

I dial him next. When he answers I cut him off. "Don't say anything. I'm going to be there in about an hour. If you touch anything else, Gabriela will skin you alive."

"I'm not scared of her, Eric."

"You fucking should be. I am. I know what she can do and, more importantly, I know what she will do. When I say 'skin you alive,' it is not a metaphor."

"If I go back, I'm a dead man."

"Only if you go back empty handed," I say. "Take down Sun Yee On's necromancer and you'll be fine."

"Are you out of your fucking mind? The man pulls ghosts out of his goddamn asshole."

"Let me worry about that. You worry about how we're gonna find him. You and Bo were hunting this guy down. You must have gotten some lead. I mean shit, you got a name, right? Naga Fang?"

"Nanong Fan," he says. I can hear the disgust in his voice at my horrible mangling of the name.

"Dude, I've had a long night and I've spent the last

four years trying to remember how to pronounce my in-laws' names, so cut me some fucking slack."

"I don't know where Fan is, but I know one of the places where Sun Yee On does business. He might be there."

"You know if there are any other mages who might be there besides this necromancer?"

"Just a bunch of guys with guns, meat cleavers, bad attitudes. Dude, how the fuck should I know?"

"I'm the tourist here," I say. "What do you know?"

He closes his eyes, takes a deep breath. "I'll think of something. Make a few calls. There's still gonna be guys with guns there. Probably the same ones that shot up your motel room last night."

"Hey, don't forget your boss," I say. "They shot him, too. He bounced around like a water balloon on a live-wire. I mean, goddamn. That was a lot of blood."

"Hey, thanks for that reminder, man. It almost slipped my mind, but with that vivid image in my head, I'll have nightmares the rest of my life."

"Least I could do, pal. All right, see what you can find out. I'll be at Gabriela's soon. Don't do anything that makes her want to kill you any more than she already does."

"Yeah, I'll just sit in a corner like a good little boy."

"Perfect. You've even got that toddler whine down to an art."

"Oh, fu—"

I hang up on him.

It takes me more than two hours to get anywhere near presentable. The gash from the dental pick is too ragged to close with butterfly bandages, so it's needle-and-thread time. I wish I didn't suck so badly at healing magic. I'm more likely to tear my face off than knit the skin back together if I try it. Vivian tried to teach me some, long time back. Had me try to close a slice on a dead pig.

The pig popped. Yes, popped. And the less spoken about that the better.

I've stitched myself up before. More times than I can count, actually. But this is the first time I've had to do it on my own face.

A shot of Xylocaine together with a couple of Oxy-Contin to dull the pain and Adderall to keep me moving because goddamn I am tired. It's slow going because my left hand keeps cramping and though I can't feel the needle going through, I am looking at it in the mirror and can feel the tugging every time I pull the thread taut.

At one point my vision doubles and I almost stab myself in the eye, but it snaps back just as quickly. I decide to blame it on exhaustion, but I'm starting to get the feeling it might be more than that. I close the gash in my face eventually. The stitching isn't pretty, but it's good enough that I shouldn't look too much like Al Capone once it's healed.

The rest of my face is another matter. It looks like a well-used punching bag. My nose isn't broken, but damn near. My left eye is swollen, the color of meat gone bad. I've got a fat lip, and a couple teeth feel a little loose. I think I might have bruised a rib in the fall through the hotel, and I definitely did something to my knee.

I can't help any of that stuff right now. I'll have to find a mage doctor when I have time. I'm exhausted, I haven't eaten, and I'm beat to hell. But I don't have time for this shit.

When I'm up, dressed, and about to head through the door, I remember the nails. I lost the ones that were lodged in my hand when Letitia yanked them out with a claw hammer, but I've got these new ones Peter had on me. When I touch them I can definitely feel the effect. But anything between me and them and there's nothing.

I wrap duct tape around the bottom half of them, so the nails stick out about an inch or so. It takes me a little while but eventually I find a knife small enough in the suite's kitchen and attach them to the blade. One stab and they'll pop off, but if just touching them to someone's skin can disrupt a spell, it could be useful. I slide it into a pocket in my messenger bag, my hand brushing the Browning.

Immediately I get a vivid image of violence and blood and a question. Images, sensations, but not words. Well, that's new. I get vague impressions from time to time, but this is a whole new level. I was warned that as long as it doesn't start talking to me I should be fine, but this is a little closer than I'd like. I pick the Browning up, make sure it's loaded. Wonder if maybe I should get another gun. Again there's that sense of a question.

"Yes," I say. "You're probably going to kill a lot of people today." I get nothing else. Somehow that sudden mental silence is even more disturbing.

Chapter 16

I pull up to the gate and there's Billy waiting for me. He's cleaned up, got a change of clothes, though fuck knows how. There were times in Hong Kong I wondered if he was made out of Teflon. Always looked put together, not a hair out of place. He slides into the Honda's passenger seat.

"You couldn't have stolen a better car?" The look of mild distaste turns into wide-eyed shock when he gets a look at me. "Holy shit, what happened to you?"

"Walked into a door."

"Big door," he says.

"Not really, just sharp corners. All right, where are we going?"

"Chinatown. Ghee Kung Tong runs a mahjong hall on Yale near Alpine."

"I thought the tongs were like the mob."

"No. Okay, Ghee Kung, yeah, they've run into some problems. But most tongs are . . . look, *tong* is just a word that means, like, a meeting hall, a social gathering place. Think of them like the Elks Lodge"

"With the occasional racketeering."

"Ninety percent of them, no. They help their communities. They help with immigration, English classes, that sort of thing. They're a lifeline for the Chinese coming to the U.S."

"You seem to know a lot about this for somebody who isn't a local."

"I'm new on this scene, mate. I only know what my bosses told me to watch out for. I know who the players are, yeah, and where some of them hang out, but not much more than that. Like this mahjong hall we're going to. I know that officially, this one's run by Hop Sing Tong, which is squeaky fucking clean."

"And unofficially it's run by Ghee Kung?"

"Parts of it, yeah. And unofficially unofficially those parts are owned by the Sun Yee On Triad."

"Wheels within wheels, huh?"

"You have no idea. Thing is, that's where my knowledge begins and ends. I don't know anywhere else they hang out. I don't know if there will be anybody there. I don't even know if the place is still standing. Somebody could have firebombed it last night for all I know."

"Fair enough." I have to take a more roundabout way to get to Chinatown. There's only the one working bridge across the river to Downtown and the traffic's already backing up.

This is a good sign, actually. For a while there wasn't anything but police and military vehicles on the road. But now it's mostly personal cars and commercial traffic. Road and bridge repairs are happening, more and more burnt-out buildings have been razed, and new construction has been sped up to get people back into homes. L.A.'s a city that constantly reinvents itself, just not usually in such a blunt force trauma sort of way.

L.A.'s Chinatown has been through more than a few reinventions itself. It's been around since the mid-1800s, a tenuous haven for the Chinese who came over to build the railroads. Took the usual shit immigrants get: racism, violence, death, and then some.

In 1871 about five hundred white workers went on a rampage and murdered nineteen Chinese men. Hung them from lampposts. Their ghosts are still there, angry and vengeful haunts judging passersby who can't even see them.

We pass under the Chinatown arch hanging over Broadway, a billboard-sized sculpture depicting two gold dragons facing each other. One is untouched save for soot, but the other is half-melted, giving the impression that it's slowly oozing down the supports and onto the street.

Chinatown was hit by the fires as badly as any other place in L.A., but somehow it feels different. Maybe it's my imagination, but it feels like the people are tighter knit, more insular. They had their own tent cities set up before the city or state came in. Already they've made more progress than most of the rest of the city has in cleaning up and rebuilding.

There are ghosts here, of course. So many more Wanderers confused at the state they've found themselves in, Echoes replaying being burned alive. A few razed lots are thick with them, men and women who don't know what hit them. One in particular where four men play a rapid game of mahjong, so absorbed in their game that they either don't know they're dead or don't much care.

We cross over to Yale and I slow down to see the devastation. As we get closer to Alpine I can see two buildings next to each other, the only ones left standing on this block. A Buddhist temple that looks deserted and a wide building with a sign in gold Chinese characters, topped with a red pagoda. Large double doors up a few short steps are opened to the street.

It's completely undamaged, which isn't too surprising, since I can see and feel multiple protection spells laying one on top of another. Some I recognize: earthquakes, fire, scrying. Somebody wanted to make sure this place stood no matter what happened.

There's a pretty big nullification spell built into the doors. I doubt magic would be dampened inside—that would screw any mage in there—but any spell that isn't strong enough to push past it is going to fizzle out.

That means no Sharpie magic. I had thought I might be able to get in posing as a fire marshal, but the second I pass through that door, the whole spell would collapse. With this much thought put into the place's defenses, I'm betting every other entrance has the same problem.

The place is packed. There are so many cars parked on the street, we have to drive another block over to find a space for the Honda.

"Popular place," I say.

"Popular game. I heard there were a couple more mahjong halls around here but that they all burned down in the fires. This is the only spot in Chinatown where you can play. Not everyone there's a member, but I heard they opened their doors to anyone who wants to come in for a game." He glances at me. "Well, anyone Chinese."

"So business is good."

"Business is very good," Billy says. "But not because of mahjong. People play for money, sure, but the hall isn't officially in any of that. The mahjong makes enough to keep the lights on and look legit. Any profit is through the drinks. And the money laundering."

"Oh, yeah. Can't forget the money laundering. You seem to know a lot about it."

"Ran a couple in Hong Kong. Gambling's illegal in China, but Hong Kong is its own little world. Technically, it's illegal there, too. But not so illegal that they can't operate out in the open. That much cash changing hands, it's easy to shift it around."

"And Fan is in there?"

He shrugs his shoulders. "Don't know. Maybe. Best place I can think of. How do you want to play this?"

"Depends. What are the odds everything goes south and bullets start flying?"

"Nobody's gonna start anything on the main floor. Too many civilians. Things are kind of a no man's land these days, but they start gunning people down in their own house, it's gonna raise some eyebrows. There'll probably be rooms underneath, though. Kind you won't find on any legal blueprints. Might even have some sewer access, maintenance tunnels, something. That's where shit's gonna happen."

"Okay. We can't sneak in, at least I can't. They've got wards that'll keep me from walking in with any magic that'll hide or disguise myself. No matter how we play it, they're gonna know I'm there. How about going in and playing a game?"

"You won't get through the door," Billy says.

"Chinese only?"

"Not officially, but yeah. This isn't your place. You can't walk in there and not expect to run into some hostility. This is where the community goes to not have to deal with any gwáilóu bullshit. You go in, nobody's gonna say word one to you. Hell, some of them don't even speak English. I've heard your Cantonese. It sucks. Know any Mandarin?"

"Nothing I can say in polite company."

"Thought so. Okay." Billy drums a beat on his thigh. I remember this from Hong Kong. The more he drums, the harder he's thinking. "Shit. I'll get you in, make some introductions. You can't sneak in, might as well just step in and announce yourself."

"Aren't you a member of a rival triad?"

"Yes, which is why I'm not crazy about this. But they don't necessarily know that, and nothing's going to happen on the main floor. Just be ready for anything. We'll go in, tell them we're looking for Fan. One way or another it'll get his attention."

"It's a plan," I say.

"Yeah," Billy says. "A stupid plan, but I got nothing else."

I get out of the Honda and dig through my messenger bag. The Browning goes in a holster at the small of my back where it itches in anticipation. Jesus. I need to melt that thing down as soon as I fucking can. My pocket watch and my straight razor go into an inside pocket of my coat.

"A pocket watch?" Billy says.

"Sentimental value. Belonged to my grandfather."

He shows me his wrist with an ugly-looking digital monstrosity. "Maybe consider upgrading."

"Mine's classier," I say. And a lot more dangerous. "You carrying?"

"Whenever possible." He shows me a Glock in a shoulder holster. I don't know what kind of trouble we're going to run into in there, so I grab a couple HI, MY NAME IS stickers and a Sharpie. I might not be able to use them before I get in, but that doesn't mean I can't use them inside. I grab whatever charms I have rolling around in my bag. A couple that I got from Gabriela look like marbles. They're, well, grenades is probably the best way to put it. They should come in handy.

I shove the messenger bag under the driver's seat and lock the door with a spell. I wonder what it would be like to own car keys.

"I hate that," Billy says. "Stupid magic shit."

"What? A lock spell?"

"Yeah. Frivolous shit. It's like if you used magic to wipe your ass."

"Go big or go home?" I say.

"Yeah. Otherwise, what the hell's the point?"

"Take a look around you," I say with a sudden anger I didn't realize was there. "See all these burnt buildings? Vacant lots? Collapsed freeways? There are corpses being kept in fleets of refrigerator trucks off the 5 Freeway all the way up to Castaic like sides of beef because there are too many to bury or burn. Ten million people are traumatized. That's what big magic gets you, Billy. We're lucky that most people with magic can only do the frivolous shit. If it were up to me, magic wouldn't even exist. But it does and there's fuck-all I can do about it. Don't go wishing for big magic, Billy. You *really* don't want it."

Billy's backed away from me, eyes wary. "Sorry, man. Didn't mean to step into a minefield. We cool?"

I take a deep breath, center myself. "Yeah," I say. "We're cool. Let's get this over with." I knew I was angry. At myself, at my knack, at my role in all this devastation. But I hadn't realized I was angry about magic itself.

I let Billy take the lead. He's my introduction to this place. Right now I just want to find this other necromancer and figure out what's going on. The last thing I need is to cause a shootout in a room full of people just trying to play a game.

As we get closer I can hear the loud clacking of tiles snapping together, like a thousand skeletons being built one bone at a time. The games are a clattering wall of sound, voices of the players a steady murmur, seashells tumbling in ocean waves.

I wouldn't call the man at the door a bouncer per se; he isn't giving off the air of menace required for the job, but he definitely has the muscle. He sits on a folding chair that gives him a view of the inside and the outside. When Billy steps in he's all smiles. When I step in behind him, the air of geniality disappears.

I can feel the wards at the door triggering. The nullifier is a momentary thing. There's a split second where I feel the magic in my tattoos snap off like a light switch and then right back on as I step in. If I'd had a disguise on it would have winked out of existence.

I can also feel the alarms going off. Ripples of magic spread out, inaudible and invisible to anyone who isn't a mage. I don't feel the bouncer starting a spell, or tapping the local pool, so I don't think the alarm's for him. I'm alarming enough all on my own.

Billy says something to him in Cantonese. The bouncer responds, brusque and dismissive. Billy says it again, less politely, voice going up. This is going downhill fast.

I put my hand on Billy's shoulder as I feel the stirrings of a spell. It doesn't feel threatening. I get a sensation of being prodded at. Whatever it is, it's trying to get a read on who or what I am.

Billy stops to look back at me and I shake my head. "Give it a second." The bouncer starts in again, more forcefully than before, but Billy silences him with an outstretched hand. The man looks more surprised than anything else.

Before he can get really mad at us, his phone rings. He sees the display and quickly answers it. He listens for a minute, a wary eye on us. He finally says "Hěi" and hangs up.

"Wait here," he says. "Someone's coming for you."

Our presence hasn't gone unnoticed. Most of the players are ignoring us, but the ones closest to the door are sneaking furtive glances. Awareness spreads and soon the pace of play has slowed, creating an eerie silence that crawls across the floor.

"This is uncomfortable," I say.

"Told ya," Billy says. He nods over toward a door in the back as an older guy steps through. Graying hair, laugh lines, jeans, a fading Hawaiian print shirt. He makes his way over to us, smiling all the while. He's definitely a mage. I can feel the spell he has running—protection maybe? Hard to tell.

He steps up to us, the bouncer backing away to give him some space. "Hey, Billy," he says. "Who's your friend?" I've been watching the mage, not Billy. A quick glance tells me more than I really wanted to know. Billy looks terrified of this guy. Awesome.

"I'm Eric," I say, putting out my hand. He looks a little surprised, but takes it anyway.

"Gordon Chow. I'm sorry to have to ask this, and it's quite awkward, but can you come downstairs with me? I can't kill you up here."

Chapter 17

"Or, and here's an idea," I say, "we stay up here, have a chat, and nobody kills anybody."

Gordon sighs, pinches the bridge of his nose. "Look, I don't know who you are or why you're here, but Billy is at the top of at least ten different shit lists around here. Now, if it would make it easier, you can walk away. Thank you for bringing him to me, we really appreciate it, etcetera and so on. Or you can come downstairs and I can kill you, too."

"Your self-confidence is inspiring," I say. Billy's rooted to the floor, too stunned to move. "But you might find that a little more difficult than you think."

"Fine, I'll kill him and beat you to a pulp. Looking at that punching bag on top of your neck, I'd say you know how to take a good pounding. So what'll it be?"

There are at least fifty, maybe sixty normals in here. I don't like a lot of my options, all of which are messy to one extent or another, but I like threats even less.

"Look, Mister Chow, I can explain," Billy says.

"You don't have to, Billy. I don't want to know. Let's keep this simple. We both know the story. That way you won't have to tell any lies that I'm gonna have to remember later."

Then I get it. "Billy was with Sun Yee On and then bailed for 14K." I'm beginning to see how this is probably going to play out, and with every second that passes I'm more and more sure.

Chow laughs. "Is that what he told you? Billy, you little scamp. I can neither confirm nor deny anything, but if he says he's with 14K, then he's with 14K. That just makes everything worse. All I know is that he had an attack of conscience. Took a buddy of his along with him. Went looking for some shit-hot necromancer he kept saying was his friend. Billy here is so full of shit he sweats brown."

"Aww, Billy," I say. While Chow has been talking I've palmed one of the marbles from out of my pocket. "I didn't know we were friends."

I step in close to Chow, my left arm going around his shoulders and pulling him close like we're best buds who haven't seen each other in years. With my other hand I slam the marble into his mouth and cast a small push spell that rams it down his throat. He gags on it, but it goes down.

"Nod and smile," I say, quiet enough that only he can hear me over the clacking of tiles. "You've just swallowed a grenade and if I think the trigger word it goes off." He freezes and waves his hand at the bouncer before the man can move on me. "Good call. In case you were worried, none of these people will get hurt. Well, I don't think they will. It's designed to clear out a room. So the explosion won't go outside its boundaries. Any size. A box, an auditorium, an esophagus. At least that's how it worked on the last guy I did this to. But that's not even the best part. Do you want to know what the best part is?"

"Not really," he says, maintaining the rictus smile on his face with increasing difficulty.

"Well, I'm gonna tell you anyway. See, once it destroys everything in a room, then it cleans up after itself and implodes, pulling in all the debris and— You know, I don't really know what it does with it all."

"What do you want?" he says. He's starting to sweat.

"Oh, that's not really important just yet. What is, though, is the fact that it takes about seven or eight seconds for food to go through the esophagus and reach the stomach. So right about now that little marble o' death is floating around in a soup of your digestive juices. I honestly don't know what that'll do to it. I'm told these things are indestructible. Until they go off, I mean. Then, boy howdy, they are destructible as fuck. Ya know what I mean?"

I slap him on the back, laughing, like I just made the funniest goddamn joke. I glare at him until he starts laughing, too. He's not very convincing, but he's making an effort.

"I shoved one of these babies so hard into a guy's eye one time that it punched through the socket. When I set it off, it cooked the entire inside of his skull. His head swelled. Really, like twice its normal size. I guess it jacked up the bone too much because the implosion just sucked the whole head in. Five seconds tops and his headless body hit the floor like a cow in a slaughterhouse. If they actually cut off the heads of the cows. They don't do that, do they? That's a pretty shit simile. Anyway, there was a lot of blood. Do you find that's the case, too? I never really know with decapitations how it should go. I think there should be a lot of blood, but I'm still always surprised. Or do you just shoot people in the head? That would make more sense."

I turn to the bewildered bouncer, who's looking between me and Chow, not sure what to do. "How about you? You ever shoot anybody in the head? Do you put plastic down? I usually don't have time for that kind of planning."

"What," Chow says, voice shaking with fear and rage, teeth clenched, "do you want?"

"I dunno. Peace in the Middle East? A really good club sandwich? Pony and a jetpack? How about we start small. Take me to Nanong Fan. Oh, and anything goes weird, and I mean *anything*, I set that bomb off. If things go well, then I'll leave you alone, and you can shit it out later. Sound good?"

"I don't know where he is."

"Oh, now that is a pity. What do you think, Billy? Isn't that a pity."

"That—that sure is." Billy's starting to look even more nervous than this guy. Looking back on our time in Hong Kong, it occurs to me that back then he was the crazy one, not me.

"I can find him," Chow says. "I just need to call—"

"Yeah, see, we can't do that. On account of I don't trust you to make a phone call. If you don't know where he is, then that means he's not here. If he's not here, then where else might he be?"

"The guest house," the bouncer blurts out. He's damn near shitting his pants. "There's a guest house in the Hollywood Hills for visiting VIPs."

"Thank you," I say. "I like you. I probably won't kill you." I turn back to Chow and give him my most disappointed look. "Now, Gordon, you weren't gonna try to keep that from me, were you?"

He shakes his head. "N-no. I didn't think he'd be there."

"So, you were going to call ahead and let them know we were coming?"

"No," he says. "I wouldn't—"

"That's okay. We'll all go see him together." I snap my fingers as an idea pops into my head. "It'll be just like the Wizard of Oz. Oh, I want to be the Tin Man. Can I be the Tin Man? I've always identified with him, probably says something about my emotional problems. You can be the Lion if you want. Billy is definitely Toto. Wait. No. We can't go off to see the Wizard. We're already wizards. So, really nothing like the Wizard of Oz at all. And I wanted to be the Tin Man. So who wants to drive?"

———

Chow's got himself a sweet ride. Mercedes S560. Moves like it's floating on air. Chow's driving, the bouncer's got shotgun. I'm behind Chow dropping the occasional bit of trivia about the human digestive tract, and making him play a game of "What do I have in my bag?" Billy sits behind the bouncer, his Glock pressed against the back of the seat.

"Is it bigger than a fish?" Chow says nervously. I look inside my messenger bag. I made them stop off at the Honda to grab it.

"What kind of fish?" I say.

"T-tuna?"

"Gordon, I don't think you're taking this seriously. There's no way I could fit an entire tuna into this bag. Try again."

"A— trout?"

"You've got a thing for the T fish names. Let's see. No. It is definitely not bigger than a trout."

We do this back and forth for a while as he drives us north up Laurel Canyon into the hills. The fires destroyed so much of this area that the trees are nothing more than cracked and blackened fingers jutting into the sky, and the ground is a patchy quilt of black and gray char.

Whenever it rains, a ridiculously rare occurrence these days, Laurel Canyon turns into more of a waterslide than a street. Curving up and over the hills, water sluices down either side, taking debris with it, sending cars with bad traction spinning into each other.

When it happens again all the canyon roads are going to be deathtraps more than any other place in the city as everything turns to mud. No brush to hold the soil, no trees with roots strong enough to hold anything down.

Everywhere I look all I can see is how much worse everything is going to get. Been thinking lately that the city should just be walled off and evacuated like in that Kurt Russell movie. Nobody here but the die-hard Angelenos, the ones too stubborn or too stupid to get out. I'll probably be right by their sides.

"So, Gordon. It is Gordon, right? I'm horrible with names. You and Billy here have some history. How'd you two lovebirds hook up? Was it a meet-cute at a laundromat? It must have been adorable."

"I—" Billy starts, but I cut him off.

"I'm asking Gordon, Billy." Until now Billy's been a lead, nothing more. I could ignore the fact that I know fuck-all about him besides our time in Hong Kong. Now that we've gotten this far, and I'm deciding if I actually need him, I want to know a little more about who he is and how far I can trust him.

"We met in Hong Kong," Chow says. He's really sweating. I can see his eyes flitting to the road and back to us. Correction, back to Billy. Interesting.

"You don't say? Same here. Did you meet him in a bar that was being attacked by ghosts out of the Walled City, too? Because that would be one hell of a coincidence. Where in Hong Kong? What were you doing? I am really interested."

"I— We met at a Sun Yee On meeting," he says. "He was looking to become a member. Thought he had potential. So I backed him."

I'm starting to wonder more and more about Billy. I remember Gabriela saying she found him snooping around the warehouse. I'd expect him to do that. But he'd specifically gone for that freezer car? Why would he do that?

"Are triad meetings like Girl Scout meetings where you learn to make daisy chains, braid each other's hair, the best ways to dump a body in Victoria Harbour? Were there cookies and punch?"

"I don't—"

"Yes or no, Gordon. It's a simple fucking question. Were. There. Cookies. And. Punch?"

"Come on, man, quit fucking with him," Billy says. "You're gonna give the guy a heart attack before you get a chance to blow up his colon. The guy I talked to about getting you those pallets of ghost money was in Sun Yee On. So after all that bullshit, I already had a contact. After you left I tried to get in on it. Guy I knew sponsored me, got me in front of Gordon and they brought me on board. It's that simple."

"And then you went and did something that really pissed them off," I say. "What was that?"

"Nanong Fan happened. He started asking me questions about what happened in the Walled City. What you did, how you did it. I gave him what I had. Wasn't enough. Said he'd eat my brain so he could know everything I knew. I jumped ship, joined 14K. They had a better deal, and nobody wanted to eat my brain."

"That right, Gordon?" I say. "You want to add any personal color to that? Or I could just think about blowing up that marble. It's gotta be in your small intestine by now. I wonder if fire will shoot out your ass."

"You won't do it," Chow says. "You do and it'll crash the car."

"What, a ride like this? This car's built like a tank. Dual side airbags, we're all belted in. We'll be fine. Except for you. You'll be shitting fire."

Chow's breathing is getting labored. His eyes in the

mirror are locked on Billy's. A glance over at Billy doesn't reveal much. He's glaring at Chow, which could mean anything. But I bet I know what it means.

"I gotta say, Billy, your bullshit skills are second to none."

"The fuck are you talking about?"

"Gordon there really looks like he's getting his cues from you. Really nervous. Why would that be?"

"I don't know. Maybe because you're threatening to make him shoot fire out of his asshole?"

"What's really going on, Billy? You working with Gordon here? Fan?"

"Oh, fuck you," Billy says. "I came to you, you sonofabitch. You think I'm working with him? Why the fuck would I have a gun on him, then? I could have shot you any time since you picked me up."

"When we hung out you always had an angle. What's your angle here? What game are you playing?"

"Not dying," Billy says. "That's what my game is. I've got two triads who want to take me to a farm and feed me to the pigs. Yes, Gordon and I know each other. Once I got into Sun Yee On he was my boss. When I bailed, he got punished for it. I like the guy. I don't want to see him blown up. I also don't want to be turned into pig shit. Is that reason enough for you?" It should be, but something's wrong. I just can't quite place what.

No one talks after that. We're all thinking how we're going to get out of this. Chow doesn't want to explode. The bouncer, I still don't know his name, probably wants to leave and never see any of us again. Billy says he doesn't want to get killed. That I believe; it's the rest of his horseshit I'm not buying.

If I kill Chow and Billy's actually working with him, can I stop him before he puts a bullet in me? Or I could take Billy out and trigger the bomb at the same time. Gordon's sort of right, though. I can set it off while he's driving, but I don't want to. I want him to get us up to this house in the Hills.

Chow pulls off of Laurel and heads deeper into the canyons. Soon he turns onto a private road that ends in a gate about a quarter mile up. An intercom stands on a pole near the driver's side.

"We're here," Chow says. "To get in I have to talk to the people inside to open the gate."

"Go ahead. I trust you," I say. "If you can't trust a guy with a bomb in his intestines, who can you trust?"

Chow lowers the window. Presses a button on the intercom. "It's Gordon," he says. "Open up." A few seconds later the gate opens and he drives through.

Time to give everybody their marching orders. "Okay, now this is what's go—"

And then everything goes black.

Chapter 18

Context is everything. For example, waking up hand-cuffed to a chair with a hot blonde in leather in front of you and no desire to use your safe word is one thing. Waking up handcuffed to a chair with half a dozen triad thugs pointing guns at you and looking at you like they really, really want to pull the triggers is something else entirely. Considering how often I run into the latter and how little I run into the former, I should probably rethink the circles I run in.

The room I'm in looks a bit like one of those police interrogation rooms. Gray, industrial paint, bolted-down table and chairs. That's where the similarities stop.

Runes are painted on the ceiling, floor, walls, and door. They're not nullifying spells, which is interesting because you'd think they wouldn't want to put a mage into a room where they couldn't control the magic. No, these are spells for binding ghosts. Looks like I'm in the right place.

Instead of a one-way mirror, there's a large plexi-glass window set in one wall, behind which stand Chow, looking downright terrified, the bouncer, looking not-quite-so-terrified but making a good showing for second place, and an Asian man I've never seen before. Gaunt, somber, black suit. Kind of like an undertaker. I like the look.

I give Chow a wink and blow him a kiss and he steps back like I've slapped him. Oh, don't you worry your pretty little head. I won't blow you up. Yet.

My messenger bag is open and the contents spilled across the bolted-down table in front of me. My Browning, pocket watch, straight razor, and the ring I got off Peter's corpse are set aside from the rest of my gear: stones, notes, amulets, necklaces, bullets, baggies of dirt, a couple bottles filled with OxyContin and Adderall.

"That's quite the collection you carry around, Mister Carter," the undertaker says. "I've always found that the things a man carries say a lot about him. I look at that, I know a lot about you."

"Unless it's murderous-yet-punctual drug fiend who has a thing for grave dirt and assorted trash, you might be overthinking it."

I hear a groan behind me. Each of my wrists is cuffed to an arm of the chair, so turning is a little difficult, and any sudden moves seem to make the gunmen nervous, but I can stretch around enough to see Billy cuffed the same way in his own chair.

He doesn't look so good. He's taken a few good punches to the face. Dark purple bruises bloom on his cheeks and around one swollen eye. He slowly comes to consciousness, blinking in the glare of the caged fluorescent lights in the ceiling.

"You look like shit," I tell him when he comes to.

"You look worse," he says.

"No I don't."

"Fuck, man," he says, voice thick and slow. "You should see your face. That shitty stitch job you got is tearing open and you're bleeding all down your shirt."

"Hey," I say to one of the gunmen. "Yeah, you. Which of us looks more fucked up? Me or Billy?"

"Uh—" He looks nervously back at the plexiglass at the undertaker, who hides a laugh and gives him a nod. "You do," he says.

"Pfft. You're just biased."

"Mister Carter," the undertaker says, his voice piping in through a loudspeaker on the wall. He has a slight accent, but it's barely noticeable. "It's good to see you awake."

"It's good to be awake," I say. "Nanong Fan, right? Nice place you got here. I assume I got in here because your front gate was trapped and it took me down before I could blow up your boy Gordon back there."

"You assume correctly."

"Pretty bold having him standing out there like that. A guy could get ideas."

"I think you'll be able to keep your ideas to yourself," Fan says, gesturing to the nasty-looking men with guns. "I'm sure we wouldn't want any misunderstandings."

"God forbid we have a misunderstanding," I say. "Who knows where that might get us. Hell, we could have an event. Or worse, an incident."

"Just so," Fan says. "I understand you wanted to see me."

I know there are at least the two mages on the other side of the glass. There's no way to tell if the others are mages, short of them pulling power or letting it loose. I could get a shield up before anyone could pull a trigger, but then I'd have to deal with the mages.

Chow's easy. One thought and his intestines pop like a balloon animal tied by a schizophrenic clown. But Fan is an unknown quantity.

I could pop to the other side, but in theory I won't be able to leave the room that way. The sigils on the walls are designed to prevent any ghosts from coming into or leaving this room. As far as those spells are concerned, if I'm on the other side I'm a ghost.

Except that they should be on the other side of the veil. They're designed to be written over there. And they work on ghosts that have broken through. I learned that in Hong Kong. One of the few bits of luck I had there. I have a feeling things aren't quite so cut and dried as I thought.

"I think you got that backward," I say. "Seems pretty clear you wanted to see me more than I wanted to see you. I mean, you went to all this trouble to get me here, and stupid me, I went along with it. How long has Billy been with you guys stringing me along? Since he showed up at my motel room? Or did you get to him after I cut him loose?"

"You're right about some of that," Fan says. "I did want to see you. But Billy isn't one of ours. Not anymore. Hasn't been for years. And I imagine you wanted to see me about the ghosts that have crossed through the barrier."

"I'd say it's more like they'd been yanked across the barrier. And I don't for a minute believe you about Billy."

"Would this help convince you?" He nods to one of the men, who pistol whips Billy. Billy lets out a cry and blood pours from a gash in his forehead.

"Look at my face," I say to Fan. "Does this look like the face of a man who's going to be impressed with a little pistol whipping?"

Everything on and in my head hurts. I've got lumps on the back of my skull. The stitches where Peter dragged the dental pick down my face have popped and crusted over. Every time I talk, little dribbles of blood run down my cheek. I'm still having some trouble focusing one of my eyes because it's so swollen.

"You'd like to see him punished more?"

"More? Nah. Just convincingly. Cut him up a little. Break a finger. If you're gonna sell it, then sell it."

Fan looks irritated. "Would it convince you if we shot him in the head?"

"Oddly enough, probably not. But it would cut down on the number of motherfuckers in this room I'm gonna have to kill."

"I think you're bluffing, Mister Carter. I think you care more than you let on."

"Oh, sure I do," I say. "I care about lots of things. Doughnuts. I care a *lot* about doughnuts. I'm a cruller man myself. How about you? I'd tag you as a, hmm, maple bar kinda guy?"

"The fuck is your problem, man?" Billy says, a whine creeping into his voice.

"Hush, Billy," I say. "Mommy and daddy are having a conversation. And don't ask me which of us is which, I honestly don't know. So, Fan. I know why I wanted to talk to you. Why did you want to talk to me?"

"The ghosts in the Walled City," he says.

"That much I figured out. What about them?"

"When you bound the ghosts in the Walled City, how did you ensure they didn't go feral when you set them loose?"

Of all the questions he could have asked me, that one wasn't even on my list. "What's your shoe size?" or "Hey sailor, wanna dance the hornpipe?" were pretty far down that list, but they were on it.

"Come again?"

"The ghosts you bound into the joss paper. When they were released on our side of the veil they were compliant. Took orders. Killed who we wanted." The ghosts I bound became servants of whoever let them loose? This is an interesting development. I don't think I like it one bit.

"I could tell you," I say, though I have no idea how

I did it, or even that I had, but they don't need to know that. "But why would I?"

"Because we'll kill your friend if you don't."

"And who would that— Oh. You mean Billy. Knock yourself out."

"We could torture you," he says. "Do you prefer that?"

"Not particularly, but if it'll make you feel more virile or something you're welcome to try. How about this—you give me some answers, and I give you some answers."

"You're not in a very strong bargaining position, Mister Carter."

"Oh, I disagree," I say. "You want what I have more than I want what you have." I'm starting to think Fan doesn't have anything I want at all. The sigils on the walls are telling me a lot more than Fan is. The Skid Row ghosts, some shit Billy has said. It's all pointing me at something, but I'm still missing pieces.

"Is that so? You don't want to know how to stop the feral ghosts, or what we plan to do with them?"

"Doesn't really matter," I say. "Once I kill you it's kind of a moot point. So, give me answers and I'll give you answers."

"All right. Ask your questions."

"First," I say, "and most importantly, which one of you fuckers is bathing in Drakkar Noir? Good fucking Christ, can you take it down a notch? Seriously, Fan, how do you let these guys get away with it?"

Fan nods at one of the guards, who slams his pistol into my head. Blood runs down my scalp. "Oh, you really shouldn't have done that," I say to the guard. I turn my attention back to Fan. "I'm assuming Billy told you about the trapped ghosts. How'd you get the notes across the barrier?"

Fan looks offended, as though I've wounded his professional pride, but whether that's pride in his abilities at magic or acting, I can't say. "I'm a necromancer," he says. "I cross the barrier all the time."

"No you're not," I say.

"Excuse me?"

"The sigils you have painted all over the walls," I say. "They're not supposed to be here. Sure, they're supposed to work, and I get the feeling they have so far, but if you were a necromancer, you wouldn't have painted them here. You'd have crossed over and put them in place there."

"How do you know I haven't?" Fan says. He's trying to sound convincing, but I can see I've got him rattled.

"Because a real necromancer wouldn't put them in both places. They'd cancel each other out. Only an amateur who didn't know what the hell he was doing would try something like that. You're not a necromancer."

"You don't know anything," Fan says. "I should just have you killed."

"Oh, I know a lot," I say, pieces falling into place. "You tried to reverse engineer the ghost money from the Walled City, figure out how I did it. I know you went to talk to the ghosts on Skid Row to make them cross over to our side, but you couldn't do it well enough to snag more than a few. But then you got better at it. Figured out how to pull them over and trap them, but you couldn't get them to do what you wanted.

"But then you figured out a way to train them to feed or not feed. I'll admit, as a professional, that's a neat trick. Bravo. Hadn't seen that one before. Is this the room you did it in? How many bait dogs you go through before you figured out how to do it? Or have you figured it out? I think you still might have some bugs to work through."

The same guard pistol whips me again, the sharp crack of metal on bone ringing through my ears. For a second I see double. Takes me a moment to find my voice again. It's thick with blood and ragged breath. I'm getting real tired of being hit in the head.

"Just so you know," I say to the guard, "you're not walking out of this room." He laughs.

Fan's good at hiding his tells, but Chow's standing behind him sweating like he's in a sauna, so even though I know I have gaps and probably have some of the details wrong, I'm not far off.

"Since you're not actually a necromancer," I say, "how did you get the joss paper out of the Walled City?" And then it hits me. Fan isn't a necromancer, he couldn't have taken the money from the other side of the veil. So how'd he get it? No necromancer in their right mind would share something like that, so he didn't get it from one. That leaves only one person besides myself who could have grabbed it.

"Oh, fuck me."

A sigh behind me. "Eric, do you make everything this goddamn difficult?" Billy stands up, the cuffs falling away from his hands. One of the guards hands him a towel. He wipes his face and fake blood and bruise makeup smear off with it.

Billy. The guy who helped me set the trap.

Chapter 19

I knew Billy was lying to me, even if I hadn't twigged to how, but this blows my mind. Not that he had me fooled, or that he stole the money—I totally buy that—but that he's in charge of people. Who the hell let that happen? When I knew him he was a two-bit drug dealer who could barely tie his own shoes.

"How much did you take?"

"Couple stacks," he says, leaning against the table. "Hundred bills a pop. I didn't know how, but I figured they'd come in handy someday. You know, I figured it out completely by accident. I was out of rolling papers and grabbed the closest thing to hand."

That sounds like the Billy I remember. "Why aren't you dead?"

"Fan wasn't lying about everything." He finishes wiping fake gore off his face, tosses the towel, holds his hand out for a fresh one. One of his men obliges. "The ghosts you trapped, they're gentle as lambs. Completely safe. Unless you tell them not to be."

I think back to the ghosts at Keenan's house. Everyone could see them for a short time. The Walled City ghosts must appear like that, too, or Billy wouldn't have known anything had even happened when he'd lit that joss paper.

"You conjured up your own personal hit squad?"

"Oh yeah. And I knew just who to hit, too. By that time I was already in Sun Yee On. I was nobody. Cannon fodder, really. But I took out some competition. Not the guys above me, not at first. The ones at my level, the rising stars. I'd hit them after they pulled a job and take credit for their success. Took a while. Years, in fact, but I got there. And I couldn't have done it without you."

"So you're the Grand Poobah now?"

"The title's Shan Chu," Billy says. "But that's about right."

"Okay, wait a minute. There were thousands of bills on that pallet," I say. "Why are you trying to make more?"

"Because there still are thousands of bills on that pallet," he says. "I couldn't go back and get them. And I sure as shit wasn't going to find somebody who could. That's not a secret you share with a lot of people."

"But you did eventually," I say.

"A few. Loyalty needs to be rewarded. Fan and Gordon are the only mages I've brought into this. Fan's good, but he can't step over to get the notes unless there's a gap he can push through, and he tells me all the holes around the Walled City have sealed themselves up. I remember you being worried about that. That the holes would be permanent. Well, they're not. I'll be honest, I'm not happy about that."

"We all have to live with disappointment," I say.

Billy says something in Cantonese to the guards, and all but the one who has a hard-on for pistol whipping file out of the room.

"You're running out of ghosts, aren't you?" I say. "Your people can't get them, and even if they could, can you really trust them? Bring a necromancer on board and you're fucked. They'd be able to do a lot more with those ghosts than turn them into errand boys. Kind of cuts down on your options."

"Oh, it's more than that. I'm trying to save lives."

I can't help but laugh. "Wait a minute. Making ghost assassins is going to save lives? I can't wait to hear this one."

"You saw what those ghosts did inside that house and the garage in Burbank. They didn't discriminate. They can't. They went after whoever was closest. Tried to kill everyone who was nearby. Calling them grenades isn't a far cry from what they are, but that's not what I want. I need compliant killers, not uncontrollable nightmares. These new L.A. ghosts don't take orders."

"But you can train them," I say. "They can feed or not feed at your command. Some of your handiwork is sitting in a freezer in Gabriela's warehouse."

"You call that training?" he says. "I can't tell them where to go. Who to kill. I can't say, 'Eat this, don't eat that.' They're useless to me that way. I need to target the right people at the right time. Those things are like starving sharks."

"Let me get this straight. You're going to save lives by having more accurate assassins."

"I don't want the killing to look like an assassination. I want it to look like an accident. Makes limiting collateral damage kind of important."

"Are you crazy or just stupid? You want assassins, hire some goddamn assassins. That's gotta be cheaper and easier than this."

"And if I'd known that at the start, I would have. But I figured it'd be a cakewalk. Fan told me if he could get a good supply of ghosts, ones that were easier than most to get hold of, he could figure out how to pull them across and trap them."

"So stop," I say. "Call it a failed experiment. Go home a little wiser."

"Can't," Billy says. "I've sunk too much into this. I'm stretched too thin. I don't make this work, I don't live very long. The minute I started down this path there was no going back. Research costs, scouting missions. I didn't even know where I was going to find a large enough supply of ghosts."

"And lo and behold, Los Angeles beckoned," I say. "Fan figured that out for you, didn't he? That there'd be a fuck-ton of them here after the fires and there'd be cracks he could wedge open to pull them through and throw them into more traps. Only he fucked it up and they all came out wrong. Sloppy work, Fan. Very sloppy." Fan glares at me behind the glass. I don't think Billy realizes just what he's gotten himself into with Fan, or how big a problem he has on his hands.

"That's why I need you," Billy says. "I knew you wouldn't just tell me how you made the Walled City ghosts so docile. The plan was to either beat it out of you, or, if that didn't work, play on your friendship with your old pal, Billy Kwan. Rough me up a little, make it look like the big scary triad thugs were really gonna kill me."

"That would have been an excellent plan," I say. "Except for the fact that I don't like you. I don't remember if I liked you much in Hong Kong, but after not thinking about you in almost twenty years I can say with absolutely zero doubt that I give a rat's fart in a high wind what happens to you these days. Come on, Billy. I figured you were dead in a ditch and good riddance."

"You've gotten bitter in your old age, you know that?"

"I've always been bitter. Let's say I give up the secret. What makes you think that the second Fan has that information he wouldn't make his own little army and take you down with it?"

"I thought of that. Fan, how's your sister doing?"

"Very well, thank you," Fan says, his voice strained, tinny over the speakers. "We talk every day."

"I'm paying for her cancer treatment," Billy says. "She's in a state-of-the-art facility somewhere in the Swiss Alps. Even I don't know where it is. And she's very, very well protected by some of my most loyal people."

"I had a sister somebody used against me once," I say. "I didn't like it. I killed them and everybody who got in my way. If you think for a moment that Fan is just gonna play the good lapdog and shit where you tell him, you're in for a big surprise. But you know what, I'm gonna do you a favor, Billy. I'm gonna help an old buddy out. I'm gonna kill you before Fan does, and I'll do it quick. He'd take his time."

Billy laughs. "I have two loyal, powerful mages standing there ready to fry your ass the minute you try anything."

"You sure about that?" I say.

"You mean that 'bomb' you put in Gordon's stomach?" He says it with air quotes and laughs. "If it existed, why haven't you used it yet?"

"Because timing is everything," I say, and trigger the bomb in Chow's guts.

The explosion is a muffled pop, ripping his entire midsection open. His body can't contain the blast. Guess when I used one on a Russian thug's skull the bones were hard enough to keep it contained. Intestines and whatnot don't stand up to as much of a beating. The blast severs him in two, spraying gore all over the room. Fan puts a shield up, but not fast enough to avoid getting covered in Chow's guts.

At the same time I drop the cuffs off with an unlocking spell and throw a shield in front of me before the pistol-whipping thug can get his shot off. The bullet ricochets as I shove the shield into him with as much power as I can put into it. It slams into him like a freight train, crushing him against the wall. I can hear bones crack, but he doesn't drop the gun.

Fan isn't stupid. Somebody must have told him what else that little bauble I shoved down Chow's throat will do. He pulls his shield around himself like a bubble, bracing for what comes next.

Now that Gabriela's bomb has blown open Chow's intestines, the space it has to work with has gotten quite a bit bigger. When the implosion happens, it pulls everything inside the observation room into itself. It's like watching a sewer pipe burst in reverse.

Fan strains against the pull, holding his own. But anything not bolted down, and a few things that are, get sucked into the vortex. Chairs, tables, the sound system, Chow's corpse, the screaming bouncer from the mahjong hall, all the blood coating everything in that little observation room gets vacuumed up into nothing, until every surface is spotless, the room empty and sterile. Except for Fan in his bubble looking shell-shocked.

I take a second too long to appreciate Gabriela's quality craftsmanship and Fan's tenacity. Billy takes advantage and punches me in the kidney, dropping me to one knee and breaking my concentration. My shield sputters out, the gunman falling hard to the floor. He's not dead, and he won't be out of commission for long.

I duck out of the way of Billy's next punch and counter it with a jab. It's just him and me, but things are about to get a lot more crowded in here when his men bust through that door. I kick at him to gain some distance and turn, scooping my pocket watch off the table.

My shield did a number on the gunman. His right arm looks broken in at least two places, and his left hand is a mangled mess. He doesn't bother with the gun, rushing me instead.

I spin the crown on the pocket watch as he barrels into

me. Before I lose the fight with gravity I manage to shove
the watch face into his eye, and press the crown with a
click.

He screams, pushing himself away, but it's too late.
The pocket watch's magic burns into him. A hundred
years shred through him in the time between one heartbeat and another, and he falls to the floor, aged into a
withered, shrunken husk.

Billy tackles me, knocking the watch out of my
hand. It skitters under the table. I go to reach for it,
but Billy aims a kick at my head that I only barely
block. I roll to my feet to get some distance. When I
come up, he's aiming the Browning at my head. He
grimaces, stares at the gun in wide-eyed horror, then
flings it to the floor like it's a rattlesnake. I wonder if
it talked to him.

I take the opportunity to body slam him, both of
us going to the floor. I get my forearm onto his throat
and press down. He's not going quietly. He manages
to get an arm out from underneath him and use the
leverage to roll me off.

We both stagger to something resembling upright,
wheezing and unbalanced. He runs for me like a
drunken toddler. There's only one way I can think of
to get out of his path. I flip over to the ghost side and
watch Billy's glowing shape pass through me and
bounce off the wall, falling backward to the floor.

I slide back next to him on the living side, kick him
in the face. There's a loud crunch, and he screams as
his cheekbone pops out of place. I catch sight of Fan
stepping out of the observation room. "How loyal do
you think Fan is?"

"Loyal enough," Billy says. He sounds like he's
talking through cotton, and his cheek is already beginning to swell. Billy reaches for me quicker than I expect and grabs my ankle. I hit the floor hard, my vision
going black for a second before coming back. By that

time he's halfway to standing, using the wall to crawl his way up. I could throw a spell at him, but I'm having trouble concentrating well enough to do that right now. Anything I can think of to do to him might very well take me down, too.

"You a betting man, Billy? I am. And right now, I bet your pet mage who just walked out the door isn't coming to help you."

"His sister—"

"Fan's not stupid, Billy. He doesn't need you, anymore. He knows his sister's gonna be fine because I'm gonna kill ya."

"He—" Billy winces at the pain in his face. "He hasn't perfected the—"

"Are you really that stupid?" I say. "He doesn't have to make an army of ghost assassins. Ghost bombs will do just as well for him."

Running footsteps in the hall. Billy's face cracks into something that's more rictus than smile, then falls when he hears multiple gunshots. The shots are getting closer. While he's listening to figure out who's shooting who, I take advantage, stumble over to him and somehow get him into a choke hold.

The door breaks open. One of Billy's men sees me strangling his boss. I manage to spin around and get Billy between us just as he's pulling the trigger. Two rounds, center mass. I throw Billy's corpse at him and he drops the gun trying to grab him.

I shove my foot against Billy's back, pushing them both out the door, but physics being what it is, this throws me onto my back. Chatter of a submachine gun. Then a single shot, a scream, and the thud of a body hitting the floor. I hope whoever just won isn't on Billy's side. Doesn't necessarily mean they're on mine, but I'll take what I can get.

I feel a flare of someone pulling magic from the local pool out in the hall. Dammit. This might actually be worse than more reinforcements. I'd hoped Fan would get the hint and bail. I'm in no condition to take him on after all this.

Billy's man manages to throw Billy's corpse to the floor and gets his gun up and pointed at me. There's fuck-all I can do at this point. I was too beat up when I got in here, and I'm in even worse shape now. If he wants to kill me, well, be my guest, pal. Was bound to happen eventually.

But instead of a gunshot, I hear a sharp crackling sound, feel a spell going off nearby. Arcs of electricity dance across the gangster's body. He jerks, every muscle and nerve fiber firing at the same time. A couple seconds later he falls to the floor, his body smoking, revealing his murderer behind him.

"Jesus, Eric. What the hell?"

"Letitia? What are you doing here?"

"Following you. Gabriela called me a while back saying you were going to find the guy who's been making these ghost bombs. They really did a number on you."

"Only some of it," I say. I try to stand but that's not working. "Most of this is from a demon and a psycho with a dental pick I ran into earlier."

"You'll have to tell me about it," Letitia says, running in and getting my arm over her shoulder. She starts to half-walk, half-drag me into the hall.

"Hang on. I need my stuff." I grab the Browning and the pocket watch from the floor, scoop everything else back into the messenger bag. A string of Chinese coins and Peter's ring fall to the floor. I fumble for them, almost say fuck it and leave them there, but Letitia grabs them and tosses them back into my bag.

"How many did you kill this time?" she says.

"Six? I think? One of them got away. And I suppose I didn't technically kill Billy. Wish I had, though."

"Wait. The guy from Hong Kong? I thought he was your friend."

"Turns out not so much. Mind if we get out of here? I'm not feeling so good."

Vertigo grabs me and tries to pull me down. My stitches have popped and I can feel blood running down my face. The collar of my shirt's already soaked in it. "This is the third set of clothes I've ruined in the last twenty-four hours."

"That's not a bad thing," Letitia says as we come to the foyer where three gunshot corpses lie on the floor. "You could use a new wardrobe. Maybe something with a little color."

"What color goes well with bleeding out?" I say.

"A dark red, maybe?"

"I dunno, seems a little . . ."

"Hey," Letitia says, giving my face a slap that I can barely feel. "Stay with me. Fuck, I think you're going into shock."

"Shock's not so bad," I say. "It's a cheap high."

"Come on, we gotta get you patched up." She pours me into the passenger seat of her car. I start to feel guilty about bleeding on the upholstery, but then I remember that this is one of those unmarked LAPD cars, so fuck 'em.

"I got a guy in Venice," I say. "Mage doc. Decent enough."

"Red hair, thick beard, glasses, stinks like a hobo?"

"You know him."

"Jesus. Yeah, I know him. That guy's batshit crazy, high all the time. If he worked on you I'm surprised you're not dead. Besides if we have to make the trip all the way down to Venice, you are gonna be dead. We're gonna get Vivian to look at you."

"No," I say. "I can't do that. We're—"

"Shut up," she says. "I know. You've always been . . . whatever the fuck you two are. You're like a couple of goddamn children and it's time to get over yourselves and act like adults."

"Says the woman who lied to her wife about magic."

"Shut the fuck up." She pulls out her phone and punches a number on speed dial. Two rings, then: "I found him. He was inside a triad safe house." Pause. She looks me up and down. "He's pretty fucked up. Like more so than usual. Way worse than usual. Is Vivian there?" Another pause, longer. "Oh, for fuck sake. I'm not asking her to get back together with the guy, I just want him to stop bleeding all over my upholstery." She hangs up, gives me a dirty look.

"Fucking children, both of you."

Chapter 20

The second Vivian sees me she tells me to take my shirt off and get onto the exam table. Decades ago I might have said something snarky back that would end with us banging in a supply closet. These days she prefers not to talk to me at all.

Seeing her, long red hair, vivid blue eyes, tall and sleek, I wonder why I ever left. For a long time after I left L.A. and for a little while after I got back, I had this little fantasy that would play out in my head. I'd come back and it'd be like no time had passed at all. She and I would pick up where we left off. We'd hang out with Alex like we used to, and I'd reconnect with my sister, be the big brother I should have always been and never was.

Only Vivian and Alex got engaged while I was gone, my sister was murdered, and then Alex's soul was consumed by a nightmare of a ghost who broke all the rules. Vivian blames me for it. I blame myself for it, too.

I left to keep them safe. And for fifteen years it worked, and they lived their lives and moved on without me. Then I walk in like an epileptic rhino in a glass factory and everything goes to shit. So when I look at her, sure, I wonder why I ever left. But at the same time I wish I'd never come back.

She turns to the sink to wash her hands. "I want to be clear, I'm not doing this for you."

"Believe me, Viv, if I'd had a say in this, I wouldn't fucking be here."

"Letitia said you were seeing that second-rate healer down in Venice."

"Well, I looked around for somebody better, but it turns out not a lot of people like to talk to me, these days. Doc Stinky Hobo was the only one who'd see me."

"That's because nobody wants to talk to him, either. You're not scraping the bottom of the barrel with him. You're scraping through the bottom and into the floor."

"So why are you doing this?"

"For what you did for Keenan and his family. They're good people."

"They are. Was kind of surprised you recommended me."

"Not a lot of necromancers around," she says. "Trust me, I looked. I knew it wasn't demons that attacked. That much was obvious. If it wasn't ghosts, then with all the shit you've been involved in you'd at least be able to figure out what it was."

I'm not sure whether that was a backhanded compliment or not. "How's the kid?" I say. "Damien, right?"

"He's doing better. He's gonna need a lot of therapy, though. A friend of mine in San Jose's taken him in. He's a psychiatrist, a normal, who works with PTSD patients. He does good work."

I peel my shirt off, blood sticking it to me like glue. It's damn near agony, but I manage to get my arms through the sleeves. Just looking at myself I can tell this is pretty bad. Everything's bruised. Chest, stomach, arms. My right hand's swelling, and I've got cuts all up and down my arms.

"How about Keenan and the rest? I kinda got the idea Indigo wasn't one for leaving with unfinished business."

"Yeah," she says, snapping a nitrile glove over her hand. "They're sticking around, but I think it might be Indigo who's digging in her heels. She's stubborn and bloodthirsty. Kind of reminds me of you." I wince at the comparison. If she's like me, god help her.

"Yeah, I got that sense."

"Tell me you didn't rope her into whatever shit you're dealing with now," Vivian says. I can hear the warning in her voice.

"No. We talked about it, she pulled her head out of her ass at the last minute."

"Good," she says. "That family's been through enough."

She turns, tightening the second glove over her fingers, and stops once she sees me. "Jesus, Eric. How are you still standing?" she says, half in wonder, half in accusation.

"I look that good, huh?"

"Somebody work you over with a pipe wrench?"

"I think they just used the pipe. Come on, Viv, you've seen me in worse shape than this."

"No," she says, looking me over like a mechanic inspecting a car wreck. "I don't think I have. Don't move." She steps closer, puts her hands out and stops.

"What?"

"Just . . . just don't talk." She closes her eyes, places her hands on top of my head and I can feel her magic coursing through me. The spell is something complicated. I can only barely make out the shape of it. Vivian was always better at complex magic than I could ever be. When you're a necromancer, you don't really need complexity.

I recognize components of it. It's not a healing spell, but something more like divination. Underneath I can feel a cool detachment warring with red-hot rage and blanketed with a thick layer of sorrow and pity.

The spell fades and she says nothing. She opens her eyes and I can't read her expression. Almost a minute goes by before I break the silence. "How bad is it, Doc? Am I gonna live?"

"Let's talk about that," she says.

"That sounds not great. Want to unpack that for me a bit there, Viv? You're freaking me out a little."

"That was a diagnostic spell. You want the good news or the bad news?" Whenever anybody asks that question, they're stalling because the badness of the bad news always outweighs the goodness of the good. Fine, I'll play along.

"Let's start with the good."

"There is none. You're a train wreck."

"That's . . . blunt."

"You've got multiple contusions and lacerations. Those stitches in your face look like they were put in by an alcoholic coroner, by the way."

"Thanks. I put a lot of time into that look."

"It suits you. You're dehydrated, down almost two pints of blood. You've got fresh stress fractures in all your long bones. Cracks in your vertebrae from C7 to T4, as well as your sacrum. Three bruised ribs, another one broken. You've got a fresh boxer's fracture in your right hand. Almost every bone in your body has been broken at one time or another."

"How many more until I get a prize?"

"Shut up," she says. There's heat behind the words and I stop talking. "Whoever tried to fix the holes in your left hand did a shit job and damaged the nerves. Hope you weren't planning to learn the piano. All the blood vessels in your left eye have burst, but your retina's still hanging on fuck knows how."

"Okay. What do—"

"We're not done, yet," she says. "Your kidneys are bruised all to hell and you're gonna be pissing blood for the next week at least. The right lower lobe of your lung is filled with . . . something. I have no idea what. But it doesn't seem to be bothering you, so I'm not too worried about it. You need a new right hip, and your left rotator cuff is about to snap off your shoulder like a rubber band."

Jesus. I knew I'd taken some punishment over the years, but I didn't realize it was that bad. That's what I get for not getting a checkup for two decades, I guess.

"Are we done?"

"Oh, no," she says. "Now we're getting to the good stuff." She flicks up her left hand and a glowing blue image of what I can only assume is my brain appears between us. It flashes, lines glowing, areas lighting up. But there are a couple places where it doesn't.

"I take it those dark spots are bad."

"Yes, they're bad. You've taken too many hits to the head. You haven't just had a traumatic brain injury, you've had several. There are lesions all over your brain, I'm betting from multiple concussions, but I wouldn't rule out slow-growing, non-cancerous tumors. At least for some of them. You've had at least one, or possibly more, coup-contrecoup brain injuries in the last couple of days, which have caused some tiny subdural hematomas here and here." The areas she points to light up in the front and back of my skull.

"My brain is bleeding?" I say.

"That's your takeaway?"

"It's the only thing I really understood. So, again, is my brain bleeding?"

"Yes, but only a little. It's the lesions you need to worry about. Okay, yeah, you need to worry about the brain bleeds, too, but like I said, they're tiny. The lesions are stacking up. Have you heard of chronic traumatic encephalopathy?"

"No."

"Well, you get to learn about something new today. I've seen brains of dead boxers that look better than yours. Your tau proteins are through the roof, so if you make it another twenty years or so, expect to have some serious dementia. Visual and auditory hallucinations, that sort of thing."

"Like seeing ghosts?" I say.

She ignores me and moves on. "I suspect these," she waves at my tattoos, "have a lot to do with you still being even semi-functional."

"Okay. Brain damage. What do I do about it?"

"Normal people?" she says. "I'd be having end-of-life discussions. Put you on a fuck-ton of Gabapentin to control the seizures, probably get you started on Aricept now to hopefully slow down the cognitive degeneration a bit. Antidepressants and maybe antipsychotics for mood swings. Then I'd get you under the knife and carve out as much of that shit in your head as I could, but only after you decided whether or not it was worth it, because if you're not already banging on death's door, you're on borrowed time."

I sit there, stunned. All my cuts and bruises and freezer burns from pissed off ghosts seem trivial in comparison. Those are things I can slap a Band-Aid on, go to somebody like Vivian to help speed up the healing, reduce the bruising. Keep me on my feet.

"Considering that neither one of us is normal," I say, "what would you recommend?"

She pinches the bridge of her nose and closes her eyes. "Here's what's going to happen. I'm going to patch you up as best I can. It's going to take a few hours. I'll stitch you up right, especially that Frankenstein mess on your face, and speed up the healing. That'll close up the smaller wounds, bring down the bruising and overall inflammation. I can do something about your latest concussion, the brain bleed, the new fractures and your kidneys. I'll restore some of the functionality in your left hand just because I'm magnanimous."

"And the rest?"

"Just what I said. If you want, I'll give you drugs. Hell, I'll even point you in the direction of a neurosurgeon who does shit with lasers and magic that I can only dream about. But he's gonna tell you the same thing. Nobody can make damaged brain tissue suddenly whole again. This isn't going to kill you right now, but one of these days, if nothing else does first, it will."

I have brain damage. Brain damage that's going to kill me. I wonder if there are any spells I can get inked that will help with that.

"If I were normal, would I be dead by now?"

"Not necessarily. But you'd definitely have some neurological issues. You having any cognitive problems? Memory loss? Headaches? Double vision? Vomiting? Mood swings?"

I'm ticking off each answer in my head. Shit, shit, shit, shit, shit, and more shit. But what I say is, "No, none of that."

"Eric, I've known you for most of your life, even with that missing fifteen years where I don't even want to know what you did. You and I have done so many things together, closely, glued at the goddamn hip, and I can tell you, you are a really shitty liar."

"Can you do anything about it?"

"I can't repair the brain damage, no. Like I said, I can give you anti-seizure drugs, stuff for memory loss and mood swings, maybe even some charms to stabilize the damage so that it doesn't spread as quickly. But other than that, I can't think of anything."

"So, I'm okay, then?"

Vivian explodes, any pretense of friendly, or even coolly detached professionalism is gone in a heartbeat. "Have you been fucking listening to me at all, Eric? No, you're not okay. You are severely fucked up. I can spackle over the dents, but I can't help you. I don't know who can. I don't even know if you would even accept help. How often are the symptoms occurring?"

"On and off, a couple months. Didn't think anything of it."

"Has it gotten worse?" I think about that. Hard to tell. I'm not falling to the floor in a grand mal seizure, so I guess that's something.

"I think so," I say, "but only a little."

"Goddammit, Eric. A little is going to turn into a lot in the not-too-distant future. Right now, you're not expressing any symptoms other than that you're an asshole, but you've always been an asshole, and you don't seem to be any more or less of an asshole than normal. But I can say with absolute, one-hundred-percent conviction that you are not at all in any way, shape, or form okay."

"Oh, we're yelling now?" I say. "I can do yelling. The hell are you pissed off about, Vivian? Am I not getting dead fast enough for you? Is it that I keep popping up in your life? Believe me, I don't want to be in your orbit any more than you want to be in mine. Should I be dead? Yes. Many times over. I'm not. So sorry to disappoint. But hey, nobody outruns brain damage for long, right? I'll let you know when my head finally explodes and you can dance a jig on my fucking grave.

"Or is this about Alex again? Because I can only say sorry so many times. Let it out. Tell me. Tell me what your problem is with me. You clearly hate me, so why do you keep helping me? You were supposed to move to Seattle but got all chickenshit and stuck around."

"I told you—"

"Yeah, I know what you told me and it's horseshit. Why are you still here? Why are you even talking to me? Are you a masochist? Do you like having the blade twisted in deeper? I can tell it burns every time you look at me, so why are you here?"

"Oh, fuck you, Eric," she says. "You don't know anything. I could ask you the same thing. Why are you still in L.A.? Nobody wants you here. People are afraid of you. Or they want to find some way to win you over to their side, like they think your presence isn't pure poison. Then there are the ones who think they can get you to settle some score for them. Everybody else just wants to kill you."

"Then they need to speed it the fuck up."

"That," she says. "That's what I hate about you. You don't ever take anything seriously. You are dying and you make some smartass joke, let everything just wash over you and go on your merry fucking way. There are people who live in the real world, Eric. We lose the things we love. We remember who isn't around anymore. Normal people grieve. How about you? Do you even know what love is? When have you ever lost something you really grieved about? And don't say Lucy, because what you did wasn't grief. That wasn't even vengeance. That was you saving your own ass. If the only way you know how to deal with being hurt is to hurt more people there is something fucking wrong with you."

"What, like brain damage? Let's leave Lucy out of this. You think I haven't given anything up? You think I haven't lost anything? You know damn well I've lost, but you don't even know a tenth of what's happened to me. You don't get to throw shit like that at me. You're just deflecting. Stop avoiding it. Tell me. Tell me what the hell your problem is with me."

"You are all that's left." She screams it in my face and the force of it leaves me a little stunned. "Everything good in my life is dead, Eric. You are all that is left. Why? Why you? Why not Alex? Why not Lucy? I don't hate you for killing Alex because I know you're not the one who did it. I hate you because you're not the one who died. And you know why I keep helping you? Because you don't get out of this that easy. I'm not gonna fucking *let* you die. I want you to live long enough to lose more. I want you to know what it feels like. I want you to find someone and fall in love and live long enough to see it all go to shit right before your very eyes and feel it."

I stare at her, all the anger draining out of me. I offend her because in her eyes I'm winning. I'm not dead and the people she really cares about are gone. I'm getting away with something. That's how she sees me. Regardless of the things she knows about, regardless of the bruises and broken bones, the people she knows I've lost—and there are so many others that she doesn't—she thinks I'm some kind of fucking golden child.

Fine. Let her think that. Maybe she's right. I'm Mictlantecuhtli's stand-in, after all. Maybe I am fulfilling some bullshit destiny. Vivian can think about me whatever she wants. Hate me? Go for it. Think I'm the biggest monster out there? Sure. Knock yourself out.

But I'm not dead, and even if I will be with the next punch I take, that's the important thing here. I'm not dead and I still have shit to do. I've got an epidemic of feral ghosts, breaches between the dead and living sides, and a mage who knows how to exploit it all and has nothing left to lose.

"You want me to fall in love and see it go away? What makes you think I haven't, Vivian?"

"Shut up," she says, her voice quiet, exhausted.

"No. You're telling me I'm gonna die soon. We're finishing this because there might not be another time to. Is it gonna kill me to get punched in the head again?"

"Maybe," she says. "Probably. The inside of your

skull looks like a boxer who retired twenty years too late. If I didn't know it was you, I'd say I was looking at an autopsy."

"Right. I'm a dead man walking. We both know that no matter how I try, I'm gonna get punched in the head again. Probably a lot in the very near future. So, let's finish this now. I loved you whether you believe me or not. I left because I thought it would protect you and I stayed away because I was ashamed. And when I got back and saw you and Alex together it hurt. It hurt a lot. But he was a good man. A better man than I will ever be. When he died, part of me died along with him.

"You're right. I don't know how to grieve. Grief should heal. Grief lets you move on. But me? My grief is anger, and vengeance, and blood. And that doesn't solve anything, but that's what I know. My thing is to hunt down anyone who looks cross-eyed at my people and murder them as painfully and bloodily as possible. And I did that, and if I have to, I'll do it again. But I cried, too. I cried for Alex. I cried for you. I cried for Lucy, and my parents and dozens of other people you don't even know about. So don't fucking tell me that I haven't loved someone and lost them. And don't you dare tell me I don't feel it."

Silence stretches long enough between us that it begins to get uncomfortable. I've said my piece. I'm not going to break it.

But Viv will. "This is going to take a while," she says, her voice flat. She won't look me in the eye. "Even with painkillers it'll hurt."

"Good," I say. "It should."

———

I come out of the infirmary four hours later wearing a pair of jeans, a t-shirt, and flip-flops for somebody twice my size. Vivian and I are both exhausted, but I'm definitely coming out with the better end of the deal. She leaves first. I give her a wide berth before following her out the door. Gabriela and Letitia are waiting for us.

"How is he?" Gabriela asks Vivian before I get into the room.

"He's fine," Vivian says. Letitia frowns at her, knowing it's a lie. That's her knack, being able to tell when somebody's not telling her the truth. It's really annoying sometimes.

"But I could go crazy at any moment," I say, coming up behind her. Vivian glares at me and shakes her head. "What?"

"Take it seriously," she says.

"Never."

"The hell is that about?" Gabriela says. Vivian nods her head in my direction.

"Ask him. If he wants to tell you, he'll tell you."

"I take it then you two didn't kiss and make up," Letitia says.

Vivian laughs, but there's no humor in it. "No," she says. She grabs her purse and heads toward the stairs. "Next time you need him patched up, call the Hobo." She looks me in the eye. "Sorry. *If* there's a next time."

"That hobo has a name, you know," I say. "I don't know what it is, but I'm sure he has one." Without a word, without looking at me, she goes downstairs. Gabriela and Letitia watch her go but don't try to stop her, or ask her about it. So they ask me instead.

"What the fuck happened in there?" Gabriela says.

"I got a clean bill of health. We cleared the air about some things. It's all good."

"It didn't sound like it was all good in there," Letitia says, which is her diplomatic way of calling bullshit. Admittedly, after we stopped yelling at each other and she started working on me it actually became less pleasant. Viv is a professional but there's some pain you can't magic away.

"You don't look like you've been through a combine thresher, anymore," Gabriela says. "That's a win. I mean, don't get me wrong, you look like hell. But better."

"And she didn't stab me," I say. "Unlike some other people in this room."

"You can't say you didn't deserve it," Letitia says. "Plus, you're deflecting."

"Somebody should make you a detective. How's your wife?"

"How do you feel?" Gabriela says before Letitia can start yelling at me.

"Like hammered shit. Just slightly less hammered." I'll give her this much, Vivian's thorough. I hadn't realized that my skeleton was as jacked up as it was and hitches in my shoulder and hip that I hadn't realized were there are gone. But goddamn, everything hurts.

"All right," Letitia says, "you're not bleeding out anymore, so spill. What the hell happened in that house in the Hills?"

"I don't want to talk about this without alcohol and painkillers."

"I'll get the whisky," Gabriela says.

Chapter 21

Gabriela cracks open a bottle of cheap scotch and pours us all drinks. She leaves the bottle on the table. I dig the Oxy out of my bag.

"That shit's gonna kill you," Letitia says. I laugh, and she glares at me. "The hell is so funny?"

"Inside joke. Tish, if I get old enough for this stuff to kill me, then I've made it to the bonus rounds."

"Then why do you do it at all? It *will* kill you."

"Everything can kill me. A lot of things are trying." Including my own brain, apparently. "I'm gonna die. You're gonna die, Gabriela's gonna die. Everybody's gonna die. We'll all be one big happy dead family. The least I can do is face my death without a migraine."

I toss the pills back with the scotch. It burns on its way down. I pour another. Letitia's question is one I've been asking myself for a while now. I didn't start taking this stuff in any serious quantities until I got to L.A. I know I'm self-medicating. It's not a good solution for the emotional, physical—fuck, probably even spiritual—shit. I haven't been worried, because I picked up a couple of detox spells over the years that have let me avoid the crushing responsibility of having to deal with my problems in any kind of healthy way. Plus my headaches are getting worse. And now that I know why, and that I'm on a ticking clock, I figure hardcore narcotics are the least I can do to face that particular fate.

"Billy was supposed to help you find the mage responsible for the ghosts," Gabriela says. "Letitia tells me he was jerking you around, and he was running the mage who was trapping the ghosts, instead."

"Plus the mage got away," Letitia says.

"Thank you for the continued pointing out of my inadequacies. Appreciate it. Yeah, it's been a fun day. When we were in the Walled City, Billy snagged some of the ghost traps before I got us out of there. He's been using them to kill his opposition and rise through the Sun Yee On ranks. Burns a note, ghost pops out, kills who you tell it. But he's running out of them, so he brought on a mage in Hong Kong named Nanong Fan to try to reverse engineer what I did."

"That was stupid," Gabriela says. "It didn't occur to him that once this guy had it, he'd just kill him to get him out of the way?"

"Right?" I say. "I pretty much told him the same thing."

"The hell is wrong with you two?" Letitia says.

"What?" Gabriela says. "That's how I'd do it."

Letitia walks a weird line. Working with the Cleanup Crew to keep magic as under-wraps as possible as well as being an LAPD detective, her moral compass is constantly getting twisted around. At least she has one. That puts her above ninety-nine percent of us right off the bat.

"Don't look at me," I say. "I'd have done the same thing. Seems Fan had that plan, too. Billy could be clever, but overall he was never a strong thinker. When shit went down, Fan bailed and left Billy holding the bag."

"So Fan can create these assassin ghosts?" Gabriela says.

"No. He can't get it right. The ones I made turned out to be docile and don't kill anybody unless you tell them to. These new ones are feral nightmares who go batshit the second they hit the air. Instead of assassins, he made bombs."

"How did you do it?" Gabriela says. "Make them docile?"

"No idea. I didn't even know I had until Fan and Billy told me about it. I left those things in the Walled City, and good riddance."

"There's gotta be something you did differently," Letitia says.

"Obviously, but I don't know what Fan's doing. He might have taken a whole different approach to the problem. It could be as simple as the fact that I made them across the veil and he made them on this side. But I don't know."

"He's going to make more," Gabriela says. "That'll be fun."

"And do what with them?" Letitia says. "Billy's already dead. He could just slide into his place."

"Not that simple," Gabriela says.

"I know," Letitia says. "But for once I'd like it to be simple."

"We've all seen this shit before," I say. "It's the same as when I killed Jean Boudreau. Cockroaches came out of the woodwork to carve it all up. When Ben Griffin finally got the whole thing back together, I showed up and broke it all up again."

"Yeah, that went well," Gabriela says. I know what she means. One of those factions grabbing power was a crazy Russian mobster who got hold of a skinning knife that could steal someone's whole identity. Memories, looks, mannerisms. He came after me in her hotel, burned it to the ground.

"Sorry about that."

She waves it off. "If it hadn't burned then, it would

have burned a month ago. Point is, Fan's going to need to consolidate Billy's power base. He might have access to some of Billy's resources, but not enough to step into the big man's shoes. To do that he's going to need a lot of money fast."

"He's going to sell the ghost bombs." Letitia puts her head in her hands and groans.

"I think she's wishing she'd killed you in high school," Gabriela says.

"She's always wishing that. The way I see it there are two problems. One, yes, he'll make more, he'll probably get better at it and a lot of people will die along the way whether he's successful or not."

"Is the other problem stopping these things from getting out onto the black market?" Letitia says. "Because it's pretty high on my list."

"No," I say. "There are still holes in the veil all over the county and I don't know how to close them. From what I'm hearing about the breaches in Hong Kong, they eventually sealed themselves up, but I don't know how long it took. It could be years."

"So even if we stop him, ghosts might still be able to come across," Letitia says.

"Right. And if Fan has figured out a way to pull them across and trap them, some other mage might, too. Somebody who's a hell of a lot better at it than he is."

"And what about our mutual friend?" Gabriela says.

I glance over at Letitia. "You sure you want to talk about that now?"

"She already told me about what's going on with Darius," Letitia says. "Is he a third problem?"

"Maybe. Probably. Unrelated, though." I tell them about my run in with Peter and Hank, the Demon Private Eye who Darius owns. Or if Hank's telling the truth about being unbound, doesn't anymore.

"How bad off was Peter?" Letitia says. They'd

worked together at one point. Though she wasn't privy
to most of what was going on, and she's angry David
and Peter lied to her like they did, she still knew him.

"Bad," I say. "He should have been in a burn ward.
The fire really did a number on him. I don't know
how he survived. But he did and he eventually made
a deal with Darius. Things got . . . messy."

"He's dead?" Letitia says.

"Afraid so."

She waves it away. "I just worked with him. Doesn't
mean I liked the guy."

"So, this demon," Gabriela says. "He obviously
can't be trusted. He's a demon. But does he really want
to see Darius dead?"

"He did some song and dance about how he wanted
to kill him, and I think he might. But I don't buy for
a second he's got the same motives we do."

"That's a safe bet," Letitia says.

I knock back my second glass of whisky and pour
myself another. I top off Gabriela's, but Letitia begs
off. "So this is where it gets complicated."

"This is the complicated part?" Letitia says.

"I told him I knew where the bottle is and that I had
a guy who could break it open. Not release the spells
on the seal, but actually break the bottle. I don't know
if he bought it, but he perked up when I told him that
Mictlantecuhtli put in a failsafe so if the bottle breaks,
Darius dies."

"How much of that is bullshit?" Gabriela says.

"Most of it. He knows I have it, but then at this
point Darius does, too, so it doesn't really matter. But
I have no idea if it'll kill Darius if it breaks, or even if
it can be broken."

"What about opened?" Letitia says. "It's locked up
tight, isn't it? Nobody can get in without removing the
wards that . . . I'm not even gonna try to say his name,
that death god put on it."

"Yeah, about that," I say.

"Eric can open it," Gabriela says, regarding me over the rim of the glass with a look in her eye—I can't decide whether it's dangerous or not. "Can't you?"

"That's kind of a leap," Letitia says. She looks over at me. "It is a leap, right?"

"No, she's got it. I am now the official stand-in for one dead death god. And that comes with the perk of seeing how he did his magic."

"Handy," Gabriela says.

"A pain in the ass," I say. "Peter wanted the bottle, Darius wants it to be found. I don't know what Hank's angle is yet, but I don't trust it."

"The fact that Darius wants the bottle in play so badly worries me," Gabriela says. "He can't open it, but if he's trying to get control of it, he's got some plan to get it open."

"Hang on," Letitia says. "Can we go back to the 'Eric is the death god who can open the bottle' thing?"

"You knew about this. When we talked to the Santa Anas." Letitia and I had run into the spirit of the Santa Ana winds in Downtown L.A. I had thought I had made the deal with them to burn down Mictlan, but it was Quetzalcoatl speaking through them, playing them like puppets. They weren't happy about that. I convinced them that if they could at least not make the fires worse—which was a tough sell for the Santa Anas—then I'd get Quetzalcoatl for them. "They called me King of the Dead."

"You said you were more like the Groundskeeper of The Dead," Letitia says. "So when they called you King of the Dead, they really meant it?"

"Apparently. I'd been avoiding thinking about it. The deal was that I spend three months a year in Mictlan as Mictlantecuhtli to help get the place back in order."

"Like Persephone?" Gabriela says.

"Supposedly it doesn't have to be all at one time, so not quite. Same idea, though."

"And when you're not in Mictlan?" Letitia says.

"I'm just me," I say. "Boring old beat-to-shit Eric Carter. It's not like last time where I could use some of Mictlantecuhtli's power. That felt, I dunno, shoved in. Like overstuffing a suitcase. Now it actually feels like a part of me, but I can't seem to do anything with it. Figuring out the wards on Darius's bottle just sort of happened. But knowing how they're all laid out and intertwined, I should be able to unlock them pretty quickly."

"Should be?" Letitia says.

"Well, it's not like he's tried," Gabriela says. "You haven't tried, have you?"

"I'm stupid," I say, "but I'm not that stupid. Right now there should be no way anyone but me can get the bottle. And I'm planning on keeping it that way until I figure out what the hell to do with the thing."

"At least one of us should be able to get hold of it," Gabriela says.

"No," Letitia says. "He's right. If only one person can get to it, there's less chance it can be stolen."

"Then at least we should know where it is," she says. "Whether we can get to it or not, knowing that can help us keep it safe."

"That I agree with," I say. "Besides, at this point I'm pretty sure Darius already knows." I tell them about the ghost of the Ambassador Hotel, the connection to my grandfather's safe room in some other world. I hold back the storage facilities, though. I know there must be other people who know about them, but I don't know who they are. I don't want to muddy the waters by letting that information out.

"It's sitting on a dining room table," Letitia says, "in a 1950s hotel suite inside the ghost of the Ambassador, a hotel that was torn down and has had a school built over the site."

"On another world."

"Right. On another world. Hmm. Can you do me a favor and lie to me?"

"I think keeping your wife in the dark about magic was the best possible decision you could have made," I say. "Ever."

"Okay. One, fuck you. Two, my knack is *not* broken, so you're actually telling the truth. I hate you. Have I said I hate you, lately?"

"Not since we got here," I say.

"I hate you."

"Duly noted. Our Mutual Friend isn't as high a priority at this point. He can't get the bottle, not any time soon at least. Fan and the ghosts are the problem. I'm running on a deadline. I've only got a couple of days to stop him. I've been putting off Santa Muerte for a while now, and she's coming to collect whether I like it or not. I can't stand up to her out here. She can drag me all the way to Mictlan if she wants to."

They both take this news in stride. I guess once you accept that there's a djinn's bottle in an extra-dimensional hotel room inside a ghost that my grandfather made a deal with, hearing that a death goddess and folk saint is coming to take me away is no big thing.

"So that brings us back to the big question," I say. "Where's Fan?"

"He's working on a timetable," Letitia says. "Has to be. News will travel fast about Billy, and if he doesn't get his act together he won't be able to take power."

"Presuming that's what he's doing," I say.

"It's what he's doing," Gabriela says. "If he doesn't, he's a dead man. Whoever does take control is going to clean house and anybody who was close to Billy is as good as dead."

"Okay," I say. "He's got a deadline, too. So he's going to want to be where there's a large concentration of ghosts and holes he can push through to get them. It's also going to have to be wherever his traps are. We find one, we find the other."

"There's something we're forgetting," Gabriela says. "Power."

Of course. When I trapped the ghosts of the Walled City it nearly killed me, and I had topped off from the local pool and then some. I almost wasn't able to flip us back because of it. I don't know how many ghosts Fan's planning on pulling over, but he's going to need a lot of power to do it. Just pulling out the ones he's gotten so far would—

"Have either of you felt any big draws on the pool lately?"

Magical energy concentrates around people or places that have some sort of significance. Cities, churches, landmarks. I mean, you should see the one at Disneyland. It's sort of an unwritten rule that nobody tries anything there because there's so much to draw on that everybody nearby will feel it and get nervous. Nervous mages are one step closer to becoming violent mages. Nobody wants a mage war in the middle of the Magic Kingdom. Lightning bolts and gunfire on Space Mountain, slinging fireballs from the spinning Teacups, bringing all the animatronic characters to life as bloodthirsty golems, controlling the weather from the top of the Matterhorn and raining fire down from the skies to slag Sleeping Beauty's castle below—not that I've ever spent several hours at a time thinking of doing all of those exact things.

Okay, almost nobody wants a mage war in the middle of the Magic Kingdom.

"I haven't felt anything," Letitia says. "I don't like this."

"Me either," Gabriela says. "With so many people

dead, the list of missing persons must be through the roof. Who's going to miss a few more here or there?"

There are a few ways to power spells. Use your own power, draw from the nearby pool, use magic that's been stored like a battery, or use somebody else's energy. That last one, though certainly popular with a particular subset of mages, is usually frowned upon by the rest of us. It's not that we don't understand the practicality of it, it's that it usually goes by the name "blood sacrifice."

"It would have to be a lot of people," Letitia says.

She's right. Normals just don't have that much power in them. And then there's the problem of burnout. A mage can only channel so much power before they overload themselves and the results are . . . bad.

But there are ways around that problem, too.

"That sonofabitch," I say. "He's using other mages."

Chapter 22

Indigo picks up on the third ring. "Eric," she says. "You find the guy yet?"

"Looking for him now, actually. I know who he is, I just don't know where."

"What do you need?"

"The guy who showed up at the house and let the ghosts loose, he offered you all a place to stay, but he only wanted the talents."

"Yeah," she says. "Said we'd have rooms, food, running water, the works."

"Did he happen to say where?"

"Hang on." She puts the phone down and a few seconds later she's back, but the sound is different. "You're on speaker. I got Keenan and Aaliyah here."

"Do any of you remember the ghost guy telling you where he wanted to take you? Even if it's not specific, anything will help." I have a suspicion, and if I'm right at least I'll have a place to start looking.

"No," Keenan says. "But I got the sense he was talking about Downtown. Just some things he said. Lots of room in a fireproof hotel, that kind of thing."

"Fireproof?"

"Yeah." The twins sound so alike I can't tell if it's

Indigo or Aaliyah. "Like those brick ones off the freeway with the big signs saying they're fireproof. Like it was a big selling point. He even said, and I'm not kidding, 'convenient freeway access.'"

"Right," says the other sister. "I remember that. Like he'd memorized a brochure."

"This helps," I say. "Thanks." I'm about to hang up, but one of the sisters yells for me to wait.

"If you're taking this asshole down, I want to be in on it."

"This Indigo?"

She laughs. "Yeah. Aaliyah's too delicate for this kind of thing."

"Oh, shut up," Aaliyah says. "These people need to be watched over. Nothing wrong in that."

Keenan chimes in. "I'm with Aaliyah. We've got things to cover here, but nobody's stopping Indigo."

"I need this, Eric." I recognize the venom in her voice. She wants vengeance. She wants to see the motherfucker who killed her mother with ghosts and put his head on the end of a spike.

Thinking back to Vivian—I'd told her that Indigo had pulled her head out of her ass at the last minute when I headed to the chop shop. I'm not going to begrudge someone a little revenge. Fuck knows I'm not one to judge. If Vivian hears about this, it's not like she's going to hate me any more than she already does. Indigo's an adult. She can make her own choices.

"Know where the Bradbury Building is?"

"Yeah."

"Meet me on the corner of Broadway and Third at seven. If I'm there and you're not, I'm not waiting. And come loaded for bear."

"Oh, believe me," she says, and I can hear the smile creeping into her voice. "I will."

The last time I saw the Bradbury Building it was on fire. Historic building, lots of metal stairs and open air elevators. You might not have heard of it, but believe me, you've seen it. It's one of those L.A. locations that keeps showing up in movies.

Right now it's covered in scaffolding and tarps. Through the gaps I can see the empty windows, the charring reaching up from each one. I pull up in the Honda to the corner Indigo's standing at and lower the passenger window.

"Hey, sailor," I yell. "Wanna date?"

"I dunno. I was hoping for something classier," she says. "You look pretty cheap."

"Yeah, but I got a shotgun with your name all over it," I say. "I know how to show a girl a good time."

"You had me at shotgun." She slides into the passenger seat and shuts the door. She shows me a massive .50 Desert Eagle. "You said come loaded for bear."

"That I did. Two others are doing a sweep up from seventh." I describe Gabriela and Letitia to her. "And we've got about a dozen runners scouting out the area. Guys who work for Gabriela."

"Gabriela," she says. "The Bruja?"

"The one and only."

"You travel with pretty powerful company. She's a legend."

"Well, don't tell her that," I say, "or she'll never shut up about it. We're starting at Third and looping around. Keep your feelers out for any magic, no matter how insignificant. We think he might be killing other mages for their power and at the same time using the surviving ones to hold that power so he doesn't burn out."

"Jesus. And he's making more of these ghosts?"

"Yeah. It'll be a shitshow if it works. His boss is dead and he's got to be at least a little bit desperate."

"So we're looking for somewhere he could be holding a crowd of mages. Like a warehouse? This doesn't seem the right place."

"It also needs to be near a source where enough people died that there are holes in the veil. A lot of ghosts, a lot of holes, and a big enough space to hold and kill a lot of people."

"And Skid Row lost a lot of people?"

"Percentage wise, the most in the county. The numbers are stupidly high. At least five thousand people died within a handful of blocks that night when a fire tornado blew through. Caught everybody who was outdoors and roasted them alive."

"Got it," she says. "If he's anywhere, he's here."

"That's what I'm hoping." I turn on San Pedro and park the car. "Gotta make a stop first."

She follows me out of the car and into yet another burnt-out building. This one's nothing but blackened sticks, the stink of char still lingering in the air. I pull a small silver dish out of my messenger bag, my straight razor, and a Maglite.

"What are we doing?" Indigo says.

"Talking to some people who might give us a direction. If we're lucky, some of them will have enough brains to answer some questions."

I can still feel the ghosts of Skid Row around me. A lot of them are hiding, sliding between the gaps in my perception. I can feel them, but I can't see them yet. They're laying low, like spooked fish when a shark's around. The street is pitch dark. The streetlamps are all still out, and the surrounding buildings are all abandoned. I need some light.

I flick on the flashlight, its spotlight-strong beam slicing through the dark. "Hold that and point here."

I give her the flashlight and put my left forearm into
the light.

"Should we be lighting things up?" she says.

"I'm not worried about it. There's nobody on the
streets, and if Fan is nearby he's not gonna be here. The
bigger tears in reality and the greatest number of ghosts
are a few blocks down. And I would like to see what I'm
doing so I don't accidentally slash my wrist and bleed to
death on you. That would be embarrassing."

"Can I just go on record and say necromancy is
fucked up?"

"Not gonna get any arguments from me." I cut into
my forearm and the blood wells up. I let a few drops
hit the silver dish, pump a little magic into it, and call
out to the restless dead.

"Hey. Soup's on. Who's hungry?"

A handful of Wanderers emerge into view in front
of me. None of them look like any of the ones I saw
last time I was down here.

"Are they here?" Indigo says.

"Yeah," I pull a Band-Aid out of my pocket and put
it over the cut. This one's got superheroes all over it. If
you're gonna bleed for the dead, no reason you can't be
whimsical about it. "You can shut off the light. They
give off enough of their own."

"I think I'll keep it on," she says. "I'm a little creeped
out right now."

"Suit yourself. All right, listen up. I need to know
if anybody's seen an Asian guy, looks like an undertaker, trying to yank you lot over to our side. Anybody?" They all stare at the dish, mesmerized. I snap
my fingers in front of them and a couple look at me.

"I did," one of them says. "I'd seen him before. He
tried to get us to cross over to his side last week. Said
we could eat our fills. But he couldn't do it."

"Yeah, I know about that. How about more recently?"

"Yesterday," the ghost says. "I think. I can't see the sun here. Why can't I see the sun?"

"Because you're dead."

"Oh. What did you say?"

"Have you seen this guy more recently? Chinese. Undertaker-looking guy."

"Yesterday. He was able to do it that time."

"And that would be . . ."

"Taking us. I don't know how many he took, a hundred? They screamed. Like they were being torn apart."

"That doesn't sound good," I say.

"What doesn't sound good?" Indigo says. "I'm only getting half of this conversation."

"Fan was here the other day and yanked about a hundred ghosts over. Hey, how did he look afterward?"

"Who are you talking to?" the ghost says.

"Nobody you need to worry about. Focus. What did this guy look like after he pulled all the ghosts across?"

"Sick," it says. "Tired. Then he left."

"Did he have anything with him? A jar, a box, a bunch of money, anything?"

"He had the dead with him."

"Yeah, I got that. But in what? Did he shove them in a suitcase?"

"He took them inside him," the ghost says. "Can I eat now?"

Okay, that's probably not good. I wonder if that's how he's been trapping the ghosts in the first place. If so, he's crazier than I thought. Or this might be the first time he's done it, in which case he's stupider than I thought. I've taken half that many at one time and it nearly killed me. I can't imagine what that would do to someone who isn't a necromancer.

"Sure," I say. "It's all yours." The ghost descends

on it like a starving bobcat on a deer carcass. Indigo
jumps back a little as the dish bounces and rattles as
the ghost laps up the life in the blood.

Once the ghost has pulled whatever meager life it
can from those few drops of my blood, I pick up the
dish and wipe it out with a handkerchief.

"What the hell was that?" Indigo says.

"You want something from a ghost, you have to
bribe it. I just gave it a snack. It eats life. What you
saw was as much of a crossover from the other side to
this side as we should be able to get. When I call
them, the dish and the blood exist on both sides for a
bit. Doesn't need to be a dish. Black rams work surprisingly well."

"It can feed on the blood in a dead animal?"

"Oh, no. Animal's still alive."

"What would that do to a person?" Indigo says.

"Nothing you really want me to tell you. You said
it, necromancy's fucked up."

"Fuck. Are we done?"

"Yeah." I'm not sure if things are better or worse
than I thought. If the ghost's sense of time is right,
would Fan have been here before or after the house in
the hills? And why did he do it? That can't be how
he'd made the other ghost bombs.

We head back to the car. I take a yellow two-way
radio off the dashboard and click the talk button a
few times to get everybody's attention.

"I have Indigo," I say.

Used to be that if something happened Downtown,
Gabriela was the first one to know about it. As the
Bruja she was the word on the street. She was the go-to
mage everybody wanted to do business with. Somebody farted in City Hall, she'd know about it.

"Copy," Letitia says.

"Roger," I say back.

"You don't say roger," she says. "You say copy."

"Why?"

"Nobody cares, Eric," Gabriela says. "Hi Indigo, I'm Gabriela. Glad to have you with us. Sorry you're in the clown car."

"Uh . . . thanks?" Indigo says. I hit the talk button.

"Indigo says thanks. We made a pit stop so I could talk to some ghosts." I tell them what the ghost told me.

"Is that bad?" Letitia says. "Won't they eat him?"

"Not if he did it the way I think he did," I say. "He might be batshit crazy and think he's a hundred different people all at once, but it probably won't kill him. Not for a while, at least."

"Great," Letitia says. "Now everybody shut up." I toss the radio back on top of the dashboard.

"So what now? We're looking for lights?" Indigo says.

We're driving slowly down San Pedro with the headlights off. Not only would they tell people we're coming, but they'd fuck any night vision we might have. There are only a couple of streetlights working, and it's almost as dark as it was on Third. Like the one where we stopped, all of the buildings we pass are either derelict or dark.

"Or if you feel any magic, but yeah, lights. Clusters of cars, a big gaggle of rough-looking gentlemen standing outside a conveniently lit-up warehouse with a sign that says 'Bad Guys Inside.' You know, the usual."

"And when we find them?"

"Improvise violently and with little to no regard for property damage."

"I can get behind that. So tell me more about this guy."

"A mage who learned a few necromancer tricks and improvised a couple of his own. His boss is dead now and we figure he's going to want to make more of those ghost bombs as soon as possible."

"I'm gonna kill him," she says. "In case you were thinking of anything like taking him alive."

"Do I look like a 'taking them alive' kinda guy? Reduce him to a chunky pink paste with my blessing."

The radio clicks on. It's one of Gabriela's people. "Think I got it," a woman says. "Sixth and San Pedro. Big building. Burnt all to shit, but there are lights on one side of the top floor."

"I see it," Gabriela says. "And feel it. Something's going on in there."

I grab the radio and answer. "We'll be there in a minute," I say and gun the engine.

Chapter 23

Gunshots in the distance. I can see Letitia's car and the flash of gunfire and spells coming from the top floor of the building. They couldn't have waited a goddamn minute?

"Let me out here," Indigo says when we're a block away. She's loading a shotgun, one of the Benelli M4 tacticals I had in the back seat with her. Between that and the Desert Eagle she should be able to take care of herself pretty well.

"What, you gonna fly up the side of the building?" I say, and pull over. She gets out and slings a bandolier of shells over her shoulder.

"Ha. No. I'm gonna run up it."

"You never told me what your knack is," I say.

"You never asked." She turns to the building and bolts. I can feel the magic as she picks up speed. Then, with a sensation like ears popping, the magic reaches some crucial point and then she's up the side of the building. Goddamn, she must go through a lot of shoes.

"Where the fuck are you?" Letitia's voice over the radio. "We're getting hammered over here!"

I don't bother answering. I gun the engine and head down San Pedro. Some of the gunfire is coming from the building's lobby now. I can see three guys with submachine guns blazing away at the car. I can see Letitia's got a shield up, and Gabriela is hunkered down putting something, a bandage maybe, on her left arm.

I aim the Honda for the gunfire in the lobby. As I hit the curb I throw on the high beams and hit the horn. I slam into the gunmen doing about fifty. The Honda crashes into the far wall, crumpling the front end and setting off the airbags. I black out for a second.

Right. I'm not supposed to do shit like this anymore.

I get out of the car as Letitia and Gabriela run up to me. The guys who were shooting at them are under the front of the Honda, at the end of thick smears of gore.

"Where's Indigo?" Letitia says.

"She went up without us," I say. "She runs. Really fast. And she has a shotgun. And a sweet Desert Eagle."

"We need to get up there," Gabriela says. "How are you doing?"

"A little woozy. How about you?" She's got a quick clot bandage wrapped around her left bicep.

"A little woozy. How do we get up?"

"It's ten stories," Letitia says. "We're going to walk into a bullet hose if we try the stairs."

"Hang on." I dig through my messenger bag until I find Peter's ring. "Either of you seen one of these before? Pretty sure it's supposed to make portals. I have no idea how to use it."

"I've seen ones like it," Gabriela says. "If it's like most of them, you put it on, think about where you want to go, and tell it to open a hole."

"All right," I say, sliding the ring over my finger. "Let's give it a whirl."

It works. A space opens up in the wall in front of us

that looks out onto the top floor of the building. Fan's men are shooting wildly at something just out of sight. Either they can't see us or they haven't noticed us. I pull the Browning and put three of them down, while Letitia takes two, before the rest of them realize there's someone on their flank.

I close the portal with a thought and open up another one somewhere else on the top floor. Gunfire around the corner. Indigo zipping back and forth. I yell for her and she glances over and runs to us.

"Neat trick," she says.

"Yeah, it's kinda nifty. How are you doing?"

"I don't think they like me," she says, reloading the Benelli. They're still firing, not realizing that she's ducked around the corner. That's not going to last very long.

"You're in good company," Gabriela says. "They don't like us, either."

"How about we all go be unlikable at them together?" I say and step through the portal. Gabriela follows, and Letitia looks at it a little nervously, like she expects it to snap closed and cut her in half, before hopping through.

This is a pretty potent little trinket. Makes me wonder what else I could use it for. It also makes me wonder why Darius gave it to Peter in the first place.

"How do you want to work this?" Indigo says. I look to Letitia. She's got more experience with this sort of thing than I do.

"Call in a SWAT team?" she says. "This isn't exactly my area of expertise."

"Jesus, you people," Gabriela says, and strides toward the corner. They've stopped firing. I can hear reloading and a few tentative steps from behind cover.

Gabriela puts her hand on the wall and closes her eyes. At the touch, a ripple goes through walls and floors like they're water. A loud ripping and crashing noise, like a jet engine and a woodchipper having a shredding contest, comes from around the corner. Water bursts from pipes, sparks explode from the shattered fluorescent lights, throwing the entire floor into darkness. Screams. Gunfire. Silence.

I give it a few seconds then peek around the corner. I cast a light spell over the remains of the hallway and let it float downward, revealing a path of destruction going five stories down. The entire hallway from one end to the other and down through half the building is missing. A pile of debris and bodies lies at the bottom.

"Tell me we don't have to go down that hall to find Fan?" I say.

"Back the way you came," Indigo says. "There's an office and I think it passes around through to the other side. Are we sure this is the right place?"

"Fuck, I hope so. Why?"

"I can't feel any magic," she says. "If he's killing people to power his spells, we should be able to feel him drawing the power out of them, or at the very least whatever spell he's working on."

She's right. I can't feel anything happening. And then I can, but it's not magic. I trigger the ring for the lobby and push all three of them through it while yelling at them to get the hell out of there.

I snap the portal closed and turn just as the first of the feral ghosts comes screaming around the corner.

———

The first time I remember seeing a ghost, I was seven years old. My power had already manifested and, like how you lock up every scrap of food when you have a puppy you can't trust not to counter surf and eat it all, my family had to take precautions to make sure nothing died in the house. Because it would never stay dead, or at least unanimated, for very long.

Later, when I had more control, if something did die, like the few times cats would go under our porch and keel over, I'd prop them up and march them down the street and let them fall over there. It was like trash that took out itself. But I hadn't seen ghosts, yet. I was vaguely aware of them, had the feeling there were more people around, that I was never really alone.

My parents didn't really know what to expect of a kid who can see the dead. When my invisible friends started telling me things like how they were murdered, it kind of threw them for a loop.

They couldn't find another necromancer to apprentice me to, so all they could do was teach me how to use magic as best they could and hope I didn't get myself killed using spells they couldn't even understand.

But that first ghost. That thing terrified me. I was at the park with my dad on a swing set, trying to blend in with all the normal kids. And all of a sudden this guy with half his face ground down like he just spent an hour on a belt sander appears in front of me and starts screaming.

So, of course, I start screaming, and not knowing what the hell is going on, my dad starts screaming. So now there's me, my dad, and a dead guy with the worst case of road rash ever, all screaming at each other. I probably peed myself or something, but I did something else then, too.

I killed it.

That's how I saw it at the time, killing it. Before I knew what ghosts were and how they worked. It was instinct. It scared me, so I sort of grabbed it with my mind and squeezed until it popped. And then I wasn't afraid of ghosts anymore. I kept not being afraid until I had to face a dozen of them on the other side of the veil and they were trying to kill me.

And then I was terrified all over again. Kind of like now.

There are ten of them, and I can feel more manifesting nearby. I wonder if Fan isn't even bothering to trap them, just wedging a hole open and letting them through.

These are like the others, feral, nothing left of them but hunger and rage. They've been stripped of so much that I don't know if I could really call them ghosts.

The first two I squeeze until they explode, and the two after that I eat. They go down like lemon juice and razor blades and it takes everything I have to not fall over puking again.

The other six are right behind them, and I get my shield up and around myself just as they get to me. They slam against it, scratching and screaming. I can't keep this up forever. My shield's going to crack eventually. And there are more ghosts coming behind them.

I need something I can use as a spirit jar. Something big enough to hold them all, like back at the Montecito Heights house. I don't think a trash can's going to do it this time. Or even a dumpster.

How many ghosts can you fit into a single spirit jar? Like how many angels can dance on the head of a pin. It'd be an interesting philosophical question if I wasn't about to get eaten.

The few times I've been in a situation where a fuckton of ghosts are on my ass I've either had to make a run for it, which has gotten me tagged enough times that there are still places on my body I just can't feel, or I've been lucky enough to have somebody conveniently nearby I can throw at them to eat instead.

But this time it's just me. Going through them isn't an option I'm all that crazy about. Especially after hearing from Vivian that I'm living on borrowed time. A spirit jar seems my best bet. But what to use?

Huh. I wonder if anybody's tried making one out of a building. Let's find out.

I push the shield further out, giving me some space. I'll have to make this quick, and it'll be sloppy. If it works at all I'll be amazed. I pull a can of spray paint out of my messenger bag, shake it up. This one's light, running low. I used more than I necessarily needed to at the Montecito Heights house and I haven't replaced it.

With the trashcans, I painted sigils to lock the ghosts into the can on each of the walls, plus floor and ceiling. I don't have that luxury now. I can only touch the floor, and that's only because the shield is descending down through it in a bubble below. If it were more powerful, I could slice through the floor itself, which would be kind of counterproductive, not that I know from personal experience or anything.

I focus on each sigil, what they do, how they interact. A shape snaps together in my mind. I step to the side and spray the new sigil on the floor. The paint can sputters out just as I'm finishing up. I pump magic into the sigil until I'm starting to see spots and the shield flickers.

If I haven't totally fucked this up, if I understand my magic half as well as I think I do, then I should be . . . maybe fine? I don't really know, but at least I should still be alive.

I get behind it, as close to the wall as my shield will let me, then take a big, deep breath—not so much to calm or center myself, more hoping that during those last few seconds somebody would show up with a better idea than being bait for a ghost trap that might not even work.

I drop the shield.

Chapter 24

Broken claws and shredded faces. The ghosts burst toward me, a draining lake behind an exploding dam. But as soon as they get near the sigil, they stop as though they've reached the end of a very long leash. And then the trap activates and they all start pouring into it.

The trap fills and fills and it feels like it has to stop any second now and the remaining ghosts will tear me to ribbons. But it doesn't. And then the torrent of ghosts turns into a river, then a stream, and then nothing at all. I cast a sealing spell and lock the trap. The spray-painted sigil fades away.

They're a part of the building now. Stuck in the plaster and the wood, trapped in joists and nails and drywall. I don't know what will happen when someone tries to demolish this place. This is L.A., so that's a when, not an if. If I tear a chunk out of a wall will I bring a ghost with me? I don't think it would set it free, but burning it might. Good thing that already happened, huh?

I lean against the wall and slide down until I'm sitting where the trap was.

I hear a noise at the end of the hall that still has a floor. When the ghosts were coming at me, I could see in the dark just fine. They lit the place up like an arc welder, even if I was the only one who could see it. But now, my eyes haven't adjusted to the darkness, and I might as well be blind.

"If you're here to kill me, can you hurry it up? I'm tired."

"What the fuck was that, man?" Indigo walks toward me, shotgun at the ready. "I don't know what the hell you did, but we could feel the spell down on the street."

"Ghosts. A whole fuck-ton of ghosts. It was a setup. Fan isn't here. Probably never was."

"Are they still—?"

"Have you been sucked dry like a mummy or covered in freeze-dried claw marks?"

"Don't fuck with me."

"I'm not. I turned the building into a ghost trap. You are now standing in the most haunted building in Los Angeles."

"Can we sell tickets?"

"Sure. We'll even make t-shirts. 'I Went To The Haunted Nightmare Building In Skid Row And Didn't Shit Myself.'"

Indigo sits down against the wall opposite me. "I don't think a lot of people will be able to buy that one in good conscience. So what now?"

"Fuck, I don't know. If Fan didn't know someone was coming for him, he sure as hell does now. That's gonna make him harder to find, and worse to go up against. He'll be dug in."

"Is that what you think he was doing with those ghosts you heard about? The ones he pulled into himself?"

"Possibly. Hopefully. If that's the case, then he might not have killed a bunch of low-power mages and built a few thousand ghost bombs to sell to, fuck, terrorists? I don't know."

"Why are you doing this?" Indigo says.

"What, going after this guy?"

"All of it. Going after these ghosts in the first place. Helping me and my family. Don't get me wrong, I appreciate it, but what are you doing it for?"

"I think I just hate myself."

"That much is obvious. Have you tried Prozac?"

"I'll stick with narcotics, thank you."

The radio on Indigo's belt squawks. "Are you dead?" Letitia says.

Indigo stifles a laugh and answers. "No. He's not either. I'll let him explain it when we get downstairs. It's fucked up."

"Copy," Letitia says.

I take the radio and hit the talk button. "Roger," I say and turn it off before she can answer me. Indigo laughs as I hand the radio back to her. It's nice to hear laughter.

———

"It doesn't matter how much you stare at a map of L.A., it's not going to suddenly tell you what you want to know," Letitia says. We're back at Gabriela's warehouse and Gabriela is pacing back and forth.

"He is out there somewhere. He's in fucking Skid Row. Where the hell else could he be?"

"Vernon?" Indigo says. "That was a big explosion. Didn't it kill a lot of people?"

Big explosion. That's putting it mildly. Vernon is nothing but industrial buildings and toxic chemicals. When it blew up, the flames were five hundred feet high and blew out windows five miles away.

"Yeah, but most of them died from chemical exposure," I say. "The blast itself didn't take out that many people. There just wasn't anybody there. There are a couple hundred new ghosts in that area. That's not nearly enough."

And besides, there's no going into that area at all. The air's a chemical soup of poison so thick that nobody can even see into the area. And it's a big area. The blast sent all those chemicals into South L.A. Displaced families, killed hundreds. It's all a quarantine zone now, though the cops don't really enforce it. Trespassing in there is pretty much a self-correcting problem.

"What's the next highest?" Gabriela says.

"In order after Skid Row, as far as I've been able to tell, it's Watts, Pico-Union, Boyle Heights, Echo Park, Highland Park, Hawaiian Gardens, Beverly Hills, Pacific Palisades, Malibu, and Santa Monica."

"That sounds weird," Indigo says.

"No, it makes perfect sense," Gabriela says. "The most deaths were in places where the median income was below fifty thousand dollars. They wouldn't have had access to as many emergency services." She looks around at us. "What? I've got a Masters in sociology."

"What about the rest of them, though?" Letitia says. "Malibu? Beverly Hills?"

"I think those were personal," I say. "They're some of the richest neighborhoods in L.A. County. Quetzalcoatl wouldn't have cared, but his pet sicaria would have. I saw her FBI file. She was not a fan of the rich and famous."

"Well, then why not one of those areas?" Indigo says.

"I said they were the greatest number in order after Skid Row, not close to Skid Row's numbers. It's got about four thousand new ghosts in it. About a third of them were homeless. Most of them are too freaked out to show themselves, but trust me, they're there. In comparison Watts only has a few hundred."

"It's concentration," Indigo says. "Okay. Well, he can't be hiding in too many places, there just aren't that many buildings left standing. What does that leave? The sewer?"

"Fuck me," I say. "Of course."

"He's in the sewer?"

"No," Gabriela says. "Goddammit. He's in the fucking tunnels."

"What the hell are you talking about?" Indigo says.

"Downtown is riddled with old maintenance tunnels," I say. "Train access, bricked over Red Car depots, all sorts of things. A lot of the tunnels aren't used for anything anymore, and most of them are sealed off. But they're still there, and some of them you can get to pretty easily. A lot of them were used to move booze during Prohibition. There's an entrance in the basement of the King Eddy Saloon. That's how they'd get bootleg liquor in the thirties."

"He could be anywhere down there," Letitia says.

"No," I say. "He couldn't be." I get up and grab a bunch of pushpins from Gabriela's desk and go to the map on the wall. Goddammit why didn't I think of this sooner? I mark areas on the map. I don't know exact locations, but I only need approximates.

"These," I say, pointing to the new pins in the map, "are all the places where I've found thin spots in the veil. If he's doing what we think he's doing, he needs to be near one of them."

"They're all within a block or two of San Pedro," Indigo says. "But none of them are near the building we were at."

"Yeah," I say. "Because I'm an idiot. Fan made a bet that we, that I, would jump the gun, and he was right. He pulled ghosts from another part of Skid Row to pack into traps and stick into that building, then put a big sign out front."

"It didn't even need to say Bad Guys Inside," Indigo says, echoing our conversation in the car.

"It might as well have," Gabriela admits, fuming. "It was too easy." I don't know if she's pissed off at me or herself for not catching it. Possibly both.

"From what one of the Skid Row ghosts told me," I say, "we know he moved a fuck-ton of ghosts from one place to another by bringing them into himself, and he looked sick afterward. I'll bet it damn near killed him. If he knew that would happen he might have placed the traps to buy himself time."

"Or just kill us," Letitia says.

"Or just kill us, yes." I tap one of the pins in the map. "We need to find out what's underneath these spots. That'll narrow it down."

"And if we figure it out?" Letitia says. "What then? We went into that building with no fucking plan, and I can't believe I went along with it. I'm not doing the same thing again."

"Yeah," Gabriela says. "There's no way to know if he's set up more traps down there to defend himself. He'd be stupid not to."

"Don't forget the guys with guns," Indigo says.

"If he has armed guards down there," I say, "it might actually work to our advantage."

"How so?" Gabriela says.

"They're probably normals," Indigo says, seeing where I'm going with it. "They may not know what's going on, and even if they do, they probably don't understand it. It's probably freaking them out. Prime chance to sow some chaos."

"We can't count on that," Letitia says. "We need actionable intelligence. Proof. I'm not going anywhere down there without it."

"This isn't an arrest," Gabriela says.

Letitia snaps back. "No, it's potentially a suicide. I don't need something rock solid, I just need enough to know that I'm not going to walk in and get murdered by shit I can't even see."

"I get it," I say. "And I agree with you. We need more information. We're also on a clock. Fan's not going to sit on his ass and wait to do this." I don't say anything about the other clock, the more important one running on Mictlan time. I've got until sometime tomorrow to get this shit wrapped up, or they're on their own. I give Gabriela a look and she nods. From her grim face she knows what I'm really talking about.

"So what do we know about these spots?" Indigo says. "Why are they special?"

"These three were shelters," Gabriela says, pointing at each pin in turn. "They all ran soup kitchens and had beds for about five hundred people, total. They would have been packed when the fires hit. Then there are the people who camp out near the missions. Safer for them, relatively speaking."

"What about the others?" Indigo says.

"Nothing special about them that I can think of," Gabriela says. "People concentrate around the services, or at the edges where the cops push them out. There aren't any shelters or large groups of people in them that I know of."

"Community outreach," Letitia says. "That big building on San Julian's got an auditorium. There was a hearing to talk to the community about new homeless shelters in other parts of the city. It was packed with residents, activists, folks who don't even live in the neighborhoods impacted. I heard it wasn't just standing room only, it had spilled down the street."

"Okay, yeah, that's a lot of people who died in those areas," Indigo says, "but were there enough in each of them to open a hole?"

"From what I've been able to find out, it's a little more complicated than that," I say. "The breaches don't necessarily appear where the greatest number of people died. The breaches from the Walled City were about a block away from it. I think it's a matter of over-all concentration putting stress on already weak spots."

"So it doesn't matter why those spots had holes."

"Not really, no. What's important is what's under-neath those spots. If it's just sewer pipe we can cross it off the list. But if there's tunnel access we need to check it out."

"Do we even have a map of these tunnels?" Letitia says.

"Better," Gabriela says. "We have guides."

Chapter 25

It takes the better part of an hour to get hold of Gabriela's guides. She has to track them down, pass word from one person to another, until she finally gets hold of a vampire and a ghoul who used to live in her hotel together. After the hotel went down they went off the grid for a while and then popped back up doing real estate. Sort of.

There are a lot of things in L.A. that don't want to be seen. They can't pass for human, or can't pass very well. Gabriela was trying to make a safe home for as many of them as she could in her hotel. But even if it hadn't burned down I don't think it would have lasted.

The problem was that there was no community. Everybody was under Gabriela's roof, and there at Gabriela's sufferance. They knew full well that she could kick them out at any time.

And that's where Frank and Gary came into it. They'd been looking for out-of-the-way locations throughout the tunnels under Downtown for years and turned sections of it into squatter's paradises. Running water, stolen electricity, Wi-Fi. All these little forgotten nooks and crannies, comfortable, well hidden, easily evacuated. They'd gone through and rehabbed dozens without anyone knowing about it until they went public to the supernatural community and opened it up as the premier—or rather, the only—underground apartment complex for homeless supernaturals. To hear them talk, it was a huge success at first, then it was a bust.

"What happened?" I say. Frank, the vampire, lifts a cup of tea to his lips with shaking hands. Like all addicts who can't get their fix, he looks like hell. Too thin, brittle hair, eyes sunk deep in their sockets.

There's some weird schism between the vampires in L.A. Some of them are at the top of the food chain and doing just fine. Others, like Frank here, are cast out onto the street and aren't allowed fresh blood. If they try, the others come down on them like goose-stepping Nazis. I don't know why they don't fight back.

"We got too popular," he says, his voice thin and reedy. He sips his tea and puts it down. All of his movements are slow, considered. He's trying really hard to avoid dropping anything and embarrassing himself.

"Our clientele was . . . impulsive," Gary says. Where Frank is tall and thin, Gary has the build of a fireplug, and a voice to match, a raspy rumble like a burst pipe. Ghouls always look a little bit off. Their musculature is different, particularly around the neck. When they eat, they unhinge their jaws. Their mouths and throats are lined with hooked, inward-pointing teeth like a snapping turtle, and their throat muscles can swallow a freshly bitten arm in under a second. If something goes in, it's not coming back out again. Together they look like a horror show Laurel and Hardy.

"A lot of them are violent by nature," Frank says. "They could defend themselves just fine. But they could attack each other just fine, too."

"Then there were the ones on the waiting lists," Gary says. "We had a backlog a mile long. There just wasn't enough extra space we could turn into housing.

And when we did find a good place, it took a long time to get set up. People got upset. Some of them forced the issue."

"They would break in and murder the current tenants just so they could move up the line. And they accused us, *us*, of price gouging." Frank's eyes suddenly fill with red. Gary puts his hand over Frank's and Frank immediately calms. "Thanks, honey."

"We only ever charged them what it cost us to put together and maintain," Gary says. "Setup costs were amortized over five years with an assumed fifteen percent maintenance per year and rolled into the rent. Rents never went up, even when we had people willing to pay twice as much. We weren't doing it for the money. We didn't make a dime."

"How long did this last?" Indigo says.

"Two years," Gary says. "Then the shit hit the fan. We had a full-scale war break out. At first it was invaders from the outside wanting a spot, and then neighbors turned on each other. We'd hired extra security, some trolls, a couple of gorgons—"

"There are gorgons in L.A.?" Indigo says.

"Of course," I say. "We're a very metropolitan city."

"They were useless," Frank says.

"They were not useless," Gary says. "They were overrun. The fighting went on for two weeks. Got to the point where the normals were getting suspicious. City infrastructure was getting hit too often and it was bringing workers into the area."

"How'd the fighting stop?" I say. Frank looks nervously at Gary, who takes a deep breath and steels himself.

"We killed them," Gary says. He doesn't like saying it. Doesn't like that he did it. But he knows what he's done and he owns it. "We set up traps designed to hit all the weak spots we could think of. Poisoned blood for the vampires, cursed stone for the trolls, that kind of thing."

"It cost us a fortune," Frank says.

"Not really the point, honey," Gary says. "Once everyone was out we burned all the apartments and cut off all the utilities. There might be a couple spots down there that still have power and water, but we did what we could."

"After that," Frank says, "we let the scavengers in." Frank looks at Gary with sudden panic. "Oh my god, I'm so sorry."

"It's fine," Gary says, and it's clear it isn't and that they'll be having a discussion on race and appropriate language later on. "We brought ghouls in to clean up. After that there was nothing else to do. We had some money left, but not much. I was able to get a bank loan to open a carnicería in Boyle Heights. We did okay. Before the fires. Now we're just waiting on the insurance like everybody else."

"Can you tell us what's under some places in Skid Row?" Gabriela says.

"Oh, sure," Gary says. "We mapped those tunnels out with so much detail I'm surprised it didn't take us longer to do it."

"My OCD helped," Frank says. "Show me the spots, I can tell you what's under them." Gabriela walks them over to her map and points out the different locations. "Oh, they all have some space under them," Frank says. "Not a lot of space, mostly infrastructure tunnels."

"Which one is the biggest?" I say.

"Oh, this one, definitely." Frank points to the building on San Julian where the community outreach meeting was held. "That's where we put our main hall. We wanted it to be a gathering place, like the building above it. It was nice. Big, good ventilation. We had to tear down a couple of load-bearing walls, but not enough to cause a problem."

"The problems came later when the fighting happened," Gary says. "It's all open plan, and big. So no cover but lots of places around the edges to hide. It saw one battle that almost wiped everyone out on both sides."

"Any others about that size?"

"Not under any of those spots, no," Frank says. "The city could have done something since we pulled out down there, but I doubt it. They never move fast on anything."

"How do we get to it?" Gabriela says.

"Easy." He grabs pins and puts them into the map. "These are tunnel entrances. Power substations, maintenance crew staging. Some are just designed to connect city buildings together, like one further north at the Hall of Records. There's an elevator in the back. Most of them are in buildings. But this one on Wall is a DWP equipment yard. They have a freight elevator outside in the back for taking down heavy equipment. It's under a pair of big metal doors in the ground. Best thing about it is that it doesn't have a lot of security. There's usually a couple of night guards, but they're easy to get past or bribe."

"You think the elevator still works?" I say.

"Yeah. This place wasn't hit during the fires," Gary says. "It's also a substation for the grid, so they've got plenty of power. Saw them running it the other day."

"This helps," Gabriela says. "A lot. But we need to know how to get around down there."

"Thought you might," Frank says. He digs a smartphone from his pocket with shaking hands and sends a text. Gabriela's phone dings. "I just sent you the map. You're going to want to download it. Cell service will be spotty down there at best."

Gabriela looks over the map on her phone. "This could get ugly."

"How so?" Letitia says.

She points out our route and I immediately see the problem. The tunnel we have to travel down has several branches going out from it to connect to other areas. Great spots to set up traps and ambushes.

"It's worse than that," Gary says. "We made a point of knocking out a lot of the lighting down there. None of our tenants needed it and it added a little more security to the area."

"You got any night vision equipment?" Letitia says.

"Yeah," Gabriela says. "But we don't want to use it. You might know what you're doing, but I haven't put nearly enough hours into working with it. I doubt these two have, either. That's just going to get us killed."

"Magic," Indigo says. "There's got to be a spell that'll let us see in the dark."

"And the second we get close he'll feel it and know we're there," I say. "We can't go in with any active spells or we won't get anywhere near him."

"I know it's not our business," Gary says, "but I know you're going down there for a hunt. I don't know what or who's down there anymore or what you're after. But some of them, if they moved in after we cut the place loose, they might be friends of ours." He gives Gabriela a pointed look. "Or friends of yours."

"We're going after one of our own," she says.

"Should we be worried?" Frank says. "I was around for the last mage war in the twenties. A lot of good people died." I don't get the feeling he's talking about humans or mages.

"This won't go that far," Gabriela says. "If anything, it'll stop some things from getting worse."

"But I'd suggest you spread the word, quietly, that there's shit going down tonight," I say. "Believe me when

I tell you it's in everybody's best interest that we get this done."

Gary and Frank exchange looks. "Do you need backup?" Gary says.

"Yes," Letitia and Indigo both say just as Gabriela and I reply, "No."

"We could be running into a deathtrap," Letitia says.

"Which is why we can't ask them to risk their lives," Gabriela says.

"We also don't want to get in each other's way," I say. "It's gonna be bad enough with the few of us down there wandering through the dark and trying not to shoot each other. We invite more party guests and things are gonna go downhill fast."

"Thank you," Gabriela says to Frank and Gary. "I know what it took to ask."

"You helped us out when we were in a bad spot," Frank says.

"And I didn't do it so you could do me favors," she says. "What you've given us is more than enough. And your payment is in the infirmary in the large refrigerator. Take whatever you need."

Frank's eyes start to tear up, and he leans heavily against Gary. "Be careful," he says. "Please. And thank you."

"Come on, hon." Gary pulls Frank in the direction of the infirmary. "Let's get you fixed up, okay?"

I wait until they're both gone. "Anybody want out?" I say. Gabriela and Indigo are a resounding no. Letitia looks hesitant. "Annie know you're here?"

"No," she says, her shoulders slumping. "Annie left. We're not divorced. But she needed to leave for a little while and figure some things out." She sees sympathy on somebody's face, probably Indigo's. "She'll come back. I want to make sure I'm still here when she does."

"Your call," I say. "No matter how this plays out, it's gonna suck. And we all know there's no guarantee we're walking out of there."

"Is this the part where you say you won't think less of me if I don't go, but it's really a lie and you'll think I'm a coward?"

"Yes," I say. "Kidding. I'm on borrowed time. Whether I walk out of there or not's irrelevant. Nobody gives a flying fuck about me. I can't speak for Gabriela and Indigo, but, well, Gabriela's impossible to get along with on a good day, so I doubt she's got anybody, and Indigo specifically came out here to slake her bloodthirsty lust for vengeance. We got nothing to lose."

"How do you know I don't have somebody?" Gabriela says.

"Because you'd skin them the first time you had a fight."

"Oh. Okay, fair enough."

"I'm going," Letitia says. "You people will die without me there."

I want to argue with her. I want to argue with all of them. This is my problem, my fight. I'm responsible for it. I should have killed Billy twenty years ago. I should have burned Mictlan so L.A. wouldn't. I should have been here all the years I wasn't and maybe things wouldn't be so fucked up now.

But I don't. Because much as I don't want them to be down there with me, I know one thing. I need them.

Chapter 26

The plan is simple. Simple plans have the best success rate. You can improvise your way around them when things go to hell. You don't get caught up in complex bullshit that'll break down if you look at it funny. But even simple plans can be stupid plans.

"That's the only entrance that we can easily use," Letitia says. "He's going to expect us to come that way."

"And if we come through one of the other entrances it's going to take three times as long to get there," Gabriela points out.

"And if we don't get a move on we'll all be swimming in feral nightmares," I say. "Look, split the difference. Indigo and I go the long way through the entrance under the King Eddy. Looking at that map, it's gonna take us an hour to get to the main hall. You two come in the DWP route half an hour after we go down and we should sync up."

"And if something goes wrong?" Gabriela says.

"Something always goes wrong. Whether we're together or split up, something's going to go wrong. It doesn't matter."

"We probably won't be able to communicate with each other," Letitia says.

"Like we'd be doing a great job of communicating in the dark sneaking through tunnels as one big mob. We're going to have red headlamps and two people are less likely to blind everybody than four people. We'll have the radios with headsets, so if they work we won't be squawking all over the place."

"The lights are going to give us away," Indigo says.

"More likely Fan and whoever he's got down there with him will be giving themselves away with their lights. He's going to need a lot more light than we will."

"So why you and Indigo?" Gabriela says.

"That's up to her, but it's my vote. She moves really fast, Letitia whines too much, and we've seen what happens when you and I team up."

"That was one time," Gabriela says.

"I'm fine with it," Indigo says. "It's after midnight, and I'd really like this to be over and done with before the sun comes up if that's all right with everybody."

"Before sunup would be good," I say. I know that tomorrow is the last day before I take a three-month trip to Mictlan, but I don't know how Santa Muerte's going to count it. Beginning of the third day? End? Random time in the middle at the most inconvenient moment?

"I still think we shouldn't split up," Letitia says. "It's like those horror movies where one guy's in the attic and the other's in the basement and the ghosts attack."

"Technically, we're all going to be in the basement when the ghosts attack."

"You know what I mean," she says. "What if we run into them and you're not with us? We won't even see them."

"Gabriela, I know you know how to flip over to the other side. How's your sensitivity?"

"Not great, but I'll know something's wrong a second or two before it happens."

"Just enough time to scream and run. Fantastic. Okay. Give me ten minutes. I'm going to make a bunch of traps. You get the vibe that something's not right, you toss one on the ground and get a shield up. At that point it's not going to matter if we give ourselves away with magic, Fan will already know we're there. Does that work?"

"Good enough, I suppose," Letitia says. "And I do not whine."

"You're right. That was unfair of me. I'm sorry. You pout. Now somebody point me to a big pile of paper."

———

It takes me more like half an hour to make enough traps that I'm comfortable with. They're just paper charms where I've embedded an intention trigger. Whoever throws it down can set it off, but they'll have to want to set it off. I wad them up into tight balls and put them into Ziploc baggies to pass out. I don't know how many ghosts they'll hold, but I tell everybody to assume no more than one each.

After that we suit up, looking like a bunch of rejects from an eighties action comedy. I've got the Browning holstered and an M4 over one shoulder, my messenger around the other. Indigo looks badass with her own M4 and a bandolier and a foot-long Bowie knife in a sheath at her hip. Gabriela doesn't have a gun, telling us if things go to shit she'd rather use her magic.

And then there's Letitia. She looks like exactly what she is, a cop. She's wearing LAPD body armor over her uniform, knee-pads, combat boots, a holstered Glock 22 and an HK416 automatic rifle slung over her shoulder. I didn't even know cops could use those.

We set out in two cars. Letitia and Gabriela hitting the DWP south of the site, and Indigo and I hitting the King Eddy Saloon to the west of it.

The King Eddy Saloon has been in place for over a century at the base of the King Edward hotel, back when Skid Row was called the Nickel. Theodore Roosevelt drank there. Bukowski drank there. James M. Cain drank there. John Fante drank there. Half the famous drunks of the last century probably downed a cheap scotch at the King Eddy at one time or another.

No matter what happens, no matter what universe it's in, there will always be a King Eddy Saloon. But it won't always be the same King Eddy. It was a bar, a speakeasy, a dive, and as Downtown got more and more gentrified, as the homeless walked the streets below $5000-a-month converted lofts, the King Eddy found itself in the same straits as all the other dark, wild places in the bowels of the city that tried to stand in the way of "progress."

It got sold to hipsters.

So it's still the King Eddy, but you won't find vomit in the bathroom stalls, the stink of old beer and older alcoholics. You can't get a scrambled egg for a quarter anymore, or sausage, biscuits, and hash browns for three bucks, and you're sure as hell not gonna find an eight-dollar pitcher of beer.

"Bar's still open," Indigo says after we park across the street. It's on the outer edge of Skid Row. A lot of the damage here was limited to some of the newer buildings. There's power here and some of the street lamps are on. And people. I haven't seen this many parked cars down this way in a long time. It looks almost normal. From the sounds inside, seems this might be the only place this far east in Downtown where people still hang out.

I'm offended. I know I shouldn't be. This is normal, everyday life. People going out and drinking to try to forget the shitshow just outside their window. Except I bet most of these people still have windows.

They've still got houses, or lofts, or own apartment buildings, or whatever.

"They will be another hour at least."

"I don't like that cop car," Indigo says. "I don't like cops in general." The LAPD squad car sitting out front has two cops in it eating taco truck burritos. Things are definitely returning to normal.

"Yeah. That could get messy. We should be able to use magic up here, but once we reach the entrance to the tunnels we'll want to drop it." I pull a couple of HI, MY NAME IS stickers and write I'M NOT HERE on each one in thick, black Sharpie. I slap one on the breast pocket of my jacket and hand the other one to Indigo. "Put this on."

She looks at me like I've just handed her a spatula and told her to take the castle. "This works?" Indigo says.

"Against normals, yeah. Against mages, depends on how much juice I put into it, or how good the mage is." I push a little more into the stickers than I normally would just in case Fan's got anyone watching this entrance to the tunnels.

I get out of the car, sling the Benelli over my shoulder. I'm halfway across the street when I notice Indigo's not following me. I turn to see her staring at me like a deer in headlights.

"What's wrong?" She can't hear me, so I yell it at her.

"You're carrying a fucking shotgun into a bar," she says in a stage whisper, like we're in a comedy heist movie. She's pointing at the police car. "You can't just walk past cops with a loaded shotgun. This isn't Texas."

"Nobody can see it," I say, which isn't strictly true. It's more that people will see it without *noticing* it. It's a lot easier than trying to make things invisible. "Just trust me, okay?"

"No. This is nuts."

I go up to the cop car and knock on the window. The two officers just keep eating their burritos. I look back and, if anything, Indigo looks even more horrified. So I jump on the hood. No response.

Tentatively, she gets out of the car. She puts the shotgun and bandolier over her shoulders and hurries across the street, ducking down like she's going to take fire any second, never taking her eyes off the police. I get it. She's black in a city known for racist cops and race riots. Mage or no, her radar's getting pinged about all sorts of threats.

"If I get shot at by some white asshole in there who freaks the fuck out because I'm carrying this thing, I will be really pissed off."

"If you get shot at by some white asshole in there, it'll be because he was shooting somebody else and you happened to be standing in the way. Nobody can see you. Promise."

"I'm trusting you," she says.

"Good lord, don't do that. That'll get you killed for sure." I head into the bar before she can say anything else.

The King Eddy still has a dive look, if not a dive feel. Like a Disney version of what a dive bar should be. Black-and-white checkerboard linoleum on the floor, barstools that have no tears, a bar top with no cigarette burns.

There are a lot of people here, and I can guarantee none of them live in this neighborhood. They're loud, brash, drunk, and moneyed. Bankers and lawyers from up around Bunker Hill, law clerks and paralegals from the nearby courts, aspiring politicians from City Hall.

Of all the fucked-up things about Los Angeles, the fact that City Hall is about half a mile from one of the largest homeless populations in the United States is the one that pisses me off the most.

"I don't like these people," I say.

"Do you want to shoot the place up?" Indigo says. "Because I'm down for that if you want to."

"That would be counterproductive," I say. "How about afterward?"

"It's a date."

We make our way through the crowd. They part to let us by, not even conscious that they're doing so. Soon we're behind the bar and heading downstairs. The basement is pretty boring as basements go. It's not very large and most of the space is taken up by steel kegs stacked one on top of another. One wall is old brickwork, and in its center is a large steel door with a chain and a padlock on it.

I pop the lock with a spell. I keep it small so I don't have to tap the local pool. If Fan is waiting for us, he shouldn't feel any magical disturbance. I pull the sticker off of my jacket and Indigo does the same, handing me hers. I break the spell on them, crumple them into a ball, toss them into the corner.

We put our earpieces in for the radios and I toggle the talk button. We should all be on the same frequency so we can all hear each other. Letitia answers. "If this is another goddamn baby monitor interfering with this signal so help me—"

"It's us," I say. "We're heading down now. You in place?"

"Yeah," she says. "We'll give it half an hour and head down. Meet you in the evil genius's secret ghost lair. If we don't die on the way."

"Yeah, don't do that," I say.

"I'll do my best." She clicks off.

I swing the door open. It groans on unoiled hinges, revealing a dusty set of steps. A heavy switch turns on industrial cage lights lining the wall to the bottom of the stairs.

"Huh."

"What?" Indigo says.

"I always heard this place was haunted," I say.

"You didn't know?"

"Oh, I knew, I just never really paid attention to how haunted it might be."

The tunnel is filled with Haunts, walking back and forth, slamming themselves against invisible walls trying to get free. Some muttering to themselves, others threatening unseen assailants, a few screaming. The Echoes are more disturbing. A lot of bootleggers died on this staircase, gunned down and bled out from the look of it. There are so many falling down the stairs it's actually hard for me to see the steps.

"Thanks," she says. "Thanks for making an already nerve-wracking trip that much creepier."

"It's a talent," I say. She pushes past me and heads down the stairs.

"So's puttin' my boot up your ass. Let's go. And I don't want to hear any more about how fucking haunted these tunnels are."

"I know a story about a mad axeman."

"Fuck you."

"Ol' Hookhand?"

"Not listening."

The tunnel continues on for about forty feet then hits a T. The lights dim down the halls until there's nothing but darkness in either direction.

"This is where we earn our keep," I say. I check Frank's map on my phone to be sure of the route. It's farther from where we think Fan's holed up than the DWP entrance, but there aren't as many branches or weird turns. I hand the phone to Indigo. "This the right way?" I say. It's good to have an extra set of eyes to make sure you don't walk right into the tiger's mouth.

"Yeah," she says. "We pass, eight, no, nine branches then turn left at the tenth." We put our headlamps on and fire them up. The LEDs light up the hall for a good twenty or thirty feet ahead of us.

"These lights are either going to come in real handy, or they're going to get us killed," Indigo says. She unslings her Benelli and checks that it's loaded and ready to go. "If anything, and I mean anything, jumps in front of me, I am blowing it into paste."

"I'll remember not to jump in front of you," I say, and we walk on down the hall.

Chapter 27

Ever driven through Texas? It's miles and miles of nothing but miles and miles. This tunnel feels the same way. It just keeps going. We pass the first five branches pretty quickly, but there's a long stretch before we hit number six. So far nobody's tried to jump us, and I'm not sensing any ghosts that shouldn't be here or magic being used. Aside from the tension and near-certainty that someone's going to start shooting at us from the darkness, it's a pretty boring walk.

"You run, huh? I've seen you pull a car door off its hinges. Do anything else?" I say. My voice is a whisper. I'm close enough and it's quiet enough that we can hear each other just fine. Hopefully our footfalls and whispers will be masked by the sound of ventilation running, water dripping, power boxes humming.

"Fuck you. I do lots of things."

I can tell I'm fidgeting. I need to do something to keep from just heading as fast as I can down the hall, screaming and firing the shotgun at anything that moves and a few things that don't.

"That's not . . . Look, I do death magic. All the other stuff I'm either okay at, suck balls, or can't do at all no matter how I try. Letitia's a human lie detector.

I haven't seen her do much else, so I don't know if she can do much else."

"I know what you meant." I can hear the tension in her voice. She's itching for a fight, too. "She can tell when you're lying?"

"Yeah, but I don't think she can tell which parts of what you're saying are a lie unless it's a direct statement, and she can't tell you're lying if you just leave stuff out. So if you ever have to keep anything from her, either don't say anything, leave lots of gaps, or make it so goddamn complicated she can't tell which part of it is bullshit."

"This is your friend you're talking about," she says.

"It's not my friend so much as my 'not-enemy' I'm talking about. I don't really do friends."

"That's sad," she says.

"Beats making friends and seeing them die," I say.

She says nothing for a long while, and at this point I'm not interested in making small talk.

"Moving fast is the thing I'm best at," she says. "I can lift a lot of shit. Anything like that I can figure out or just do on instinct."

"I noticed your shoes weren't smoking, and none of your clothes tore when you ran."

"And my bones didn't shatter, my muscles didn't shred, and I didn't give myself a hemorrhage, either. Means I hit like a motherfucker, too."

"All that in one spell," I say. "Nice. Complex. And that's all self-taught?"

"Damn right it is," she says. "Run fast, hit hard."

"You ever consider getting training?"

"You looking for an apprentice?" she says. I can hear the distaste in her voice.

I have to stifle a laugh. "Oh, hell no. I wouldn't know what to do with you. Talk to Gabriela when we're done. She'd know somebody."

"If we ever get done," she says. She stops in her

tracks. I take a step before I notice and turn to her. Her eyes are hard. She's gripping the Benelli with white knuckles.

"This is bullshit," she says. "Walking in the dark trying to sneak up on somebody who might not even be here. And if he is, he isn't stupid enough not to know we're coming. He's waiting for us. Probably figures this sneaking around shit is exactly what we're doing, and while we're stumbling in the dark, he's sitting there laughing his ass off."

I agree with her, but I don't want to tell her that. Impulsiveness gets people killed. I should know. "What do you want to do, then?"

"Fucking run in there and kill everything."

"I'd like to say I'll be right behind you, but you'll be leaving me in the dust. And as soon as you start running, he's gonna know for sure we're here."

"No, he'll know I'm here. And I can dodge anything he can throw at me."

There's a point where self-confidence turns into cockiness turns into stupidity. We're already well beyond that point, so I say, "Let's do it."

She looks at me in surprise. "Seriously?"

"I'm not well known for my impulse control."

"I'll see you down there, then."

"Good hunting. Don't hit any traps. If I notice any of his ghost bombs going off, I'll try to let you know through the radio."

She nods, clutches the shotgun hard in her hands, and lowers into a runner's starting stance.

"One more thing," I say. "Don't die. I'll never hear the end of it."

"Gotcha," she says. I feel her magic go up like a flare and she's gone.

"You may have just sent her off to her death." A smell of smoke and roses fills the hall. Santa Muerte fades into being in front of me.

"I think I did that when I asked her if she wanted to come along."

"It's the third day, Eric."

"Yeah. But the third day ain't over, yet. If I don't see this through I'll be pissy the entire time I'm in Mictlan, and you really wouldn't like me pissy. I'm like a fucking toddler. Everybody'll be, 'This clown's in charge?' and then they're going to wonder about your taste in men."

Santa Muerte shifts, shrinks. Flesh flows over bones until Tabitha takes her place. "My taste in men is just fine," she says. "All right. Finish this. But if it's not done by midnight tonight, you're coming whether it's finished or not."

"Is that midnight Pacific?"

"Eric."

"Fine. Midnight. I'll see you then. Oh, you wouldn't happen to know if he's actually down there, do you?"

"Yes. He's down there, still preparing everything. And you need to hurry. He's felt Indigo's magic, and he's going to try to rush through his sacrifices. Here, let me help."

"How—" The hallway blinks out, the headlamp-lit hall suddenly replaced by a wide chamber, industrial lights ringing the edges and feeding from a generator in a corner.

There are bodies on the floor. A lot of bodies. Forty? Fifty? Some of them look homeless. Some look like they were taken coming home from work. There are people in street clothes, police, and fire and National Guard uniforms. A couple in lab coats. Quite a lot of Chinese men, some of whom I think I saw at the mahjong hall. Seems Fan is cleaning house and sweeping out the old guard. They're all unconscious but alive. So they've got that going for them.

Every person is connected to the others along a complex sigil on the floor in silver paint, each at a point that branches off to multiple others. In the center of the sigil is a pallet filled high with stacks and stacks of joss paper. The pile looks to be about two or three times more than I used in the Walled City. Over on one side, hemmed in by a silver circle with spokes that radiate out to the rest of the sigil, is Fan.

He doesn't look particularly happy to see me. Pity. I'm overjoyed to see him. I raise the Benelli and fire off a couple rounds of buckshot. The pellets stop in the air with a pulse of magic as his shield comes up, then clatter to the ground.

"How the fuck did you get here before me?" Indigo says, coming to a sudden stop by my side.

"Caught a ride with my wife. I think the fireworks are about to start."

She sees Fan and unloads her Benelli's entire magazine at him. It has the same effect. "Goddammit."

"I would have told you not to waste the ammunition but I didn't want to break your flow. You looked really determined."

I hear running from the other side of the room, Gabriela and Letitia coming into view. Letitia does the same thing with her Glock, and sure enough the bullets stop dead and fall to the floor.

I wave at them. "Hey! You're not dead." I have to yell over the sound of the generator, plus there's the ringing in my ears from having a 12-gauge go off next to my head when I wasn't expecting it.

They head over to us, skirting the sigil. "He had a couple of IEDs in the tunnel but that was all," Gabriela says. "You?"

"Clear path. Got halfway through and Indigo ran the rest of the way."

"And he still got here before I did. I don't know how."

"How about we focus on him for a bit?" I say. I can see Fan's lips moving, though I can't hear him. The magic in the area is growing and he's already starting to sweat. I can feel the Skid Row ghosts trying to move farther away, but they're being pulled in.

"What's happening?" Indigo says.

"He's reeling the ghosts in like fish in a trawling net," I say. I wish I'd known that spell twenty years ago. Would have saved me a lot of time and trouble. "Once they're close enough, and I don't know what close enough is for him, he'll trigger his spell, shunt most of the power out to all those people so it doesn't fry his brain, and then pull them across and into the bills on the pallet."

"Can we shoot at his shield until we just break it down?" Indigo says.

"I don't think so," I say. "I saw him use it to protect himself from one of Gabriela's vortex grenades."

"Vortex grenades?" Gabriela says.

"Easier than saying 'Marbles that blow everything up and then suck it into a hell dimension.'"

"He survived that?" She gives a low whistle of respect. "Damn. He's better than I thought. Vortex grenades. I like the sound of it."

"If we can't get him out of there, what do we do?" Letitia says. "What if we focus all our magic on him? He can't fight us all off."

"I have a better idea," I say. "We wait."

"And what?" Gabriela says. "Glare at him a lot to make him feel all self-conscious?"

"I don't like that idea," Indigo says, and empties another magazine at Fan. Though the shield stops the pellets, he flinches from the blast. So do the rest of us.

"Could you warn us before you unload like that next to my head?" I say.

"Sorry," she says. I think. It's hard to tell over the ringing in my head. "I could punch it a lot."

"I'm telling you, we wait."

"And then what do we do?" Letitia says.

"Oh," Gabriela says, looking at me, realization coming to her. "Of course."

Indigo reloads her shotgun. "What?" she says. "What 'of course'?"

I tell them.

"That's fucked up," Letitia says. "Even for you."

"Trust me, I've done worse. He's almost done reeling the ghosts in. Anybody got a better plan?"

"I can't just shoot him in the head?" Indigo says.

"I guarantee you this will hurt more and take longer."

"Fine," she says. "I'm in." Letitia's face is grim, Gabriela is trying not to laugh. They say the same.

"Great. Everybody get ready. It's showtime."

Chapter 28

We all move to different points of the room. I walk up behind Fan. He's concentrating so hard he doesn't notice until I knock on the shield and he feels the vibration. He spins to look at me.

"Hey, buddy," I say. "Whatcha doin'?"

"What do you want from me?" Fan says. "What have I done to you?"

"Cuffed me to a chair, did a lot of threatening, which isn't really all that much, actually. Did you use bad language? No, you didn't, did you? I don't really know. I don't think you've done anything to me."

"That was all Billy," he says. "He didn't understand. He never understood. But you do. You know what I'm doing." Channeling multiple spells and holding a conversation is kind of like walking and chewing bubblegum while you're patting your head and rubbing your tummy. I'm impressed.

"Oh, I know exactly what you're doing. Which is why I'm not crazy about the fact that you're doing it."

He chuckles, then goes into a full-blown laugh. "And what are you going to do about it? You can't get to me. I can hold this shield up all day and none of you can touch me."

"You are absolutely right," I say. "I can't do a damn thing to you. Instead, I'm gonna watch. Professional curiosity. Who knows, I might learn a thing or two. We're all mages here. Think of us as students. We're here to learn."

He gives me a skeptical look. "You're up to something."

"No shit," I say. "It's me. Of course I'm up to something. And aren't you curious to find out what it is?"

"Whatever it is, it won't matter soon."

"Is this where you tell me about your dastardly plan and monologue like a supervillain?"

"That would just be self-indulgent," he says. "Besides, you already know what I'm doing. After all, you came up with the idea."

"I came up with the idea to solve a problem, not create one."

"Then you have shitty problem-solving skills."

"You got me there. If you do this, you're going to kill a lot of people. Starting with all the ones you kidnapped and laid out on the floor. If you stop now, then nobody has to die."

"If I stop now, I'll die," he says. "Billy wasn't lying when he said he was a dead man if he went home without his ghosts. He's burned too many bridges, called in too many favors to make all this happen."

"And since he's gone, if you don't deliver, somebody'll have your head, too, right?"

"Yes. And why do you care about these people? I don't know them. You don't know them. They're normals and know-nothing talents. There are no real mages there. They're cattle. They're meant to be used."

I can feel the magic building. He's going to have to release it soon. If we don't get the timing right, it could be very bad.

See, we might be able to get through that shield, but it would be stupid to try. He's good. Maybe better than all of us combined. If we broke through it might take too much energy. We want to be full up. You don't go into a gunfight with a pen knife.

Easier to not fight at all.

"You say shit like that," I say, "and it makes my conscience feel squeaky clean."

He flips me the bird and sets off the spell.

"Now!" A lot of things happen all at once. The power from the spell starts to pulse through the sigil, Indigo starts running and sliding people off of the lines. On the other side of the room Letitia and Gabriela are using fire spells to burn the paint off of pieces of the sigil.

I use the ring to open a hole under the pallet full of joss paper to the ceiling of the King Eddy Saloon. It falls through—hopefully on a lawyer—and I close the hole up after.

The power from the spell, not finding other people to get shunted into, feeds back into Fan. He screams but doesn't go down. He's channeling it, a huge amount. It would probably kill me, and it's definitely going to burn him out. After this he won't be able to channel enough power to light a fart in a high wind.

That really is a horrible fate for a mage. It's like having your arms and legs cut off and your eyes gouged out of your head. I don't want to see that happen to him. All sorts of other things, sure, but not that.

All the ghosts he's pulling speed across the silver lines, hitting empty spots where Gabriela and Letitia have burned through them, doubling back and finding a better route, like rats in a maze. They don't understand what's happening, and I can hear their panic as they try to pull away from the magic tearing them through the veil and down the line to be trapped in the pallet of joss paper.

Only there's no pallet of joss paper to go into.

Like the saying "all roads to lead to Rome," in this

case all roads lead to an asshole sorcerer who's got more power than sense. Every single ghost Fan pulls through slams into him like a cannonball. They fill him up, threaten to spill over. These aren't the feral ghosts he would have created. They're normal, just on the wrong side of the fence.

But even normal ghosts want to feed. I can see them tearing into his soul, burning away chunks of his being. They're really good at this sort of thing. It's better than having a hog farm.

Fan's gone before his body gives out, his soul filled with holes like a target at a shooting gallery. His brain is still firing, his magic is still working. There's just nobody at the helm.

When his body finally dies and the ghosts burst out of him like spiders leaving a giant egg sac, I'm ready for them. His magic sputters, the shield drops.

I crank as much power as I dare into a spell to shove him, and all the other Skid Row ghosts he'd dumped into himself, across the veil to the other side. I've never moved this much across before. It's not mass, or volume, it's something else I can't define. The collective weight of so many consciousnesses threatens to pull me along with them, but I'm able to hold my ground.

The last one goes back to where it belongs intact, not torn apart like Fan's ghost bombs. They're probably shell-shocked, but ghosts never remember anything for very long. Once I'm sure there aren't any more on this side of the veil, I kill the spell.

And then I black out.

———

I come to in the back of Letitia's car, an unmarked police car that might as well be painted black and white for all the good not being marked does it. It's hot, sweaty, and smells like a campground outhouse.

"Holy shit, it stinks back here." The back seat is like every other cop car. Wire cage separating it from the front, no inside door locks or handles.

"You get used to it," she says.

"How? It smells like vomit and Febreeze."

"All cop cars smell like that. It's the scent of Justice."

"I think Justice needs a shower and maybe a dip in turpentine."

"How you feeling there, champ?"

"You ever see those late-night infomercials for stupid kitchen gadgets?"

"Yeah."

"I feel like the egg in one of those Inside-the-Shell Egg Scramblers. How about you? You didn't get tagged by any ghosts, did you?"

"No, they stayed in the sigil. Indigo got most of the people out of the way before things got really bad. Damn, that girl can move. Some of them have busted legs, a few have migraines from having caught some of the power Fan was trying to shunt off, but after finding out what happened they're okay with a couple of fractures and a headache."

"What about the normals?"

"There were like five or six of those. I took care of them. The only thing they'll remember is waking up outside of an open sewer grate."

"Indigo and Gabriela?"

"Gabriela's off with Frank and Gary. Said something about setting up those tunnel apartments again. Got some idea that with her help they can make it work or something. Indigo's pissed off at you for not letting her shoot Fan in the head."

"I'll make it up to her. Find somebody else who pisses her off and let her shoot them in head. How long have I been out?"

She looks at her watch. "About four hours."

"The fuck? Have I been in here the whole time?"

"Yeah. I figured if you pissed yourself while you were out it wouldn't make anything worse back there. And if you didn't wake up, all I'd have to do is kick your ass out onto the curb. Don't worry, I left the window cracked open when I wasn't here. There's laws against letting dogs die in hot cars, you know."

"If you ever get tired of being a cop, you should go into comedy. Give the audience somebody to boo off stage."

"I can still kick your ass out onto the curb, you know. I don't even have to slow down."

"Oh, like my getting thrown from a moving car has never happened before. Where are we?"

"Heading down to Venice. Figured your stinky hobo doc should take a look at you, seeing as the better one never wants to see you again."

"Well, you can turn around, I feel fine."

"You don't look it."

"I never do."

I can see her frown in the rearview mirror. "People don't fall unconscious for four hour stretches on the regular, ya know. Maybe we should get your brain looked at."

"Did that already," I say.

"Yeah, did they find one?"

"One with multiple lesions and a couple of bleeds. If I get knocked around too much more I'll have a hemorrhage and die. If I survive long enough I get to enjoy the fun of chronic traumatic encephalopathy, complete with more blackouts, vomiting, double-vision, mood swings, dementia, and death."

Neither of us says anything for a couple miles. It's nice. I like the quiet.

"Is that why Vivian was so pissed off at you?"

"That? No. Maybe? Mostly she wants to keep me alive so I can suffer along with her. Seems to think I

don't know what loss is like. Sounded kind of drama
queen–ish, but I can't say I don't see her point."

"But she knows about it?"

"She's the one who told me. I've been getting migraines, double-vision, blacking out for short periods.
Been going on a while now. She thinks the magic in my
tattoos has kept it from outright killing me."

"Jesus, Eric. What's the treatment?"

"Drugs, mostly. Not just the fun kind. Anti-seizure
shit, anti-psychotics, anti-whatever else I can't remember. She offered to carve up my brain, too. But
when it comes down to it, there's nothing to do. Hey,
you got anything to drink up there?"

"There's a Taco Bell up the street. Hit the drive-
thru?"

"Sure. It's not like that shit's gonna kill me. But
experiencing this car's unique odeur from back here
at the source might do me in."

"Hang on." She pulls over and lets me out of the
back. I slide into the front seat and roll down the window. Either the air conditioning's busted or Letitia
likes driving a sauna.

"What about Santa Muerte?" Letitia says.

"What about her?"

"She can do something, right?"

"No idea. Didn't ask. Not going to."

"But what if she can help?"

"Letitia, I'm fucking tired. We all go out eventually. I'm not crazy about kicking the bucket, but if this
is how I go, fine. I can think of a hundred worse ways.
Most of them I've seen. And when I do go, I have a
pretty good idea where I'm going."

"I don't remember you being this depressing in
high school," she says.

"And I don't remember you ever suggesting we eat
Taco Bell in high school, either. But people grow."

"What about the holes?" she says.

"What?"

"The breaches that the ghosts were coming through. They're still there, aren't they?"

Shit. They are. With what Fan was doing, they might even be more unstable. "You know what, let's skip the monkey-shit tacos. Can you drop me off in Skid Row? I have an idea."

"Will it work?" she says.

"When haven't my ideas worked out?"

"You want a bulleted list? Might take me a couple of weeks to pull together."

"Either this will work and we can close everything up once and for all, or it destroys all life as we know it."

"Close enough." She hits the lights and siren on the car and floors it. I look at Peter's ring and wonder if it can do what I think it can.

Chapter 29

A Klein bottle is one of those weird cannot-exist-in-nature things that looks three dimensional but really isn't. Like a Möbius strip, where you twist a strip of paper and attach the ends to each other, and voila, it suddenly only has one side.

But a Klein bottle is a lot more complicated. It's "a two-dimensional manifold against which a system for determining a normal vector cannot be consistently defined." That's math-speak for Weird Shit. Think of a tube where one end goes back into itself and feeds into the other. Except that it doesn't actually intersect itself because the intersection exists in the fourth dimension. No, really. Look it up. They're fascinating.

If I understand how the ring I got off of Peter works, and how the rifts between the dead and living sides work, I should be able to . . . do something. I don't think I can close them. But I think I can do something almost as good.

Letitia pulls over across from one of the larger breaches in Skid Row and lets me out. "You coming?" I say.

"I was thinking I'd sit here with the car running in case your plan goes tits up and I have to outrun a black hole of ghosts or some shit."

"Smart. Won't work, but it's smart. I'll be back in a bit. Maybe."

I was right about what Fan pulling all those ghosts over last night did to the thin spaces. They're larger, less stable. Riddled with holes like torn curtains. I can also sense them better. Before, I couldn't entirely make out the boundaries, but now I can see where they begin and end.

If I have this right, I think I can punch a hole through and double it back onto itself. There are a lot of things that could go wrong. Fortunately, I don't know enough about what the hell I'm doing to know what those things are. Sometimes ignorance is bliss. Though sometimes ignorance will just make you very surprised when it kills you.

I trace out the edges of the thin area in my mind. Fix them in my memory as well as I can. Then I tell the ring to rip open a hole the same size and shape and have it lead back into the one that's already there. The magic grows, the ring doing something it clearly wasn't designed for. My hand shakes from trying to keep it still. Then there's an anticlimactic pop, and the hole feeds back, sealing itself with itself.

A migraine punches me between the eyes. I figure this must be my brain hemorrhaging. Great timing, brain. But then it fades as quickly as it came on.

I head back to the car, Letitia watching me nervously. "Did it work?" She can't see it, and I don't want to have to explain what I did, so I just tell her yes and ask her to head to the next one.

We do this five more times. Each time the migraines get worse and last longer, but they still fade fairly quickly, so I'm not going to worry about it. Letitia drives back around so I can make sure everything's still closed up. I don't know if this is a temporary patch or a permanent fix. But for right now, at least, they seem to be holding.

"We good?" Letitia says.

"Looks like it."

"Now what?"

"Can you drop me off at the Ambassador? Oh, and swing by the King Eddy Saloon first?"

"Sure. Why?"

"Indulge me." A little while later we round a corner and see that all the bar's windows have been blown out and there's a plywood board where the door used to be. That pallet with the ghost money on it probably weighed at least a ton. Suddenly dropping it into a small space must have sent out a shock wave that shattered the glass and blew off the door. I might have given it a bit of a push.

She narrows her eyes at me. "Did you do this?"

"Me? No. That's a horrible thing to say and I was nowhere near the area at the time, detective."

"You had something to do with it. What the hell happened there?"

"Reverse gentrification?"

"Shut up. Don't talk the rest of the way."

"I—"

"I said shut up."

I give her a thumbs up in response.

The drive out from Downtown along Wilshire is beginning to look a little more normal. MacArthur Park was turned into a FEMA refugee camp, and as we pass by, I can see more cars leaving than going in. There seem to be fewer people outside, less activity. The National Guard presence has been replaced by LAPD and private security. It will take years, but Los Angeles is starting to rebuild.

Letitia drops me off at the school entrance. School's let out, so there's only a handful of faculty around. I find a dark corner and flip over to the other side. The Ambassador is as lively as ever. Cars driving onto the grounds, dropping off guests, or people coming for dinner and drinks at the Cocoanut Grove. By my reckoning it's only a little after noon, but over on this side there isn't any sun, and as far as the Ambassador is concerned, it's always Saturday night.

I greet the bellboy and make my way up to the room. I've only been here once since I ran into Peter and Hank, and that was for maybe five minutes to grab clothes.

I unlock the door and head inside. I want more sleep. I want more painkillers. And I want to not have somebody trying to kill me for at least a few hours.

It's good to want things. You get important life lessons in cynicism and disappointment when you don't get them.

There's a loud pop and at the other side of the room, a very familiar-looking sort of hole appears, and Hank steps through. Immediately I grab Darius's bottle from the table and throw the hotel door open.

I just make it over the threshold when Hank tackles me, wrapping his arms around my legs and slamming me into the hallway wall. The door to my room closes on its own with a click.

I pull my left leg up and out of his grip and then kick, connecting with his jaw. It pushes him off and I roll until I can get to my feet. He's already up and charging at me. I duck under and past him and as his hands sweep above me I see a very similar-looking ring on his finger.

"I see we have the same taste in jewelry," I say. I swing Darius's bottle, raking it across his face, then bring it up into an uppercut that knocks him to the floor.

I run for the stairs. I make it to the next floor down when Hank leaps over the side and lands in front of me. He's dropped the middle-aged white guy disguise in favor of a blue-skinned demon with two sets of burning red eyes. His hands end in razor-sharp talons. I know exactly what he can do with those things.

"You don't have to die," he says, his voice thick as he tries to talk with mouth full of teeth too big for it.

"Much as I'd love to have a spirited philosophical debate on the subject, I really don't have the time. So if you don't mind." I shove at him with a push spell that knocks him down to the next floor. He rolls to his feet, anger twisting his face even uglier.

"I take that back," he says. "You do have to die."

"Excuse me, sir." The bellboy appears between the both of us. "I'm so sorry, but as you are not a patron of this establishment, the management would like to inform you that you must vacate the premises immediately."

Hank looks at the bellboy and laughs. "What are ya gonna do, little ghost? Eat me?"

"Hardly anything so tasteless, sir," the bellboy says, and the staircase between me and the floor disappears. Hank plummets the remaining two stories to land in the lobby below.

"So sorry for the intrusion, sir," the bellboy says. "I thought you might use some assistance."

"Thanks," I say. "I appreciate it."

"Not at all, s—" The bellboy is shredded to ribbons as Hank flies back up and tears through him with his claws. The hotel shakes, whether in pain or anger I can't tell.

"I'm a fucking demon, you little shit," he yells, hovering over the space where the stairs used to be. The bellboy doesn't reappear. "Looks like you're on your own, necromancer."

"Just me and my good friend gravity." I step into the gap and fall to the lobby. This time, I don't try to flip to the living side, but instead I use a push to slow myself down. Running away, enjoyable as that might be, isn't really an option. Doesn't mean I can't use some distance.

I break into a run as soon as I land, bolting for the doors. Hank is faster. He flies between me and the doors and gets his hand around my throat. Not exactly what I was hoping for, but I'll take what I can get. I hold onto the bottle with one hand, wrap the other around his meaty fist and try to pry his fingers loose, slipping a couple off my neck before his strength overwhelms me and they're right back there again. That's okay, I got what I was going for.

"All I want is the goddamn bottle," he says. "Is it such a bad idea to just give it to me?"

"See, that's not really gonna work for me," I say, my voice straining past my constricted throat.

"Here's the thing," he says. "I'm not supposed to kill you. I really, really want to. And I might just take that hit if you don't hand the bottle over."

"Why don't you just take it?"

"I can. But I want you to give it to me willingly. It's a good-faith thing. Darius wants you to know there's no hard feelings, that you and he can still be friends. But you gotta show him that you're willing to work with him. So give me the bottle."

"Yeah, no."

"Suit yourself." He pulls back his other hand and the claws grow another inch out of his fingers.

"Hang on."

"Reconsidered?"

"Just a question. Was the ring I got off Peter some kind of homing signal? Is that how you got into the room?"

"Darius said you were smarter than you looked," Hank says. "He also said you weren't nearly as smart as you thought you were. Yes. The rings are linked. As long as I have one I can go anywhere the other one is."

"Convenient."

"I think so. Beats having to be summoned. Can we get this over with now?"

"Raincheck?"

"Sorry, no." Instead of gutting me, he punches me in the face and throws me onto the ground. It's like getting hit with a sledgehammer. My vision doubles and the entire left side of my face goes numb.

I pull the bottle in close, tucking it under my arm. He picks me up and slams me onto the ground again. My vision isn't double anymore. But that's only because one eye has gone blind. I also can't feel my feet.

"If you have one ring you can follow me, right? That's how that worked? And without one you can't go anywhere unless you're summoned." My voice is a slurred mess.

"What is your obsession with this? I'm trying to convince you to play ball here, and if you don't, then kill you. Or maybe I'm just trying to kill you. They both look very similar to each other to me."

"You know, I can leave this side of the veil any time I want," I say, which may be a bit of an overstatement at this point.

"Why bother? I'll just follow you."

"Right," I say. "Because you've got one of these." I show him my right middle finger, with my ring slid firmly onto it.

"You think you're funny," he says.

"Oh, I think I'm fuckin' hilarious," I say, and show him my left middle finger, wearing the ring that I palmed off him while he was choking me. "Enjoy the sights on this side of the veil. Asshole."

I flip over to the other side as Hank lashes out for me. His claws connect for just a moment, but the cut is deep enough to open up my gut.

I fumble for my phone. I've only got Gabriela and

Letitia on speed dial, so I should get at least one of them. It rings, but I pass out before anyone picks up.

———

Everything is a smear, punctuated by snapshots of sensation. Someone slamming on my chest. Hot breath into my lungs. A stab of bright light, someone—Vivian—shining a flashlight in one eye and then the other. At least I think it's Vivian. It can't be Vivian. Maybe it's the Hobo Doc. My eyes—sorry, my eye isn't focusing very well. Then I stop seeing altogether. There's a burning in my gut, the sense that everything is slowing to a crawl. There's a lot of yelling. Why is everyone yelling?

"Clear," says a voice and it sounds a thousand miles away. My body jerks in a bone-cracking spasm. It hurts. Holy fuck does it hurt. But then everything hurts and it feels like just one more log on the bonfire of pain.

"Again." Really? Do we have to? Because that really sucked. Can't you people just, I dunno, leave me alone?

No. A voice that isn't a voice, a sepulcher grinding open, stone against stone. A sense of smoke and roses, though I don't actually smell anything. I feel Santa Muerte's presence next to me, around me, through me. She is everywhere and everything. *You know they can't. They'll fight for you whether you want them to or not.*

Seems like a lot of trouble to go to.

If they thought the same, they wouldn't be doing it.

You and your logic. Will it work?

I don't know. Let's find out.

Oh, by all means. Yes, let's.

You somehow manage to sound sarcastic even when you can't speak.

It's a talent. You're a goddess of death. How do you not know whether I'll live or die?

With everything you know, and everything you've experienced, you still see death as a binary. Dead isn't always dead, Eric. Alive isn't always alive. You know this. If you die, the slab of meat called Eric Carter dies. If you live, you get to walk around in that meat a little bit longer. But you're a complicated case. You're Eric Carter, you're Mictlantecuhtli. Death doesn't know what to do with you.

Huh. That's kind of a drag. I think I was hoping it would all just . . . stop. I know it won't. I know it doesn't. But I was hoping. How am I doing?

They've got your heart beating again. I don't know how long that will last, though. Her voice has shifted from Santa Muerte's to Tabitha's, softer, quieter, not the harsh gravelly sound of the grave.

They're both the sound of death. Sometimes death sounds like the rattle of dirt thrown on a pinewood box. Sometimes it sounds like a gentle passing in the night.

Your blood pressure's bottoming out. Not long now.

I wonder if I'll leave a ghost. A feeling of laughter from Tabitha. I like it. I haven't heard nearly enough laughter in a long time. Even if it's slightly mocking.

You're way too self-centered to leave a ghost. More than one Eric Carter? You'd never let that stand.

She has a point.

"Clear." Jesus, again? Give it up, people. I can barely feel the jolt when it hits me.

I hope no one mourns me.

People will do what they do.

Let me go. Forget about me. I've caused enough trouble. I don't see any point causing more after I'm dead. No grief.

I know grief. Everyone knows it. It eats at all of us at one time or another. I'm never sure if it's a cruelty or a kindness. It's about not knowing. About living with uncertainty. But I know what happens. I know what will happen to me. Maybe not the details, but I have the gist. But even then, mourning's a hard habit to break. It's brutal. Tears at you, gnaws on your guts, eats you alive. Missing someone hurts. I'm tired of hurting people.

"Goddammit."

Who was that?

Gabriela. And to your next question, no. Vivian isn't there.

That's good. I think that's good. I'm going to miss her.

Even the dead mourn.

Yeah. Grieving. Grieving is hard.

But dying is easy.